A Princess and the Pea retelling
of
Crystals
and
Peas
I072165

Contents

To my parents, on whose laps I learned to love stories.
Thank you, Mommy, for teaching me how to read, for reading to
me everywhere we went, and for supplying me with good books.
Thank you, Daddy, for being a walking dictionary whenever I
needed to know what a word meant, and for investing in books.
Thank you for being readers yourselves and making sure we had
books in every room of the house.
Thank you for making books a reward and giving them as gifts.
I'm writing them now because of you.

He hath made everything beautiful in his time.
— Solomon

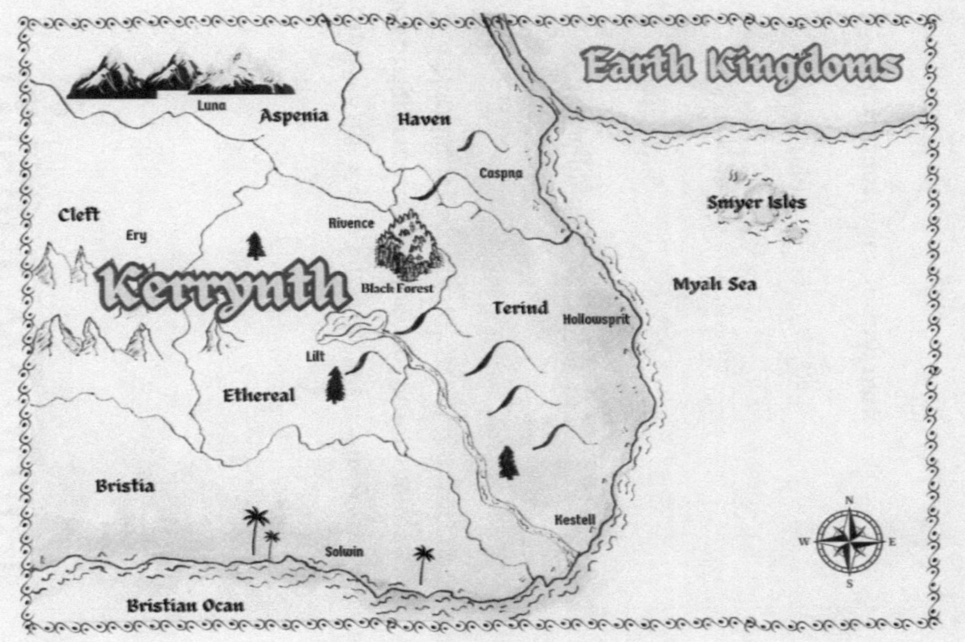

Earth Kingdoms
Kerrynth
Luna
Aspenia
Haven
Caspna
Cleft
Ery
Rivence
Black Forest
Smyer Isles
Myah Sea
Terind
Hollowsprit
Lilt
Ethereal
Bristia
Kestell
Solwin
Bristian Ocan
N
E
S
W

Trigger Warnings

I consider this a cozy fairytale, but if you are sensitive to these triggers, this story may not be for you.

Nothing is gory or explicit, but this story does mention:

- Kidnapping

- Stabbing

- Attempted sexual assault

- Abortion

- Emotional abuse/manipulation

CHAPTER 1

Paint the Skies Orange

Distant shouting awakened Avalon in the middle of the night. She blinked, trying to clear the confusion of sleep from her mind. The sky outside her window danced with a gruesome glow. Fire? She flew out of bed and flung open her door, nearly running straight into her mother.

"Mother, what's–?" Her question was cut off as the Queen grabbed her hand and pressed something into it.

"Guard this," she whispered. "Don't lose it, Avalon. You can–"

Men in unfamiliar uniforms came up behind her mother, dragging her back down the hall into the dark chaos.

Avalon's fist clasped tightly around the tiny marble her mother had pressed there, as she stood, frozen with fear, while her mother was pulled away. Where were the guards?

Before she could make herself move, more soldiers rushed toward her. They grabbed her arms and shoved her toward her bedroom. A new fear clawed around her neck, and she screamed until a large hand smothered her mouth.

"Get your things," the man commanded, pushing her forward. Bewildered, Avalon slipped her feet into her shoes and pulled a cloak and dress from the wardrobe, and then the soldiers were hurrying her out of the palace and toward their waiting wagons. No one came to her rescue, and she realized why when they stepped around a dark heap in the corridor. She spotted Jem's face in the tangle of oddly lying men. Her oldest bodyguard had blood trailing from a wound in his chest, and his eyes stared blankly at her through the shadows. Her soft shoes felt the squish of the blood pooled on the stone floor, and she threw a hand across her mouth to keep back the scream that rose in her throat. Her legs shook so she could barely walk, but the men pushed her along.

Outside the walls, someone hoisted her into the darkness of a covered wagon, but not before she caught sight of Amelie and Raine being shoved into wagons ahead of hers. Raine's eyes met hers for a split second, and the flash of raw terror on her sister's face made her blood cold.

Avalon continued to tremble as one of the men in black secured her ankle with a heavy rope. She caught sight of Cleft's light blue mountain symbol on his chest before the door cover rolled shut, and all was blackness inside, with only the heat and stench of fire and blood coming in through the small window. The wagon lurched forward, leaving the palace behind.

Terror squeezed Avalon's lungs, and she could only gasp for breath. Tears blinded her. Had her mother and father been killed? What did Cleftans want with her and her sisters? Still shaking, she melted onto the bench seat. Nausea grew as the carriage shook and hurried along, crashing over her in mounting waves. She stumbled to the window and vomited.

As she wiped her mouth with the back of her hand, breathing shallowly to keep her stomach intact, she realized she still had the glass ball in her fist. Unclenching her tight fingers, she opened her palm to reveal a small round jewel, polished smooth. It shone through the darkness with a subtle green glow. Her sickness subsided a bit, but her head pounded. She felt around for the clothes she had brought along and found them on the floor. By feel, she stripped out of her nightgown and began dressing, using her discarded nightgown to wipe at her dirty face, though it was a losing battle as tears kept rising and spilling over. For a while, she mulled over where to keep the tiny pea-sized jewel safe, finally dropping it into her dress under her chemise. She nudged it to the right, wedging it firmly between her underclothing and her skin.

Towards morning, fatigue overcame her, and she fell in and out of sleep while the wagon bumped along. When she awoke, the sun had risen high, and they had stopped. Someone slid breakfast through the door, startling her, but the door was shut again before she could react. She ate a little of the porridge. Chagrined at the smell of sweat and vomit on her skin, and the stickiness of her tear-soaked face and neck, she tried to clean and smooth herself as best she could without water or a comb. She expected to be confronted today, maybe given an explanation and told what to expect. But, other than the bowl set on the floor mid-morning, no one came near her.

CHAPTER 2

Let My Tears Roll

Now, a few nights later, Avalon waited from her seat in the wagon, listening for the sounds of the camp to die down. She leaned toward the window until muffled conversations drifted into silence and she was sure nearly everyone was asleep. The moon had risen, but clouds had soon obscured it, leaving little light to shine down on earth.

She pulled her cloak around her, glad for the cover it gave to her odd posture just in case anyone checked on her. Then she maneuvered her right ankle to rest on her other knee and strained to lean down until her mouth could reach the large knot tied around her ankle.

This was the third full night she had spent as a prisoner in this convoy. The first night was the night of her abduction, and though they had pushed on through the darkness without stopping to make camp, Avalon had been too distraught to think of anything but her grief and fear. She had trembled for hours, soaked in tears, her throat burning from the smoke surrounding the palace, and her head spinning.

Slowly, her mind had cleared. These Cleftans were not abusive. In fact, they largely ignored her, other than the guard who accompanied her wagon, and the thick rope tied to her right ankle. Both ends of it were connected to the guard, preventing her from going too far, even when she went to relieve herself. Trying to untie the knot would only tug at the man and alert him, so she hadn't dared. Besides, she could tell the knot was much too tight for her fingers to wiggle loose. Someone always came by to feed her in the morning and again at eve, pushing a bowl into the wagon discreetly, presumably so she wouldn't be able to see her surroundings. She knew her sisters had been herded away like herself, but she hadn't seen them since that night.

Her mind incessantly screamed questions at her, but she still couldn't answer most of them. She assumed they were heading toward Cleft. She'd recognized the emblem, but Cleft was all the way across Kerrynth, and she knew little about it. What did such a far-away kingdom have against Haven? Her kingdom had always lived peaceably, if not closely, with the rest of Kerrynth. What could Cleft hope to gain from a conquest so far from their land? Still, she hadn't demanded answers or spoken to anyone beyond necessity. She wasn't loud or brave, and right now she was more afraid than ever before. She could get in trouble. Or she could get her sisters in trouble and make this whole situation worse.

Avalon shook her head slightly to clear her mind. There was a lot she did not know, but the one thing she knew was that she had to be brave. *I must escape and find help for my younger sisters.* She could not rescue them on her own right now, but maybe she could persuade others to help her save them. She was going to try.

At night she had taken to painfully gnawing on the rope around her ankle like an animal. She tried to concentrate on the strands under the tight loop. *One fiber at a time.* If she could snap enough, the frayed rope should loosen easily without tugging at the guard, and she hoped she could pull it off if she ever got the chance to flee. It was agonizingly slow work, and her back and neck and jaw ached after just ten minutes of straining, but desperation fueled her. One by one, the fibers snapped, and the guard never even felt the movement.

She sat back for a minute, untwisting herself and stretching. She ran her hands up her bodice, pressing slightly so she could feel the secret gem she had hidden under her dress press into her skin. That was another thing she thought about. Why had Mother been so desperate to give it to her when they were in danger? Was the small thing worth enough that she could pay someone to help her? *But if Mother thought this gem was so important, I can't just spend it.* The only thing that scared her more than running away was getting caught trying, but she couldn't see another way out. She had to take the risk.

Amelie and Raine. I have to do it for them. That thought had become her refrain.

And now she was as ready as she could be. She did not have much of a plan beyond running and staying hidden from the men who were sure to pursue her. She hoped to find refuge, and perhaps even help, from someone she encountered in this kingdom, wherever this was. It was a risk, not only that the Cleftans would catch her again and maybe punish her for the attempt, but that whoever she met would be on friendly terms with Cleft and side with her captors. She chewed her bottom lip. It was a risk she would have to take.

And now was the time. She had been keeping her face glued to the outer window as much as possible without seeming suspiciously eager, trying to get a sense of the land and which direction to head. About an hour before they stopped for the night, she had spotted a village in a valley. Before she could get a clear view or calculate how large the town was, a thick forest had obscured it. The wagons had followed the perimeter of the forest as the road led around it. Trees still loomed, not far beyond their small camp, a shadow blacker than the darkness. The wind had picked up as night fell, and dark clouds had rolled in, hiding the moonlight. Rain threatened, and Avalon willed it to fall so her tracks would wash away. The darkness and the storm would not be ideal for her, but they would also slow anyone chasing her, and that was all that mattered.

Avalon closed her eyes in silent prayer to The One. Mother always said His presence made anything bearable, so Avalon had been praying, relying on that presence as much as she could.

Calmness filled her, now that the moment had arrived. With a deep breath, she rubbed gently at the frayed fibers until her ankle knot loosened considerably. She could ease her foot out now without disturbing the rest of the rope. She moved cautiously toward the door, looking for somewhere to tie the rope so the guard wouldn't notice the unusual slack once she was free. Slowly, she inched the door open, peering into the darkness. The guard had taken his bed under the wagon tonight, probably in anticipation of the storm. Taking tiny, silent breaths, she began sliding her heel out of the rope when she heard the guard mumble. She pulled her hand away and froze.

His head appeared, though it was hard to make out in the dark. "Girl?" he questioned. He sounded tired, but a tinge suspicious.

"I, uh, need the privacies," Avalon said, her mind pivoting.

The man mumbled something about chamber pots, but he rolled out and got up. Avalon headed toward the woods before he led her elsewhere. Surely her plan had failed. If she ran now, she would only have a few minutes' head start before the guard realized she was gone. The wind blew strongly, and she shivered. The air was chilly tonight, as though autumn was eager to come.

I can't do this, she thought in panic. *This won't work.*

She positioned herself behind a tree, trying desperately to calm her breathing. Suddenly, a small glow drew her eyes toward the ground, where something similar to a firefly hovered. But the light was longer than any bug she'd seen in the dark before, and it dashed like a little arrow, pointing behind her, deeper into the woods. Another followed, then another, a small glowing path into the heart of the woods, each tiny light flickering out as the next one came on. They seemed to beckon her, and Avalon knew at that moment she was going to follow. Hesitantly, she eased her foot out of the rope and looped it around a rock on the ground.

She groaned a bit, then said in a voice that was shaky without trying, "I don't feel well."

She hoped it would buy her a few extra minutes of time before the guard got suspicious.

Then she turned and fled into the darkness.

CHAPTER 3

A Flick of Light

Avalon could hardly make out anything in the darkness, not even the trees, and at first she feared running headlong into one. But the tiny lights were staying with her, always just a few feet ahead, and she trusted they were leading her down a clear path. She had no way of knowing whether they were on her side, but she had no other option at the moment, so she could only follow. Her blind faith gave her a speed she would not otherwise have been able to accomplish in the murkiness. The wind had picked up, though it was not as cutting here in the shelter of the woods, and she was glad for it. The rustling and creaking sounds of the swaying trees gave her footsteps some cover.

She tried to listen for a shout or some indication that someone had discovered her absence, but she could make nothing out, so either she was already too far, or it had been a silent discovery and pursuit. Rain drops hit her skin, quickly growing from a light shower to heavy sheets of water. Avalon was soaked through in just a few minutes. Her cloak grew heavy with water and tangled around her legs. She paused for just a moment to shrug out of it, slinging it around her neck and over her shoulders the way a shepherd carried a new lamb. She immediately felt the chilly rain and wind pierce her without its protection. Her little light guides blinked incessantly in front of her face, so she swiped a hand at the water coursing down her face and kept going.

The storm was in full force now, and she could hear nothing but its fury. The going was harder. She grit her teeth against the cold. The Adrenaline which had coursed through her when she escaped was wearing off slowly, leaving exhaustion in its wake. The ground was slick and sometimes muddy. Her cloak only got heavier as time went on, and the strain of trying to see in the darkness was taking its toll. She stumbled, bruising her shoulder as she careened past a tree. The rain hadn't let up yet, but neither had the lights. She would keep following as long as she could move, and hopefully they would lead her to somewhere to hide. She was sure the Cleftan soldiers would search the forest, if not now, then in the morning.

Suddenly, the lights disappeared.

Avalon stopped short, fear gripping her as the darkness swallowed her and she realized how immensely alone she was. Her thoughts swirled, and she tried to grab at one to make sense of it, to make a plan of some sort, but a crash of ground-shaking thunder made her jump instead.

And then they were back. The flash of lightning that followed the thunder momentarily blinded her, but when her eyes adjusted again, she could see them. The lights worked together to form a perfect circle. They were further ahead than before, and they seemed to be trying to show her something.

She hurried forward. The trees thinned, and as she got closer to the lights, she could feel herself leaving the woods altogether. Now she could see the lights were illuminating the knocker on a large, heavy wooden door. A quick glance told her the door was the opening in an enormous stone wall. Some kind of fortress? Was it the entrance to the city? The rain was coming down heavily, so she could not see far in any direction. The lights blinked, calling her attention to the knocker again. She raised her arm and lifted the heavy metal. The lights dimmed slowly.

"Thank you," she breathed quietly to them, whatever they were.

Haven was not a place of enchantment or magic. Avalon had heard of such things in other kingdoms, but she had always comforted herself by pretending the stories weren't real. Still, this had seemed magical all right. She just prayed it was from a kind source. Mother had always said magic was dangerous. Avalon let the knocker fall. The thud resounded dully. Who would hear her over this storm? Desperately, she grabbed the metal again, slamming it against the wood a few more times, trying to summon those behind the walls, but fearing she would only summon those behind her somewhere in the woods.

The barred window high at the top screeched open. Light flickered through it.

"Who enters?" a wary voice demanded.

"I'm—I'm Avalon, Princess of Haven. I need help."

She was met by silence. "Please," she pleaded. *I must sound ridiculous*, she realized. But it was the truth. "Cleft attacked us four days ago. They captured me. I escaped, but I need help," she repeated.

There was some movement, and a few moments later, the door opened, though just barely. Arms reached out and pulled her inside, then the door was shut again, almost before she cleared it.

Two guards sized her up, their features alert, waiting for a possible attack. Perhaps they thought she was the distraction. But nothing happened, and after a few minutes, they seemed satisfied. Behind them rose the dark stone walls of a castle. The men led her through a courtyard, then into a sheltered hall, where they questioned her.

"You say you are the princess of Haven?"

She nodded.

The two men exchanged glances. "What happened?"

Avalon pushed her sopping blonde hair off her face. "My palace was attacked four days ago. Soldiers captured me and my sisters and have been traveling with us ever since. We were heading west, toward Cleft, I think. Tonight I saw a chance to flee. I came through the forest." She pointed vaguely toward the wall where she had entered.

"The Black Forest?" The taller soldier seemed skeptical.

Avalon shrugged. It had certainly been black. She was shivering now, and she could barely control the shaking.

"No one enters the Black Forest, especially at night," the soldier continued, looking at his fellow for support.

The second soldier raised his eyebrows in agreement, but said, "Haron, she's shaking. She needs to be cared for. We can verify everything later. She seems harmless enough right now. And who would be out in a storm like this if they weren't desperate?"

Haron nodded, called another guard to take his place, and then went to alert the castle.

A few minutes later, the guards escorted Avalon inside. Candles glowed from every sconce in the entry, offering a warm reprieve from the wind. A worn red carpet extended through the main hall, and there were gold fixtures on the walls, but the gray stone walls were otherwise stark.

A maid stepped toward her. "Oh child," she said sadly at the sight of Avalon's dripping ensemble. She draped a blanket over her shoulders, and Avalon wanted to cry at the warmth.

"Thank you," she murmured.

Another figure appeared from the shadowy interior of the castle. The tall woman peered curiously at Avalon. She was pretty, though she was frowning. Lines around her eyes hinted at her age, but her brown hair was shiny and youthful, pulled into a large simple pouf.

"How strange to get a visitor on a night like this, especially one who claims to be a princess," she said, her green eyes traveling down Avalon's length. She addressed the maid over her shoulder. "She certainly needs cleaning up. See to her needs, Mava. Take her to the bedroom upstairs in the west wing. Once you have her in a bath, please come see me for further instructions."

"Yes, Your Majesty," Mava murmured.

The Queen offered Avalon a polite smile. "You are Avalon Demar, I am told. I am Queen Lilian of Ethereal. Mava will take care of you, and once you are ready, we extend an invitation for you to dine with us. Perhaps we can hear more of your plight then."

"I am most grateful," Avalon responded genuinely, finishing with a polite curtsy, though she was chagrined by her bedraggled appearance. She hadn't expected to meet royalty tonight.

The Queen simply turned and flowed back out of sight. Mava put her hand on Avalon's arm, leading her gently up the stairs and into the west wing. The upstairs hall was dark and chilly, but Mava lit some sconces along the way, lending an eerie light to their path. The bedroom was at the very end of the hall. A large window took up most of the far wall. The rain was still falling outside, though some of the ferociousness of the storm seemed to have abated.

Avalon looked despairingly down at the floor where her wet clothing was still creating puddles around her, but Mava waved her hand.

"It's just water. Nothing that won't dry. Wait a moment whilst I get this fire going, and then we will get you dried out and warm, dear."

True to her word, within a few minutes, a fire was crackling, and a warm bath had been prepared. Mava began helping Avalon peel off her dress, and Avalon suddenly remembered the pea-sized gem. She made an awkward grab at herself before it rolled away, but the action seemed to go unnoticed. Mava turned to test the water and Avalon shoved the small crystal into her mouth, holding it in her cheek.

Please don't slide down my throat, she willed the tiny thing, *even if you are like a pea.*

The warm water was wonderful on her cold skin, and feeling clean after so long was simply heavenly. Avalon enjoyed just soaking, letting the water drain away her tension, but when Mava left to see the Queen, she tried to think of somewhere to hide the tiny gem that wasn't on her person. The room was spacious. Her tub had been placed in front of the fireplace. The bed sat in the middle of the room with a small table beside it. The enormous window had shutters, but no curtains, and there was a wardrobe and a vanity on the other side. Everything was of fine quality, but there were no adornments. It was practical and comfortable, but certainly not effusive. Avalon decided on the bed, planning to stow the pea beneath the mattress once she had the chance.

Less than an hour later, Avalon followed Mava back down the stairs. Her wet clothes had all been taken away for washing, and Mava had produced replacements. The gown Avalon wore now was simple. The soft blue, lightweight fabric flowed around her legs to the floor. It was plain, but comfortable, and even the slippers they had given her felt soft. Being dry again was glorious. She had left her hair loose to dry, a headband the only adornment she wore. She was told their Majesties usually took tea before bed, and upon their request, she was to join them. Avalon's eyes were heavy, and she was surprised that their Majesties kept such late hours. But perhaps her trek through the forest had not taken as long as it had seemed. She couldn't guess the time, but refreshments sounded good. She was quite hungry.

She could hardly believe she had made it to safety so quickly and was being received so easily and warmly. With a flash of guilt, she thought of Amelie and Raine, still in the wagons. Had they heard of her escape? Did they know it was for them?

I would never leave you, her thoughts called out to them. *This is all for you. I only left to save you.*

Her warm bath and the upcoming meal made her feel even worse. Should she have forgone all that and just begged for assistance immediately? Biting her lip, she scolded herself. What a terrible sister she was. Well, she certainly wouldn't miss this opportunity. She would have an audience–with a King and Queen, no less–and she would use it to plead her case.

CHAPTER 4

Stormy Winds Blow

A footman announced Avalon's name quietly as she entered the parlor. The King actually rose and inclined his head to her, smiling widely.

"Welcome, Princess. I am His Majesty King Henry Rearevgard of Ethereal. My Queen, Lilian, and my sons, Princes Joran and Golan." He motioned to the others seated around the tea table. "You must be hungry by now. Well, Alice whips up some wonders in the kitchen. You're in for a treat!"

Avalon couldn't help but return his smile, warmed by his goodwill. Surely he would help her.

"Certainly, enjoy." The Queen inclined her head, gracious but reserved, as she had been earlier. "And we're eager to hear your story," she added, though Avalon thought it was more a challenge than an invitation.

"Thank you so much for allowing me to shelter here. You rescued me." Avalon's throat tightened with emotion, and she pulled her tumbler to her lips.

"Eat first," the King ordered gently.

And she did. Hunger ransacked her at the sight of the pudding and porridge, and she had to call on all her self control to just nibble politely.

After a few minutes, the prince–Golan, she thought it was–spoke up. She had glanced at the brothers discreetly. Joran, the other one, was tall. His hair was light and long, tossed back from his handsome face. He looked amused and sure of himself. Golan's face was square and framed by closely cropped light brown curls.

He turned dense green eyes on her now. "It's strange you made it to Blackstone and not the village, as if you entered from the rear. What road did you travel?"

Avalon willed her tongue not to stick. "I don't know the road we traveled. I was locked inside the carriage. I think we were not always following the main road." She was wary to mention the Black Forest again after the guards' reactions earlier.

She decided it was time to make her request. "Your Majesties, I am grateful to The One for bringing me to the safety of your castle. Thank you for the tea and the room for tonight. I have never been so frightened as I was before I got here."

Her gaze glanced toward the door and her mind to the storm beyond, the thick blackness that had seemed to swallow her as she tore through it blindly. "I need your help."

Queen Lilian studied her impassively, though a certain hardness crept behind her eyes. The King raised his eyebrows and nodded for her to continue.

Avalon's look covered everyone at the table. "The soldiers took all three of us, my sisters and I. Four nights ago they infiltrated our palace and kidnapped us. I don't know how they got in or what they were after. We haven't had any trouble with Cleft, as far as I know, and they have never had much connection to Haven on account of the distance."

She took a steadying breath. Despite all her lessons in conversation and speech, being the center of attention while talking made her nervous. "I don't know where they were taking us or what their plans were. They threw me in a carriage around midnight, and I saw them doing the same with my sisters, Amelie and Raine. Amelie is only twelve."

Joran sat back, regarding her from a distance. Golan tilted his head. "How do you know they were Cleftans?" he asked.

"Well, I...I just assumed because I recognized the emblem on their uniforms to be from Cleft, at least I think so," she stammered. "It's a blue mountain rising out of waves."

Golan and the King both nodded.

"How many were in the raiding band that took you all captive?" probed the King.

"There were five carriages. I was alone in mine, except for a guard who was always outside. I was tied to him. I have not seen my sisters or heard about them since the moment we were being loaded. No one told me anything about where we were going or what had happened, or, or anything." She clenched her jaw to stop the nervous stammer.

"I am not familiar with Haven," the King said thoughtfully. "Although our lands are not many days travel apart, most of my alliances are with the kingdoms south of here, Terind and such. I know of King Jasper, but I had not heard of his daughters." He broke his distant gaze and brought his eyes to her face.

"*Is he probing? He doesn't believe me!*" Avalon thought, but the King's eyes were respectful and kind, the wrinkles forming around them giving him a jovial look.

"Tell us about your kingdom," Golan said, his eyes unblinking on her face. He didn't smile, but he seemed genuinely interested.

"And how you escaped your captors," added Joran, sarcasm hovering around his statement.

Avalon's hopes dropped to her stomach. This royal family seemed suspicious, and she did not have a way to prove her story or even her royalty.

She took a breath, trying to calm the tightness in her chest and throat. "I am Avalon Demar, oldest daughter of King Jasper and Queen Heather. My father was the crown prince of Haven and has been the king since his father passed away when I was six. I have two sisters, Raine, who is fifteen, and Amelie, who is only twelve. Haven has not been involved in any disputes for at least ten years," she added. "Especially not with Cleft. Most of our trade and alliances are with the Earth Kingdoms in the North. I have not traveled to Ethereal before, nor have I been to Cleft." *Stop rambling.*

"If you need to question me, I will answer any questions you have about my family or history. You must believe me. My sisters need help. If you would just dispatch a band of guards or some soldiers, I am sure they could overtake the Cleftans, and then you would see I am telling the truth."

She tried to gauge the reactions her jumbled speech had raised. Spirits, talking was not her strength. The King nodded his head understandingly. Golan leaned slightly forward, his green eyes intense, and Joran was studying her face, his own emotions impassive. Queen Lilian's lips were slightly pursed, but then, quite suddenly, she smiled.

"My dear, of course we will help you."

Avalon glanced quickly at her, surprised that the cool queen was the first to agree.

"We will try to find your sisters and perhaps even rescue them if we are able, but it is too late tonight. Those carriages must also stop for the night, am I right?"

Avalon nodded once, suddenly wary of agreeing. Something in the Queen's sweet tone tightened her stomach.

"Then no time will be wasted. Rest here tonight. In the morning, we will discuss further scouting and rescue measures."

With that, Queen Lilian dabbed her mouth with her napkin, then raised her hand at the maid hovering in the background to clear the table. She rose, excused herself, and with a slight nod, glided out of the room.

Avalon entered her large bedroom, feeling unnerved by the long walk down the dark, deserted hall. She headed toward the bed to sink down on it, but surprise jolted her out of her forlorn reverie. The bed had grown while she was gone. Mattresses had been piled on each other, making the top too high to reach from the floor. She reached out, counting mattresses as her fingers ran over them. They were thin pallets, not the plush luxurious ones she was used to, and she realized as she reached up to finish her count that there were actually twenty. A step stool stood at the foot of the bed. Gingerly, she stepped up on one foot, surveying the top of her mattress tower.

A soft knock at the door brought her quickly back to the floor. The door opened a crack and Mava slid her head through. "Ah, you have returned already. Was the fare enjoyable?" She entered the room, a blanket over her arm.

"Yes, thank you. It was satisfying. Mava, I have never seen a bed made like this. Is this often done in Ethereal?"

Mava glanced at the tall bed, then back, not quite meeting Avalon's eyes. "It's often done here at Blackstone Castle, Princess. The Queen enjoys making her guests comfortable."

"Oh. It is almost frightening to sleep so high off the ground. But I am sure it will be pillow-soft," Avalon hurried to be kind.

"Well, child, I've brought you an extra blanket. That storm brought on a bit of a chill. Is there anything else you need before you retire? Would you like help out of your dress? There is a fresh nightgown on the table there." She motioned to the vanity.

"If you could undo the buttons, I can manage the rest."

Then, with her back to the woman, Avalon ventured, "What is Queen Lilian like, Mava?"

"My child?"

"I just want to know if she will help me. She has been kind," Avalon hurried to add, "But I do not think she trusts me, and she said we couldn't discuss any rescue measures until the morning. I don't know what my sisters are going through right now. I just want to help them, but now I'm here, and they've moved on, and I can't help them."

She had another thought. "Maybe the Cleftans are looking for me. If they came here, do you think the King and Queen would protect me? Have I put them in danger?" She swung around to face the maid.

Mava just shook her head. "The Queen is known for her good sense," was all she said, leaving Avalon's questions hanging. "Now, I'll leave this sconce burning. Just put it out before you go to bed. There is a candle and a match there on the vanity if you need it tonight."

She left, and Avalon dropped the blue dress to the floor, exhaustion making every move leaden as she put on the nightgown and ascended the step to her outrageous bed.

Although she was frustrated with her helplessness to aid her sisters and worried about tomorrow and about her family, tiredness was stalling her thoughts and numbing her senses. The Adrenaline rush of her escape had long ago vaporized, and she felt too weak to keep her eyes open. She hadn't checked her pea jewel before climbing up, but surely it was still safe under the original mattress where she'd shoved it before leaving the room. She lay back on the pillows, surveying the room from her perch halfway up the wall.

Like a bird. Her eyes fell shut.

A slicing pain shot through her arm, and she jolted in the darkness.

CHAPTER 5

Color Me Purple, Red, and Blue

Her heart thundered in her ears as she cowered in the corner of the bed. A few seconds ticked by, and nothing happened. Her arm still stung, but there was no noise or movement. Her eyes began adjusting to the darkness and the faint glow of the dying fire.

What was that? What happened? Where am I?

It took a while for her brain to place her whereabouts in consciousness. The dark castle, the impassive queen, the towering bed. She rubbed her arm gently, easing the burn, which was slowly fading. Maybe it was a dream. There was no other presence in the room. Still, she was afraid. Shakily, she climbed down and lit the candle on the vanity, holding it high to shine into the corners.

Nothing was amiss. No concealed soldier was hiding to reach out and grab her. She went to the door, put her ear to the wood and listened. All was quiet. The door was not locked, but there was no key in sight. She wished there was something she could wedge in front of the door, but all she could see except the step ladder she needed to get back into bed was the stool at the vanity. She put it in front of the door. It might at least make some noise and wake her if anyone were to open the door.

She wished she could keep the candle lit, but it was the only one, and it would burn out within an hour, anyway. What if she actually needed it later?

She let out a breath, blew out the candle, and got back into bed. No sooner had she put her knee onto the bed than pain like a hot metal rod shot through it. She collapsed as her leg gave out, pain traveling down it. Her breathing was rapid, and she whimpered against the deep burn, willing it to ease.

She lay as still as she could, barely breathing, until the pain ebbed. *What is wrong with me?*

She scooted higher on the bed, easing her leg along. After interminably long minutes in the dark, worrying, hurting, and afraid, she finally felt drowsiness descending on her again.

Gratefully, she rolled onto her side, thankful to lose her fears in sleep, but was jerked awake by the pain in her side. Though it was duller this time, it was enough to wake her, and it still hurt.

Tears trickled out of her eyes. What kind of cursed place was this, where her desperation was met with suspicion, and the only lavishment was her bed, which seemed alive and hostile?

The nightmare is not over, her mind whispered, fueling more tears to splash down to her pillow. She lay curled stiffly, afraid to move, waiting for dawn.

Mava came in not long after daybreak and seemed surprised to see Avalon sitting on the floor, her knees drawn up and her back against the bed. She was staring off into the corner and barely acknowledged Mava's entrance.

"Are you all right, child?" Mava bent forward and reached a hand to the Princess' forehead, her eyebrows pointing down.

"Princess?" she asked, when Avalon did not respond.

Avalon blinked. "I am tired," she whispered.

"Were you not comfortable last night? Were you in need? You could have rung for me," Mava said. Her brown hair, streaked with graying strands, was pulled back from her face. She spoke kindly, but there was a weariness in her posture and a flatness in her eyes that kept her from being too warm.

Avalon's chin trembled slightly, and she fought against her wobbly emotions. "The bed was most uncomfortable. Every time I moved, something hurt me. Like someone hid needles, or, or knives, all over the bed." She raised her sleeve, uncovering a swollen bruise above her elbow. "It was a long night, and I could not rest, and I am exhausted."

I'm also worried about my family, but I can't leave. I'm alone, I don't know where to go, and I don't think the Rearevgard family is eager to help me. I don't even know if they believe anything I've said.

Tears swelled in her eyes again, too deep to breathe back down. They rolled out slowly. She hid her face between her knees and arms. Her back shuddered as she sucked in a quivering breath.

Mava shook her head sadly, then gazed out toward the window, lost in thought for a bit. She pursed her lips and bent down again. Avalon felt the maid's hand run down her long, blonde hair.

"Oh, Princess. Things will come right in the end. They always do."

Avalon shook her bent head.

"They do. You have to believe that," she said more sharply. Then added, "*I* have to believe it. Now, stand up. I am going to bring you fresh water to wash up, then I'll help you dress and do your hair. And let me see what I can find for those bruises. I am sorry to hear about your discomfort. I'll do my best to remedy that." Her tone was cheery, though the emotion seemed forced.

Avalon stood, and Mava stoked the fire, then left. Avalon studied the room more closely in the morning light, trying to find signs of magic or haunting or curses, anything to explain her night.

Besides her family and the pain from last night, there was something else weighing heavily on her, something she couldn't breathe, even to the maid. Especially not to the maid. As soon as the first light had broken over the horizon, Avalon had forced her weary body up, moving cautiously on the edge of the bed until she could step down. She'd plunged her hand under the bottom mattress, pushing her fingers forward under the heavy tower of bedding, searching for the gem she had hidden there the night before.

She tensed, wary of the strange pain, and struggled to move her arm beneath the mattresses. Her fingertips finally brushed the small gem, and she withdrew it. Her eyes doubled in size as she stared in horror at the pea in her palm.

It wasn't hers. It wasn't the same. The small jewel she had managed to hide and keep safe for the last few harrowing days had shone a transparent light green and was polished smooth. Instead, the jewel that lay in her palm now was a dark opaque green, the color of a pond too long stagnant. In place of the smooth roundness, this one had tiny prismatic edges. In the center, there was a tiny pinpoint of light. It was glowing from within.

She couldn't tear her eyes away, unable to comprehend the meaning. Was it possible her pea was still under there? She shoved her hand back under the mattresses, all the way past her elbow, stretching her fingers, but felt nothing.

Was my gem stolen? When all the mattresses were brought in while I was at tea, did someone find it as they made the bed? Or perhaps it rolled out.

She got down to her hands and knees, stooping her head to look under the vanity and in every corner. Thanks to the sparse furnishings, there weren't many potential hiding places, but the early light was still dim, and she felt frustrated as she searched. Finally, she gave up, shoving the changed jewel back under the mattress, and sitting back against the bed.

She held a hand up to her forehead, thinking. *If mine is gone, then how did this one end up here? Maybe something changed my pea. Maybe it was magic I felt last night.* The edges of this pea were cut, after all. Surely something like that would hurt if she got in the way.

She pondered her situation. She had been so hopeful last evening when she had made it through the forest, through the storm, and ended up at Blackstone Castle. She thought of the small lights leading her through the trees, the ones she had trusted for her escape. Now she wondered if it had been a trap.

There were too many mysteries here. Her lady's maid spoke vaguely, and her bedroom was strangely sparse for a castle, except for the bed itself, which was ridiculous. The Queen was hard to decipher. And some strange magic had tortured her all night. She didn't know anything about magic, except for what she'd been taught. *Stay away from it. Don't talk about it. Magic is dangerous.* Occasionally, a few rumors would filter in from other kingdoms, but her mother had always discouraged them in an effort to keep her daughters' minds safe.

Now Avalon felt like she had walked onto a stage, accidentally becoming part of a play in which she didn't have a part. She had no idea what to do.

CHAPTER 6

Let Me Taste the Summer

By early afternoon, Avalon had neither seen nor heard from the King or Queen, and she was tense and impatient. Breakfast had been served in her room, and although she had been escorted to lunch, she had dined alone in a small dining room. Now she was back in her room, and she sat on the window ledge, contemplating her next move.

She could see the Black Forest beyond the castle walls. The tree line was distinct, not a single tree out beyond the others, and they grew close and tall, building a formidable wall of foliage. Even in the daylight, the shadows from within seemed strangely dark, as though no sunlight at all filtered through the canopy of leaves. The forest was large, stretching beyond what she could see. She cast her eyes in every direction, wondering exactly where she had started to run and what the route of her trek looked like from here.

The castle grounds were quiet. Although well-trimmed, they appeared little used. Except for a guard or two making rounds, and the two stationed at the gate, which was tightly closed, no one else was stirring. The gate in sight was a back entrance, she felt sure, since it faced nothing but the wall of trees a few yards beyond it, but it seemed eerie that no servants were headed into town or coming back, or even visible on the grounds.

Why hadn't the King acknowledged her all day? The Queen had said they would send out a patrol in the morning, *hadn't she?* Even if something else had come up, Avalon thought they should have at least notified her about the delay.

Finally, feeling irritated at doing nothing and all the unanswerable questions bombarding her thoughts, Avalon stood. She smoothed the long white silk of the gown Mava had brought in this morning and marched toward her bedroom door. If no one else would help her with information, she would find it herself. She had been treated decently since she arrived, and no one had insinuated that she should not leave her room, *so I have no reason to feel guilty, no reason I should not go exploring,* she told herself, trying to shake her nerves about getting caught.

She wandered more slowly down the hall than she had before while accompanied by Mava. Her bedroom was at the very end. There appeared to be four other bedrooms before it, or at least four other doors like hers in the hall, but they were all closed. The left wall was blank dark stone. The torches that were lit scantily at night were extinguished right now, although Avalon still had to peer hard to make things out in the dusky shadows. At the end of the hall, stairs swept to the left, and there was nowhere else to go unless she descended them. At the bottom of the stairs, another staircase met, the other one also ascending, but in the opposite direction from which she had come. She assumed it led to another wing, maybe the royal family's suites.

She did not want to be caught snooping too closely to their personal spaces, so she followed the path toward the room she had taken lunch in earlier. That dining room was a more intimate version of a grander one she found at the end of the hall. The big room was empty, but the doors stood open, a large table looming on a raised platform in the middle. It seemed to command her toward it, and she ventured to the doorway, furtively poking her head inside and glancing in both directions. The table could seat fifty, she estimated. Each place was set with gleaming utensils and dishes. The crystal sparkled, and the gold shimmered in the afternoon sunlight. A long red cloth draped the table and hung to the floor. Three ornate glass windows stood with pride on the opposite wall, topped with heavy burgundy drapes pulled back with braided tassels. This room, finally, looked typical of a castle.

Still, everything was eerily quiet. Sudden chills crept along Avalon's arms. *Where is everyone?*

She spotted the servant's entrance to the kitchen in the corner of the imposing room and headed resolutely toward the door. If she could not find the King himself, nor any of his family, she would speak to the servants.

Involuntarily, she breathed in relief when she opened the door and she came upon a scene of life. The back door of the kitchen was thrown open, and the window was uncovered, so light poured into the room. There were three scullery maids moving about, chatting casually. No one even looked her way when the door first opened, but when she stood there uncertainly, her silence must have descended on the atmosphere, because all at once, everyone stopped and stared at her.

"Good afternoon. I am Avalon of Haven," she said, leaving off her title at the last moment.

Surprise painted each face. The oldest woman there, a full-figured robust woman who was probably over fifty, but looked like time had stopped for her a decade earlier, was covered in flour up to her elbows and down her apron. She seemed the most startled of all. There was another woman, maybe half her age, with a clear pretty face, who smiled, despite the question in her eyes. And then the youngest, a girl really, started toward her. The girl's blonde hair floated out in tendrils from her mob cap. Her eyes were a turquoise blue, and her lips full and pink.

"Oh, you're the Princess," she said, negating Avalon's attempt at secrecy. She even curtsied. "We heard about you last night. Heard you just showed up all by yourself during that terrible storm. Did you really?"

"I, uh, yes, I did." Avalon cleared her throat.

The girl had come toward her. She was striking, the natural colors in her face bright against the white of her uniform. She reminded Avalon of a painted doll, though her features were much rounder and fuller than the little pinched noses and lips on the pewter dolls.

"I'm Alice." And she smiled, a full beautiful smile that spread across her entire face and swept up everything in its path.

Avalon smiled back.

"This is Martha." Alice threw her smile toward the larger lady. "She is the cook at Blackstone Castle. And Jenna is also a scullery maid. I am the Royal Baker," she added. "Now what brings you into the kitchen, Your Highness? Are you in need of something?"

"I only have a few questions, Alice. I did arrive here last night. I was on my own because I was seeking refuge. I had run away from a band of Cleftans who kidnapped me from my home in Haven a few days ago. They stopped for evening camp, and I got out of my shackles and away from the guard, so I headed into the woods just as it started raining."

All three sets of eyes widened. Alice leaned forward. "You went into the Black Forest?"

"Yes. I had nowhere else to go. I was desperate. I thought I could lose them there and maybe find a village and someone to help me before I was caught. I had to risk it."

She took a breath. Then curiously asked, "Is the Black Forest dangerous?"

Alice threw a look back at her friends. "Oh, Your Highness, the Black Forest is the only place magic still exists in Ethereal, but the magic there is dark. No one understands it, but it is deadly. The Black Forest is forbidden, because the few who did venture there never returned. There have been terrible stories too."

"What kind of stories?"

Alice looked down for a moment, and when she looked back, her eyes were guarded. "Even if you get too close to the forest, there is danger. I would know."

Avalon tilted her head in question.

"It is a long story. Thankfully, I'm safe. Others have spoken of strange lights, trees that grow before your eyes, that grow limbs that twist around you and hold you prisoner. And, of course, the hidden holes."

"I saw lights, Alice." Avalon's excitement rose. "I did see lights. They reminded me of fireflies, but they were different. They streaked like arrows. I followed them," she admitted. "They seemed to point the way, and I had nothing to lose. That's how I got here. It was so dark and raining so hard, I couldn't see a thing. It was hard to keep my eyes open, let alone find a path. I just kept heading toward the lights, and they showed me the way here."

Jenna gasped. Martha's eyebrow twitched. Alice's round eyes swelled rounder.

"Princess, if you don't mind my forwardness in saying so, you are either very lucky, or very special."

"Oh, well, I hope both. I was lucky to end up here, or at least I thought so."

Alice raised her eyebrows. "But now?"

"Now I feel uncertain. Alice, you are the first person to be open with me since I got here. Do you know Mava?" She didn't wait for Alice's nod. "She has been my lady's maid. She is kind, but she avoids my questions. And the King was quite kind, but I don't think the Queen believed me. I haven't seen either of them today. In fact, I've hardly seen anyone. I was beginning to feel afraid."

Martha cleared her throat and gave Alice a pointed look when the girl glanced back at her. Alice just smiled widely.

"Don't worry, Martha, the pastries will get done before dinner. I still have several hours, and I've already mixed the dry ingredients. Let me show Her Highness her way around the castle so she doesn't feel so much a stranger here. I will return in less than an hour." And without waiting for permission, she slipped through the dining room door, pulling Avalon with her.

Alice ran on light feet to the hall, pausing just outside the dining room to giggle. Avalon joined her, bewildered but amused.

"Oh Princess, you have given me a wonderful excuse to get out of the kitchen for a bit. Martha takes her job seriously. On most days, she has us there from breakfast preparations until after evening tea is served and cleaned up with hardly a break. It's amazing just how much she can find to keep us busy."

"Are you really the Royal Baker?"

"Yes, I am. I've been baking since I was ten years old, and the King is fond of my desserts. My mother works in the kitchen at home. I ended up spending a lot of time there as a child and eventually wiggled my way into experimenting with ingredients myself. The first thing I ever baked was a cherry tart, and I didn't do it all myself. I helped the former Royal Baker, Ma Paley. She was kind to me, even when I was underfoot, and thanks to her,

I learned how to bake. She died last year. That's when I was promoted." Alice's lashes softened around her eyes, shrouding them in inward sadness.

"I am sorry to hear that, but happy for you to be in such a position at a young age."

"Thank you, Princess."

"I don't mind if you just call me Avalon," the Princess said on impulse. "This isn't my castle, and you aren't my servant. In fact, I would prefer it. It's nice to just be Avalon without the title once in a while. Now, where was home for you?"

"Oh, it's still home. I was talking about the Grand Castle in Lilt. The Royal family usually presides there. This is simply their summer home. They are only here for a few weeks of the year, the hottest weeks. It's cooler here, on the other side of the mountains, and the village is smaller. Much less to worry about for such a busy family. Only a few of the staff travel with them. This castle is much smaller, and the demands here are lighter, you see."

That made sense. The lack of grandeur, the silence of the place, the casually guarded gate.

"I didn't know that. I know nothing about Ethereal. I have never been here before. My father trades only with the kingdoms north of us. My mother once said that Haven used to be closely tied with the western and southern kingdoms, even more than the northern kingdoms, but that times have changed."

They had entered another wing of the ground floor.

"This is the King's Courtroom." Alice motioned to a set of tall double doors which were firmly closed. "He conducts all his business and affairs here. It joins his library, which isn't as extensive as the one in Lilt, but still grand. I would show you, but it's usually locked. These other rooms are for private meetings, a powder room to refresh, a tea room particularly for the Queen to socialize with other ladies." She continued down the hall, pointing at doors as she talked.

Although this side of the castle seemed much more alive because of the frequent windows which allowed sunlight to flow in, most of the doors were still closed, and the emptiness was eerie. At least Alice was there to chatter.

"Alice, do you know where the royal family is today? I was quite hoping to speak to them. They agreed last night to help find my sisters. I was hoping they might even help me with the means to return home. I need to know how my kingdom is, if my parents..." She was afraid that finishing the sentence would make the horrors a reality.

She was afraid her parents were dead, but without actually knowing, she chose to keep hoping. If the attack had been minor, though, wouldn't the Havenian army have pursued the Cleftans?

"The King left at daybreak, Your Highness, and the Queen is abed. She suffers often from headaches." Alice looked apologetic.

"Will the Queen take messages? I just want to know if she or the King sent anyone out to search for my kidnappers or to find my sisters."

Alice shook her head slowly.

"When she is unwell, she refuses to see anyone or hear any matters. Even political matters that need her approval have to be put off until the next day. I'm sorry."

Avalon breathed in, trying to think. She had to control her feelings, the panic and anger that threatened to make her desperate, but she said, "It's not your fault, Alice. What about the princes? Are they here?"

"Yes, Princess. I mean, Avalon. Prince Joran often goes out, but he will probably appear for supper. Prince Golan sometimes cannot be found. He likes solitude." She giggled a little. "But I know some of his usual places. I'll show you the rest of the castle and the grounds, and if you would like to speak to him, maybe we can locate him on our way. Then I need to get back to the kitchen, or Martha will have me for supper." Another giggle.

They continued through the castle. Avalon had guessed correctly that the other wing across from her own was for the royal suites. Alice did not take her up there, presumably because even servants should not be so near the personal spaces of the Rearevgards without a purpose. Or perhaps she was merely giving the Queen a wide berth out of courtesy.

They passed the servants' quarters downstairs, and the laundry room where several other women were working. The second floor was a mezzanine, a parlor which overlooked a ballroom. The ballroom took up the center of the castle, as though it was its very heart, and despite this being a temporary summer residence, it was nearly as large as the royal ballroom at the palace in Haven.

The floor was checkered in gleaming black-and-white tiles. The pattern made Avalon dizzy, looking down on it. Golden gilding around the ceilings depicted ornate scrolling. The parlor above the ballroom was plush, full of overstuffed sofas turned in every direction, chaotic but charming. Small tea tables were also scattered between the couches, and large potted plants bloomed all around the edges of the room.

"This is unique," Avalon commented.

"I love this room," Alice agreed. "It can be full of people, and yet there is always a corner in which to be alone. Three different conversations can be going on, and no one is in anyone's way. It isn't used very often, probably only once or twice a year. Like I said, the Rearevgards use this castle as a place to refresh themselves. They do not hold many parties or meetings here."

The warm air outside felt good on Avalon's face as she stepped outside behind Alice. The sky was clear and bright, holding no evidence of the storm the night before.

"Let's visit the stables first, then I will show you the courtyard and the gardens. You aren't too winded yet, are you?"

Avalon laughed. "No, not at all. This air feels wonderful, and I am enjoying your tour."

The stables had fifty stalls, but weren't nearly as large as the royal stables in Lilt, Alice informed her. The King and Queen had their own personal riding horses, as did the princes. The others were carriage horses, wagon horses for transport, and the messengers' and guards' horses. The stable master was in the far stall, but when Alice announced their presence, he backed out, grinning. He was past middle age, lines striping his thin face, but when he smiled at them, Avalon could have believed his grin and the glimmer in his eyes belonged to a boy less than her own years.

"Alice, to what do I owe the honor of your presence?" he teased.

Alice flashed him a smile, but then grew serious. "Actually, Steward, I am escorting Her Highness here, the Princess of Haven, on a tour of Blackstone."

Steward's eyebrows rose. "My apologies, Your Highness." He lowered his head toward Avalon.

She graciously nodded in return, then added, "Alice has been giving me the most pleasant afternoon." She was pleased that Alice had the foresight to maintain the title of respect in the presence of others. Her mother would give her a pained look of disappointment if she knew Avalon was allowing servants to call her by her given name.

Alice's smile at the compliment took up her entire face. Again, Avalon marveled at the bright colors of her eyes and lips against her complexion.

"Thank you, Princess Avalon. Now, Steward, would you be so kind as to introduce the Princess to the horses? Though I forgot to ask, do you enjoy animals, Your Highness?"

"I do. I own a beautiful mare at home. She is about to foal soon. The stable master says he thought it would be before the month was over." The heavy sadness that hovered around her tried to descend, but she continued. "I would love to meet these fine horses."

Steward's face crinkled again. He looked mischievous when he smiled, and Avalon liked him almost as much as she liked Alice. He took them to each stable, greeting each horse with affection, teasing them like old friends.

"The King and Queen brought twenty horses with them this summer, so our stables are full this year. Ours here don't know what to do with all this company."

He rubbed a gray horse's neck, then pointed at the empty stalls.

"Prince Joran left about two hours ago on Fury. And the King departed this morning on his steed."

"Please pardon me for asking, but do you know where he went? Or mostly, when he will return? I was hoping to meet with him about a matter of importance as soon as possible."

Steward gazed at the sky through the stable doors, as though he were studying the time.

"He most likely won't be back until late. He had some saddlebags packed. Looked like he was going hunting, as I recall seeing his hounds following."

Had the King really gone on an excursion while she was waiting for his aid?

"If I would like to go for a ride sometime, which horse may I use?" Avalon asked, ignoring her irritation and letting the threads of a plan dance in the back of her mind, like frayed strings on a rope.

"Let's see. Gilly, here, is getting up in age. She is gentle and docile, and quite right for a young lady," he said, pointing out the gray spotted horse. "Depending on how confident you are in the saddle, there is also Acorn, and his brother, Oak, both dependable geldings." He showed her the big brown horses.

"Thank you," Avalon called to Steward as Alice waved goodbye and hurried her out the doors.

"Steward is a darling," she said. "He's not my grandpa, but I used to pretend he was, and he loved it. He played right along. He lives here year round, so I only see him in the summers. I really must get back to the kitchen now. I did promise to have the pastries ready before dinner, and the sun is not waiting. This is the back gate of the castle, the one that opens toward the Black Forest. We servants usually use this entrance, though I believe this is where you happened upon last night."

Avalon nodded, looking up at the castle to locate her bedroom window. A shadow moved inside. The interior was dark from where she was standing in the brightness outside, but she knew she had seen a movement. Although she supposed it was only Mava or a maid tidying things up, a sudden worry pricked her. The pea!

She turned to thank Alice, who was still talking.

"The gardens are quite peaceful. There is even a small pond hidden in the center. It's all surrounded by the trellises covered in ivy, so it's very private, and every good love story has a page that happens there," Alice laughed. "The courtyard is on the other side, as well as the main gates. I must run back to my duties now. Will you be able to find your way? I could walk you back to your chambers if you need."

"No, Alice, there is no need. I can see my window from here, and I know how to get back. Thank you so much for welcoming me and giving me such an enjoyable afternoon. I shall look forward to tasting your famous pastries."

An unexpected shadow crossed Alice's face. She leaned close. "And Avalon," she whispered, "Not all magic is evil. I know what I said in the kitchen seems contrary, but keep trusting the lights. I'm not at liberty to say more, but..." She bit her lip and her eyes darted around. "There are secrets here. Just be careful of the Queen."

Then she gave a little wave and ran back inside. Avalon blinked after her.

CHAPTER 7

I Remember the Sun

Avalon wanted to run after the servant girl and find out what she meant, but perhaps Mava had been in her room looking for her. Maybe she had news. Besides, she wanted to check on the pea. So she turned, retracing her steps back inside and up to her room.

Mava sighed as she pushed open the bedroom door. She had heard Alice talking in the corridor downstairs, and she had said the new Princess' name, so Mava didn't bother knocking.

It seemed Avalon had ventured her way out of the room and somehow met Alice, and, knowing Alice, the Princess would be occupied for a while. Alice was like that, never where she should be, but somehow getting away with it. The King favored her, or at least her desserts, and many of the servants loved her like family, though her only relative was her mother, who was back in Lilt. She was a sweet child, pleasant to the eyes and the spirit, and though she could do some harm with her chatter, it was unlikely that she knew anything too serious to get in trouble.

Unlike me, Mava thought.

She crossed the room, which was empty, as she had suspected. She pulled the top mattress pallet down, then hurried back to the door and locked it. She couldn't be too careful. She hadn't had the chance to retrieve the Queen's treasure this morning, with the Princess in the room, and during lunch, when Avalon had been dining, Mava had been busy elsewhere. Being the most trusted servant had its benefits but its trials as well. It meant she had to fill in as a chambermaid to the new girl for now, since she was the only one the Queen trusted with the mission. It wasn't a mission she exactly relished. She had done it before, countless times.

The Queen always came up with new and creative ways to carry out her plan to find a Gifted royal girl for Prince Joran to marry, but this one was a bit ridiculous. Mava didn't really mind, though, especially since no one had ever been found. That meant no one had really been hurt. But this girl, Avalon, and those bruises this morning...Mava had never seen anything like it. She had told Queen Lilian, of course, even though the Queen was in bed because of her headache.

She gets headaches, that's certain, but if only everyone knew why, Mava thought, chiding herself immediately afterward for the dangerous thoughts. She continued displacing mattresses until she could lift the remaining ones enough to retrieve the green jewel.

When the Queen was having one of her episodes, which often followed her use of the magic, Mava was the only one she would see or allow into her room. Mava had been the Queen's personal maid since she was twenty, which was now that many years ago.

You'd think that after all this time, I would love her, she mused.

Instead, Mava hated her. She knew forced loyalty was necessary for Queen Lilian. There was no other way the Queen could guarantee her secret would be kept and not destroy her.

Because that's what it would do, if it got out.

Even the most loyal of servants sometimes went bad. People were people, plain and simple. They could be bought. They could get distracted by grabbing power. Or they could be threatened into obedience – like Mava.

She did not love the Queen, even though the Queen was her life. For almost two decades now, the Queen had been her one focus and responsibility day in and day out. She knew her better than she had known her own mother, and she knew better than to do anything except obey. And, yet, sometimes even her very trained, very obedient mind grew wild with hopeless plots that would remove her from the Queen's power.

But she wasn't daring enough. Wasn't young enough anymore. Too much time had passed, and what had been lost could not be reclaimed. Long ago, she had resigned to this life. After all, with all things considered, she was still alive and so were her sister and nephew. The Queen had great power, and she knew how to play her cards well. Mava was afraid of her, but, as long as Mava did her bidding and kept her mouth shut, Lilian was bearable. Mava didn't dare expect more.

She held the pile of mattresses up at one corner, stretching to reach under them. There it was. She breathed a sigh of relief, as always, that the tiny pea hadn't rolled away and gotten lost, dropped it quickly into her pocket, and re-stacked the mattresses. She was out of breath and sweating by the time she was done, but she knew she shouldn't linger. She checked out the window where she heard voices floating up. It was Alice and the Princess. Quickly she drew back so she wouldn't be seen, then let herself out of the bedroom and headed to the Queen's chambers.

The Queen was in bed, but she had apparently risen to dress, because she was now clothed in a simple day gown. She was sitting up against a wall of pillows, but her eyes were closed. The room was dark. The light hurt her head, she said.

"Your Majesty." Mava quickly curtsied, the movement as habitual as breathing.

Queen Lilian's eyes fluttered open, and in the moment that she moved from sleep to consciousness, they were soft, and she looked girlish and beautiful. But, just as quickly, they were guarded again, the mellow green hardened into something darker. When Mava had told her of the girl's complaints and the bruises, she had seemed almost excited. Those same wide green eyes had pinched at the corners as she obviously worked through something in her mind, but she hadn't shared her thoughts with Mava.

"Do you have it?" Queen Lilian asked her now.

Mava nodded. The Queen glanced around the room to make sure they were alone.

"Show me and then stow it in the usual place."

Mava pulled the jewel out of her pocket. Her own sharp intake of breath matched the Queen's when she opened her palm to reveal the crystal.

She was speechless. The jewel was...different. It was smooth, as though all the cut edges had been sanded out and re-polished. And it was a light translucent green instead of the murky dark green she had seen so many times.

Queen Lilian lurched forward, then drew her neck back as though she were afraid to get too close.

"Mava, where did you get this?" Her voice was low, but it trembled with an undercurrent of something hideous.

"It was where you asked me to place it last night, Your Majesty. Under the bottom mattress, with the others stacked over it. I had to remove some mattresses to reach under there, but I felt this right away. I simply put it in my pocket so I could hurry and remake the bed while the Princess was out of the room. I didn't even look at it until now." She shut her lips tightly to curb her rambling.

"Help me get up," the Queen commanded in the same low, measured tone. "Help me get up, then please make sure the girl is gone from her chambers and doesn't come near them because I must go there myself."

She reached out slowly and plucked the little jewel from Mava's palm, turning it in the tips of her fingers. Her eyes lit with cunning, and Mava knew she was planning something.

"Summon Joran. I will make sure he keeps her busy for a while. You know, Mava, I think we may have found even more than I had hoped." She smiled, the twisted smile of power. "Yes. Yes, this is definitely the princess I want."

Mava returned to Avalon's room and found her there apparently just arrived. She seemed in much better spirits than she had in the morning because she smiled at Mava and asked, "Were you in here recently, tidying up, perhaps?"

Mava blanched. She dropped her eyes to the polished floor, trying to steady her breath.

"Ah, yes, Your Highness. I was, in fact, just coming in to check on you and see if you needed anything."

"Thank you, but I am quite all right. I had a bit of a stroll with the baker, Alice, just now."

Mava scrambled for a way to get the Princess out of the room. "Did you see the gardens yet?"

"No, actually. Alice had to return to her duties before she showed me."

"Well, I need to clean up in here a bit – change your washing water and bring you your clothes, which have been laundered. Why don't you go out and enjoy the afternoon sun while I finish up? The gardens are lovely this time of day. The walk will improve your appetite for supper tonight, too."

She practically shooed Avalon out the door.

Give Me Something Timeless

Avalon's shoulder blades tensed with the feeling something was not right. She blinked back at her bedroom door, about to turn around and march back in when she heard boots coming up the stairs.

Joran appeared. He broke into a grin and lifted an eyebrow. Her pulse quickened at the surprise of seeing him there when she thought he was still out riding.

"Just the lady I was looking for." He bowed to her. "I hardly had the chance to meet you last night, but I hope I can change that today. Would you be willing to accompany me? I was thinking about a stroll in the garden myself, but it would be dreadfully boring alone."

"I - I - of course," she managed, embarrassment climbing her neck as she faltered. Refusing would be rude, and he was the first person in the family she had encountered all day.

Joran only smiled wider and offered her an arm.

He kept her hand on his elbow the whole way. He was lithe and athletic. She could feel the bulge of his muscles against her fingertips and she...liked it. Despite her other worries, the attention of a handsome young man was distracting.

Once outside, they passed through the main yard.

"Who is training?" Avalon asked, spotting two men in armor engaged in a tussle.

Joran glanced carelessly in the direction she was looking.

"That would be my little brother. He takes things too seriously. He's afraid a few weeks away from the Academy will make him weak." Joran laughed. "First year students are all alike."

The gardens were in full bloom. The flowers were open, soaking up the summer sun.

"These are my favorite gardens," Joran said easily. "The grounds at Lilt are beautiful, but," — and he waved a hand at the leafy trellises and tall hedges creating shaded pathways, — "this is perfect for lovers, isn't it?"

Avalon laughed. Joran caught her eye and winked, leaning close to her ear. "And stolen kisses."

His warm breath fluttered over her skin, and she fought the rise of goosebumps. They reached the lovely pond at the center. She kept her eyes carefully on the water, away from Joran's face. She could feel his sideways glances, and they made her nervous. She wasn't sure how she felt about his attention.

Unexpectedly, he pulled away from her, coming to stand in front of her. He leaned against a bench and crossed his arms, studying her with amusement.

"So, Avalon, did you really escape from a hostage situation?" He leaned forward, his voice dropping low. "Are you really the Princess of Haven?"

Avalon's face fell. He was mocking her.

He stepped forward quickly, regret on his strong features. "Look, I'm sorry. That didn't come out right." He took her hands in his and rubbed his thumbs over the back of them. "I just really want to get to know you. Will you tell me everything?"

Avalon could hardly meet his eyes. He was brazen, but charming, and the way his lips pouted in apology made her heart race. She wasn't sure if she wanted to tell him everything or run away from him.

"We have the afternoon," he invited, motioning to the bench. "Talk to me, Princess."

But then he straightened, his brows furrowing as he looked at her. She stepped back, trying to unravel the sudden confusion that spread over his face. He cleared his throat uncertainly, looking around with blank eyes.

"I-I think I'd rather rest before dinner," she said, that same sense of warning pinching at her shoulders. The isolation of the garden suddenly seemed threatening.

"Of course," he said. He nodded politely, but his easy, teasing manner had vanished. A poisonous look crept into his eyes, though it seemed directed at something far away, not at her.

Prince Joran's goodbye was curt, and Avalon wasn't sure if she was relieved or hurt to be left standing alone by the water.

CHAPTER 9

Standing on Sand

Disappointment filled Avalon again at dinner that evening. Only the princes were present. At least this time, a servant gave them an explanation, saying the Queen was still unwell, and the King had not returned. Joran and Golan were painfully silent during the meal, though Avalon was aware all three of them were sending the others covert glances. Avalon kept her eyes peeled for Alice as dinner was served, but she did not see her. She ate as quickly as she politely could, eager to escape the awkwardness. Afterward, she considered going to the servants' quarters to find her friend, but it was likely Alice would be cleaning up in the kitchen for a while. Avalon's exhaustion after her sleepless night was descending on her like a weight, so instead, she wandered slowly back to her bedroom.

She fought off a chill as she walked through the long, empty hall with its strange shadows and deafening silence. This castle was nothing like the palace in Haven, her home. Things were always busy there. Cheerful. Alive. Bright. She thought of all the flowers that were brought in daily and set in vases in almost every room and corridor. Blackstone was a coffin in comparison, with little colors or furnishing to ease the starkness of the stone.

She lit the candle in her room right away, wanting to ward off the darkness that was descending. She changed without help, then felt for the pea, which still had its strange rough edges. Remembering the brutal pain of the night before, she pulled the top mattress off the stack and laid it against the wall. She felt it gingerly, pressing it with her hands, making sure none of the strange magic was present. She felt nothing but the feathers stuffed inside.

After adding a second pallet, she decided her nest was plump enough to be comfortable. She wanted to lock the door, but she couldn't find a key. She waited for Mava, who would probably appear to ready her for bed. Hopefully, the maid could locate a key for her.

Mava knocked not long afterwards. Avalon opened the door, but only a crack.

"I have already changed for bed. In fact, I am planning to retire now. I was wondering, though, is there a key for this lock? I would feel more comfortable having this door locked at night, seeing as how this is a new place for me, and I am not used to the draughts and creaks of the night."

Mava looked apologetic. "I'm sorry, Princess. I'm afraid I've misplaced the key for this room. But I can post a guard at the door." She offered.

"Yes, please." Avalon wasn't sure that would make her feel much better, but it was something.

Mava nodded curtly and turned away.

Avalon lay down, rubbing her bruises lightly. They had lightened considerably, which made her more sure that some sort of magic had caused them. Regular bruises didn't disappear in a day. But hadn't Alice said that magic had been outlawed a long time ago? Her eyes closed, and she pictured the little mysterious lights in the forest. Tomorrow she hoped the King would be back. She would speak with him. If neither he nor the Queen were available, she would take things into her own hands. She had wasted enough time here today, and she had no intention of sitting around any longer.

She needed to find her sisters. And she needed to get home.

CHAPTER 10

A Song I Remember

Golan watched Avalon leave the dining room. Her simple yellow dress, nearly the color of her hair, was tied with a braided belt around her waist. The fitted sleeves ended at her elbows, widening to long cuts of fabric that hung to her knees.

Joran blew out a soft snort, and Golan jerked toward him.

His brother smirked. "Does she catch your eye?"

"No," Golan said quickly, but he knew it was obvious. He never could lie.

"You did nothing to woo her at dinner," Joran twitched his eyebrow. "If you are interested, speaking at least is the normal thing to do. If you need lessons..."

Golan ignored him. "I saw you in the gardens today," he said, changing the subject.

Joran's smirk darkened. Golan knew his mother had used his brother, but he didn't say it out loud. Joran must have known it too, because he pushed out of his seat with a loud scrape.

"Where are you going?" Golan asked.

"Out."

"Joran, you know–"

Joran spun around, his anger throbbing in the air.

"You don't command me, little brother," he snapped. "And you may think I remember nothing about this afternoon, but I remember some." He leaned closer, taunting. "I was close enough to size the girl up pretty well, and she's too skinny to be much fun, but her breast could fill a man's hand at least."

Golan shot up, unsure why anger surged through him, but his fist was already tightened to land in Joran's face. Except his brother had already staggered away.

Perhaps he was already drunk before he even got to the taverns.

Avalon awoke on her third morning at Blackstone, again impatient to do something. She had seen the King and Queen yesterday, but she was still no closer to home. The King had apologized for his absence, but assured her he had already dispatched a letter to Haven checking on their wellbeing.

The Queen had smiled at her, her lovely face nearly radiant.

"And we sent a patrol to check the roads passing Ethereal on the other side of the Forest. They will be back with news as soon as they have it. Please do not worry about anything. You are welcome here, and I do hope you will enjoy your stay. I had no time to prepare your room before you arrived, but I'm having the servants add comforts today."

The Queen's misgivings about me must have been cleared up, thought Avalon.

Queen Lilian encouraged her to enjoy the grounds, visit the library, and go riding, as she wished. "Prince Joran would be delighted to accompany you," she promised, though his face was sullen when she volunteered him.

In the evening, Avalon had been invited to enjoy a musical performance by a famous minstrel who was scheduled to play for their own private enjoyment. They had all gathered in the mezzanine parlor, close to the short wall that overlooked the ballroom. The musician played for over an hour, waltzing and swaying with his own musical selections. It was very pleasing, and since the family seemed intent on listening and watching instead of conversing, Avalon had been free to her own private thoughts.

She snuck glances at each of the family, particularly the princes. She had to admit Joran was handsome. His flirtations made her uncomfortable, but not in a terrible way. She was still confused about his reaction in the garden, though, the way he had seemed to wake up, and he had barely spoken to her since.

Although there had been talk about her betrothal to Prince Ledhar of Aspenia, no official transaction had taken place. She wasn't against the match. She and Ledhar had gotten along when they had met on several occasions, though the last time she had seen him they had both been younger. He was handsome enough and interesting enough that she felt lucky to have such an acceptable match being made.

There had been other offers too, but since she was just seventeen, the time to take them seriously was just beginning. Most of them had been from over-ambitious parents who wanted their youngest son, much too far down the line ever to be important, to have a union with the eldest Princess of a large kingdom. Avalon had spent a lot of time with other young nobles and royals in her life. She had friends, but she had never had a love-interest, nothing more than an exciting tickle inside or a blush when someone particularly attractive met her eyes unexpectedly or paid her a compliment. She had never spent enough time at once with anyone to fall in love with them. There were numerous parties, balls, meetings, and conferences in which she and others her age had been in attendance, but when they were over, everyone traveled back to their own homes, and any embers soon suffocated.

The only infatuation she had ever experienced was with her father's scribe, merely a servant in their home. He was a few years older than her, extremely handsome, with night black hair and a long nose. He was a quick scribe, scribbling notes with ease, his long legs tucked under the table over which he hunched, and he never missed a syllable, while glancing up occasionally, and sending Avalon's young heart aflutter with a small smile of his impossibly adorable mouth.

One time he had winked, and Avalon's heart had melted. She was just twelve then, but for the next two years, the only man she had dreamed of was Benjamin. She sat with her father as often as possible, especially on busy days when he needed his scribe the most. She loved being with her father, of course, but it was most exciting when Benjamin was there. She watched Benjamin while he worked, trying to be demure and not too open about it, but she knew she probably wasn't hiding the adoration in her eyes. She lived for those secret moments between the King's thoughts when their gazes met.

Once, just before the entrance to the King's study, they had brushed against each other. It was an accident, or maybe it wasn't. Avalon wasn't sure. Perhaps she had tried a little, and perhaps Benjamin had too, but it had happened. There was a quick murmur of apology from both of them, awkward and nervous, but then they paused and looked at each other. And in Benjamin's eyes, Avalon saw the same yearning as in her own. And this time she knew, really knew, that he adored her too. For a moment, she was unable to breathe. Benjamin reached out, took her hand furtively and rubbed his thumb over her knuckles.

Then, just as quickly, he stepped back, bowed, and said, "Your Highness," opening the door and allowing her to precede him into the room. His professional face was in place, and he greeted the King as though it were any other day, but Avalon's heart was singing, even as her nerves were on fire. She hoped the

King would not notice, and, as usual, his mind was on weightier matters. He greeted her warmly, then set to work, not even noticing when Benjamin lost track for a few seconds as he and Avalon gazed at each other, and then fumbled to catch up a moment later.

But when she turned fourteen, Avalon knew it was futile. She was a princess. *The* princess. The next Queen of Haven. She could never marry a scribe, no matter how much her heart tore itself to pieces wanting him. She stopped visiting her father while he worked and tried not to be around if Benjamin would be there. It was better to break her heart now before she had to break both of their hearts, she told herself, but that didn't make it easier. She even asked to be sent to stay with her cousins for a season. Her mother complied, and the distance helped, though it didn't heal her completely. When she returned, she found out Benjamin had resigned his position, stating he had an offer of employment to a nobleman in the country, which suited him much more than the grand fanfare of the palace.

He was gone. She had not forgotten him, but she had stopped loving him. Would she ever really know what being in love was like? Could she love Ledhar?

The melody floating up from the ballroom floor was slow and sad, matching her reminiscing. The strings sounded celestial, like they were leaking through fissures in the sky, and not from a mere human's fingers. The sound filled Avalon so full that it pushed tears up to the surface to make room. She missed her mother, her slender, smiling mother, the one that seemed too girlish to be the Queen, but whose quiet convictions for protocol were the foundation for everything she did. And her father, with his seriousness and his often-distracted affection for his girls. She missed Raine, even though her middle sister's mischievousness sometimes drove her as crazy as a jester. Raine was the only one she'd ever whispered to about Benjamin. She missed sweet Amelie. She missed her bedroom, and the familiar hands of Gerta and Penli, her lady's maids. She thought of the ghastly face of faithful Jem, dead on the floor.

She tried to blink back the onslaught of tears, but some ran down her cheeks. Embarrassed, Avalon brushed her gloved fingers against her cheeks, hoping no one noticed her lack of control. The Queen's eyes focused on a distant point, her thoughts alive somewhere in her mind's eye and not in the present. Prince Golan, on her other side, glanced sideways at her. His jaw shifted, then he reached out and gently squeezed her arm, withdrawing again so quickly that Avalon blinked, wondering if she'd imagined it. His small kindness warmed her heart, and she overcame the tears. Golan kept his eyes carefully on the musician after that, but Avalon was grateful. She forced herself to focus on the music and not to think about home for the rest of the evening.

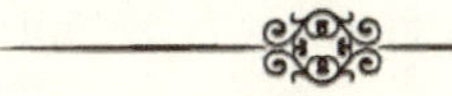

But today was a new day. Today the patrol sent to find information on her sisters should be back. She hoped she would have news from Haven in just a few more days as well.

Her breakfast tray hadn't been delivered yet, so Avalon decided to visit the kitchen herself. She would enjoy seeing Alice again. She was still wondering what she had meant when she had said to be careful of the Queen, and perhaps today she'd have a chance to ask her about it.

She was about to replace the mattresses on the tall bed, but decided to check on her pea first. Although Mava was gentle and attentive, Avalon couldn't completely trust her. Or anyone. For whatever reason, her mother, Queen Heather, had entrusted her with that crystal. She hoped one day she would discover why, but for now, she knew it must have been important, at least to her mother, and that was enough.

After a moment of feeling around, she began to worry. She pushed further. She had not even been sleeping on the bed for the past two nights. The gem couldn't have shifted that much, could it? Panic oozed in. She began dragging the mattresses down from their stack, forcing herself to be methodical and shake each one before re-stacking it beside the bed. Although the pallets were not heavy by themselves, they were large enough to be awkward, and after getting halfway through the stack, her face and neck were damp with sweat.

Finally, she got to the bottom of the pile, with just one more mattress between her and the wooden bed frame. She paused. The pea was here, surely it was here. It was just so small she had not felt it earlier. Her fingers had missed an inch, and when she lifted this last mattress, the gem would be there, safe and innocent in its spot.

But dread was coiling in her stomach, and she was afraid to look. She brushed the fly-away hairs out of her eyes, then plunged in. The space was empty.

She forced her eyes to move slowly, to search every inch, but there was nothing there. She pressed her fingers around, trying to feel any small crack or space where it could have slipped and disappeared, but there was nothing. The platform was solid. And it was empty.

C H A P T E R 11

Broken Rules Can Break Me Too

Avalon dropped to her knees, searching the floor, frantically eliminating every crevice and corner. The pea was *gone*. She chewed the corner of her mouth, fighting panic and trying to gather her thoughts.

Just then, there was a knock. Oh, no! Mava was here with breakfast, and the room was torn apart.

"I'm coming."

She piled a few mattresses back on the bed, then decided to leave the rest where they were and ask for them to be taken away. She would be honest in saying she wasn't comfortable with the ridiculous arrangements.

She flung the door open and was surprised to see Alice there. The girl was smiling as widely as ever.

"Good Morning, Princess. Mava is the Queen's personal maid, and, as the Queen needed her this morning, I asked to be the one to deliver your breakfast when we got the message in the kitchen. I've brought you a sweetbread twist from last night! And there is fruit, and toast, and cold meats," she said, setting the wide tray down and pointing to each dish.

Avalon swallowed. She didn't want to burden Alice with her problems, but she didn't feel like eating right now, and she needed help.

Alice was understanding. Avalon had whispered everything to her, starting with the last glimpse she'd had of her mother, a week ago now, when she'd pressed the jewel into her daughter's hand before being pulled away. The nightmare scene didn't feel any less frightening as she told it. And now the jewel, which she had thought was safer in her room than on herself, had disappeared.

They had looked everywhere–again–together, but no shiny green ball went rolling or winked from a corner. It was gone.

Alice seemed as upset as Avalon was. Her empathy was like a hug.

The girls concluded that, unless it had evaporated by some magic, Mava would be the only other one who might know anything about it.

After telling Alice everything, Avalon felt better and ate some fruit. She broke the sweetbread twist in half, handing Alice one piece and nibbling at the other while she contemplated her next move.

"I'll ask Mava if anyone else has been in here," she mused. "If no one has..."

Alice smiled weakly. "Mava has worked for the royal family for a long time," she reminded Avalon. "She is most trusted by Queen Lilian. I am sure she will have some information to help you."

Avalon's eyebrows furrowed with a sudden thought.

"Alice, what did you mean when you told me to be careful of the Queen?"

Alice threw a wary glance toward the door and shook her head.

"Not here," she whispered. Then, more loudly, "Do you want to go riding this morning? The breeze is lovely today. I think I could spare an hour of work to accompany you as your guide." She winked, and Avalon couldn't help smiling too.

She sent a message to the King asking for information on the patrol, since he was locked in his study, and then she took Alice up on her offer, and they went riding.

"How did you learn to ride?" Avalon asked.

"It pays to be friendly. Every summer, after I'd get chased out of the kitchen for being underfoot, I would visit Steward in the stables. He taught me."

They rode out through the front gate, an official guard following them at a polite distance. The gates were closed behind them, and Alice led her away from the main road, which she said led into the town, Rivence.

"This direction is mostly meadow and hills. Just perfect for riding."

Avalon sat on the gray horse Steward had suggested for her, her gown stretched tightly against her legs as she straddled the horse. She normally rode sidesaddle, but, then, she was normally in Haven where her decorum mattered, not a lost princess in a strange land riding with a servant girl. She enjoyed riding like this. It let her feel the horse's movements so much better, to anticipate them and flow with them, as if they were one.

She hadn't bothered to ask Mava for a riding habit. She did not know where the clothes the family had already lent her had come from or how hard they had been to find—after all, there were no other princesses in the castle. The dresses had all been a pretty good fit, not extravagant, but fine. Perhaps there was a young duchess within range who had a good heart. As long as no one else saw her like this, she didn't care that she was being improper. For the moment, it just felt good to be in the sun, with all the green openness around her, and a girl with a heart of gold treating her like they were best friends.

At home, she would have found such familiarity disrespectful. It wasn't proper for servants to look her in the eye as though they were equal, to touch her without permission, or to chatter without being asked, and she had never questioned the way of things. But for once, she was not being treated like a princess, and, with Alice, it didn't matter. Alice was happy, and she made the world happy. Most of all, Alice *cared*. Avalon liked how it felt to be cared about as Avalon, not just as the next queen. Most of the concern others had shown her had just been to gain favor with the future power, or in the Kingdom's interest and her as its head, not in her as a person.

Her mother, of course, had been different. Casual sometimes. She didn't mind her daughters running barefoot when they were little or playing outside like other children, though it was still within the palace walls. However, with age came responsibility, and it had been a long time since Avalon had felt free.

When they had ridden a distance, and were meandering through a meadow, Avalon spoke again. "Alice, I need to know what you meant the other day when you said that not all magic is evil. And about the Queen?"

Alice's lips tightened. "I am not free to speak any more about it, Avalon. I put you at risk saying anything. I put myself at risk, and many others."

She was quiet, and Avalon waited. Finally Alice sighed and continued. "I met some people from the Forest when I accidentally fell and hurt myself near the Black Forest last year. I have never told anyone else, because magic is illegal. I would betray my friends in the Forest by talking about it, or I might get myself in trouble, and then be in no position to help them when the time is right. I trust you, but I've given them my word not to talk about it. In fact, I try to back up the frightening stories about the Forest. That fear is part of what keeps them safe." She sighed. "And the Queen is...dangerous. I don't know how to explain it, but I believe she has some kind of powers. I don't want you to get hurt by her."

She didn't say anything else. Avalon wanted to ask more, but Alice changed the subject, talking about the new tea made from the yellow flowers along the road.

There was a small note of apology from the King when they returned which simply read, *No news yet, but employ patience. I will tell you as soon as there is word.*

In the afternoon, when Avalon had seen neither the Queen nor Mava, she decided to investigate the missing jewel on her own. She considered approaching the Queen's quarters, but did not want to be that rude just yet, so she found her way down to the servants' quarters instead. It was almost empty, most of the staff doing their duties elsewhere in the castle, but on a bed in the corner, a mother was nursing a baby.

Avalon asked her if she knew if anyone had gone into her room to clean the day before, but the young woman said she hadn't heard. "I kin ask tonight, if you wish, milady."

"If you could," Avalon nodded and left.

She slowed her steps as she neared the mezzanine parlor. She had been wanting to come back here alone, when it was empty, just to sit and think. Anywhere that wasn't her mysterious room would help her clear her mind, and she invited the idea of sinking into one of the large cushioned chairs, completely abandoning her proper posture, and refocusing her thoughts. It was so shadowy and quiet up here that she felt the need to step lightly.

The room waited for her, all its large furniture and abundant cushions strewn about in random order, each empty spot providing an opportunity for comfort. She glided toward the back of the room. She wanted to hide. As wonderful as the brightness of the sunshine and the open fields had felt this morning, right now she wanted friendly solitude, the kind that wrapped around her like an embrace, where she was safe to relax and let her mind wander.

There was a chair covered in black velvet in the furthest corner, its tall back to the entrance. The arms were wide and tall as well, as though it was a former throne which had been covered in softness. This was the one.

She rounded the chair and jerked back, inhaling a small scream. The dark figure hidden on the throne chair turned to her, almost just as surprised, although he didn't squeak.

CHAPTER 12

A Glitter in the Darkness

"Oh! Hello!" he said.

It was Prince Golan.

Avalon recovered herself, all except for the racing beat of her heart.

"Ex-excuse me, Your Highness. I did not know you were here."

"That is the aim of hiding back here. I like the peace when no one knows where I am," he said. He sounded amiable.

"That was my goal in coming up here, too," Avalon admitted. "It seemed like a good place to be alone and think."

"It's perfect for that."

"But I didn't mean to invade your privacy. I'll go now." She took a step back as she spoke.

"There's room enough in here for at least two."

She paused. "But maybe not for all their thoughts."

Golan stood, closing the book on his lap and bowing formally now. "Please, sit. Be comfortable. If either of us needs to leave, I will go."

Avalon peered at him. His arresting green eyes were genuine and kind.

"I didn't expect you to enjoy reading," she commented. "Your brother seemed to indicate that all you cared about was training."

Golan looked amused. "Everyone has their surprises, I guess. Would you like to sit?" He even gestured to the seat he had vacated.

She sat.

The chair *was* like a throne. She needed to perch on the edge for her feet to reach the floor, and the arms were far too high to be comfortable as elbow rests. A giggle escaped as she leaned back, exaggerating the move.

"Are the nobles in Ethereal abnormally large? Or is this a retired throne?"

Golan laughed along, then fell into a chair tilted toward hers, leaning back easily.

"Actually, when I was little, my nurse tried to scare me into obedience by telling me that chair belonged to a giant who lived in the woods, and he would come for me if I didn't behave. I believed her for a bit–until my big brothers ruined her scheme and laughed at me for being gullible. I was just six, mind you!"

Avalon laughed. With the trauma of the past week, laughter had been far from her heart, and the sudden involuntary bubbling inside felt like breathing after holding your breath for too long.

"I don't actually know the origins of that piece. It could very well be an old throne, a relic of some faraway country, but just a parlor set in a tiny summer castle in Ethereal now. My father has an affinity for unique furniture." He splayed his hand toward the room. "This is basically his collection. The Queen allows him to display it here."

"That's interesting. My bedchamber makes more sense now."

"Oh?"

"It's a...unique...room. The bed is in the center of the room, and it is very high. At least the mattresses make it so. There are twenty. I have to use a stool to get to the top." She stopped, the thought occurring to her that discussing one's bedchamber might be inappropriate.

Golan shrugged. "Like I said, my parents have some eccentric tastes in style."

Silence ensued for a moment. Avalon's training in conversation made her open her mouth to elicit a polite comment before the lull became awkward, but Golan spoke first.

"What really happened, Your Highness? How did you get to Blackstone?"

He turned to her, and his eyes were bristling with seriousness. They seemed to fasten her to her seat.

"I related my story already, at tea the night I got here," she said quietly. She had told the truth. Why couldn't this family believe her?

Golan swung into a sitting position, and leaned forward, his elbows on his knees.

"I believe you," he said, as though he'd heard her thoughts. "I could have seen you were royalty if you had been dressed in rags," he said. "No one less than a princess has training like that." He motioned to her straight back and her toes pointed perfectly together as she perched on the edge of the black chair.

"But I feel like there is more to your story. How did you get through the storm? The servants say you came through the Black Forest. I have never even been past the edge of the treeline. How did you do it?"

"I have as many questions about this past week as you do, Prince, and not very many answers."

He was leaning toward her, and his gaze hadn't wavered from her face. His green eyes were distracting. She wanted to look anywhere but straight into them. Their proximity! In this dark, isolated room! Her eyes dropped instead to his lips, and she blinked, embarrassed at her slip. That was even more improper. Her cheeks burned, even as she willed the blush to cool.

But as he waited, Avalon was struck with the desire to tell this man everything, even her secret about the jewel. He seemed interested, and she had been in distress all week. Maybe he would help her in areas where the King and Queen seemed reluctant. Maybe he knew more than Alice did and would know where her jewel had gone—or who had taken it.

She just didn't know if she could trust him.

"If there is anywhere you do not have to follow the rules, it's in this room," he encouraged.

Avalon's eyes must have widened at the insinuation, because he straightened up and stuttered, "That's not, I mean, I only meant that you don't have to hide behind your royalty in here. You don't have to pick what you are going to say based on what is proper or acceptable or necessary. You don't have to sit like you're tied to a rod or even call me by my title. Under my title, I'm a person—and you are too..." his tirade trailed off and his shoulders sank an inch.

"I'm Golan. I just thought that maybe I could help you. And I like genuineness. Being on display gets tiring," he finished quietly.

Avalon was at a loss for words. Finally she managed to open her mouth, though she couldn't quite get her eyes to meet his.

"I get tired of it too," she whispered. "In fact, I met Alice, the royal baker, a few days ago, and I was so relieved to meet someone friendly that I asked her to call me Avalon. This morning I even went riding with her, just like we were friends." She lifted her eyes to his. "And I enjoyed it," she admitted.

Golan's lips twitched in a smile he was trying to hold back. "I saw that," he said.

"You saw us?" Avalon pictured herself straddling the saddle in the same gown she was still wearing, chagrined at the way she had let the fabric rise to her knees and tighten around her legs without a care. Heavens, did she smell of horse sweat?

He broke into a laugh. "Yes, Princess of Decorum, I saw your unconventional habit from a window this morning. And I saw you toss your head back and embrace it."

"I'm sorry. I didn't realize I could be spotted so easily."

"Don't be sorry. I liked it."

Heat billowed into her cheeks.

"I enjoyed seeing someone be free to be themselves. I *admired* it."

He's serious!

She looked at him more closely. His hair was short, but it twirled in ringlets that she assumed would become too thick and wild if he let it grow longer as was the fashion. His face was wide and square and strong. His chest was wide too, and where Joran seemed to be cut from fine glass, all his tall angles just right, Golan seemed to have been cut from oak. He was strong and steady.

What would she lose by trusting him with her secrets? She was already being treated strangely in this unusual castle with mysteries, and her jewel was gone. She still didn't have any word about her sisters or her parents. Not much worse could come of telling her story, and if he wanted to help, she would lose out by *not* telling him. Besides, she felt the hurt of his parents' mistrust, and she didn't want to return the same sentiment.

"A week ago, my family's palace was attacked in the middle of the night. It was a complete surprise."

"Haven, right?"

She nodded.

"I looked it up after I met you. I'd heard of it, of course, because you're not that far north of us, but we didn't learn about it in our studies. We mainly covered our own history and those of the kingdoms with whom we do business."

"Likewise. I did not know where I was when I fled the Cleftans and arrived here."

"But my research proved that if you are Avalon, you were born seventeen springs ago, the first child of King Jasper and Queen Heather. There was no information about your sisters."

"The next sister who survived is Raine, and she is several years younger."

"The book outdates her, then. Now, back to your story."

"I didn't know what was happening. I woke up and heard s-screaming, and from my window I could only see orange light and smoke, so I knew there was a fire. I got up. There were no servants around, so I went out into the hall to find out what was happening. My mother ran up to me, and she handed me something. I took it without even seeing what it was. She just told me to protect it, and then two men, dressed as warriors, in uniforms I didn't know right away, ran up behind her and pulled her away. And then someone g-g-grabbed me too. There were several others with him, and they made me gather some clothes, but they didn't wait for me to change, they just dragged me out of the palace to where there were carriages waiting. There was so much smoke. It was hard to see. I don't know how the fires started or how much burned. I didn't see our guards, except a few who had already been killed. Right before I stumbled into the carriage, I saw other men holding Raine and

Amelie and shoving them into carriages in front of mine. Then they locked the door and sped away and traveled the whole night and some of the next morning."

Her voice had become hollow as she retold her story. She could feel the smoke burning her eyes again, and the fear that had clawed up her insides as she had been pulled through her home by force, but her voice sounded flat, as though she were reading a boring document, except for the occasional stutters that revealed her emotion.

She could feel Golan's eyes on her, felt his presence as he leaned into her story, but she stared down at her hands. A small drip splashed on her lap, and she realized she was crying.

Quickly she swiped at her face and bit her lip. "Excuse me."

"Avalon." His voice was so gentle. He reached out his hand and placed it over hers. His fingers were ungloved. Hers were not, though that didn't keep her from feeling the weight and warmth of him.

"It's okay to cry."

She shook her head a little and tried to continue. If she gave into tears now and let herself accept his concern, she might just lose control and never stop crying. And she needed to be strong. She needed to save her family.

She drew in a wavering breath. "I wasn't treated terribly. They fed me. But no one spoke to me, and I was too afraid to demand answers. A guard was assigned to me. One night I asked for privacy in the woods, and when I was out of sight, I slid the rope off my ankle. I had been working for a while to loosen the knot. I didn't know where to go, but I knew the darkness would hinder them as much as it hindered me, and it was raining, which was even better. I didn't realize how very dark it was in the woods, though. I couldn't see a single step in front of me until I noticed small lights. At first I thought they were fireflies, but they darted forward like tiny arrows, and they worked in unison. I decided they were showing me the way, so I thanked The One and followed them. The storm was furious, and I felt like the water would drown me. It was hard to walk and harder to see, but I hoped I'd stumble upon a village before my captors stumbled into me. After what felt like forever, the trees ended, and I was here. The lights even circled around the gate so I could make it out. And then I was let in and given a place to stay. I suppose it was still early evening then because you all hadn't had your evening tea yet, and that's when I met everyone."

Golan's eyebrows drew together, and his lips bunched in thought. "You said you thought they were Cleftans, the ones who kidnapped you?"

"Yes, I believe so, from their insignia."

"Do you think it could be another army posing as Cleftans?"

"I suppose, though I don't know why that would benefit them. Why choose Cleft's identity over all others? I don't even know why we were attacked in the first place, by Cleft or anyone else. What makes even less sense is how they infiltrated the palace so easily. We're not on the border, so they had to travel through Haven first, and then get through the gates and walls and guards."

"I'm sure you've been thinking about whether you heard of any unrest or disagreements lately?"

"I have tried to think, but I can't recall any."

"The thing your mother gave you, did you ever see what it was?"

"Oh, yes. It was a small jewel. It was green and round, only the size of a pea. I managed to hide it the whole journey. When I got here, I hid it in my room rather than on me because I thought it would be safer, but I was wrong. This morning I looked for it, but it's gone."

"Are you sure you looked everywhere? It sounds quite small."

"Yes, of course I'm sure," Avalon said defensively.

He overlooked her tone. "Where was it hidden?"

"Under the mattresses on my bed. There were so many of them, it seemed extra safe, but it's not there or anywhere else in the room. We searched, Alice and I. She came with breakfast this morning, and I was in despair, so I told her about it."

Golan nodded. "Alice has good sense. I'm glad you've met her. You can trust her, and she will help you however she can. Everyone knows Alice does only good."

I hope I am doing the right thing by trusting you too, Avalon thought, then plunged into the other details of her story. She told him about the strange bruising the first night, and how she had been afraid to sleep on the bed again, and even how her jewel was changed the next morning.

"It sounds like your mother gave you more than a sentimental keepsake," Golan commented. "It sounds magical."

"Does magic exist here? Alice said it had been outlawed here, as though it does exist, and it just can't be practiced anymore."

"Of course it exists. Don't you have magic in Haven?"

"No, not at all. We learned that other Kingdoms have fables of magic—you know, the fish people in the lakes of Terind, and potions that magisters create to empower or harm people, but mostly we were told that it was dangerous and evil and told not to talk about it."

"That's strange. Everyone knows there is magic in the Black Forest. That's why no one—well, not many—go near it. All magical practices were outlawed a few years before I was born, and everyone knows that most of the magical people or anyone who had an affinity for the supernatural disappeared deep in the Black Forest. We leave them alone, and they don't come out, on threat of death. It seems the magic that does reside there is dark and cynical, based on the tales of those who have been close enough to the Black Forest to see things. A few people have even disappeared inside and never returned. Only three have dared in the last twenty years since magic was banned, as far as I've heard. But you! Your experience was different. You made it through the Black Forest, and it even helped you."

He sounded amazed. Avalon pictured the lights leading her through the blinding onslaught of rain and the thick blackness. She'd always thought the stories about magic were just exaggerated, but she could not explain what had happened to her in the Forest. Then there was the jewel which had changed overnight and now disappeared. Maybe no one here was a thief, and there was something supernatural linked to the gem which had caused it to disappear.

"Why was magic banned in Ethereal?" If magic was alive here, she wanted nothing to do with it. She'd always believed it was evil, and the stories of the Black Forest only proved that. But if her pea was magical, she needed to at least know more.

"It was my parents' decision, actually. The people with magical abilities, called the Gifted, were getting out of hand. They seemed to have all become dark and violent, and there was an uprising just after my Father took the throne. For his safety and the kingdom's posterity, he declared that all magic be banished and anyone caught being involved with any supernatural creature or eliciting any supernatural power would be put to death. He said it took him several years to rid the kingdom of magic, as it is so strong and secretive, but by the time I was born, it was all gone. Or safely contained, at least."

"Is there such a thing as good magic anywhere?"

"I was taught that the Great Magister at that time began experimenting with dark magic and was infected by it. In turn, he infected all he interacted with, causing most of the magical realm to grow sinister within a short time. That's why it had to be stopped. I'm not sure if the curse spread to other kingdoms or not, but I know several kingdoms which still have a magical realm that seems healthy. It was here that there was an epidemic of evil."

"Why weren't they all killed to prevent the spread?"

"The extent of the curse wasn't known until the uprising. Many were killed in our effort for victory. The rest fled into the Black Forest, and they've been using it as a barricade of sorts ever since."

"But, if they have a refuge there, what if they just grow stronger until they are ready to come out again and take the kingdom?" She asked, appalled that the castle sat so close to the danger, and that she had been right in it herself.

"The Great Magister disappeared during the uprising, most likely dead, and many of the effects of his curse wore off. In fact, I don't know that much evil remained, but there was so much confusion and mistrust. Both sides had lost many, and tensions were high. The King made a good call when he simply banned the magic instead of inciting both sides to lose even more. I don't believe there is really a threat to the Kingdom. It has been more than twenty years, and no one has attempted to leave the Forest. I also think the frightening happenings and disappearances could be more for their own protection than because of a hatred of Ethereal's royals."

Avalon and he lapsed into silence as they contemplated the recent events. She recalled Alice saying the same thing — that those who lived in the Forest used fear as protection. She wasn't sure she was at liberty to share Alice's insights, so she stayed quiet.

Finally, Golan stood and stretched. His smile was genuine when he said, "Thank you, Avalon, for trusting me. I promise I will help you however you can. I can look through the King's library and gather books that might have information. If you want to meet here again tomorrow, we could look through them."

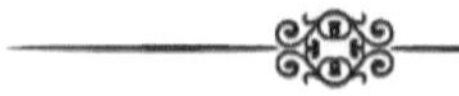

It wasn't until she was going to sleep that night—on a bed half the size as before, that Avalon realized something. Mava had found her bed in disarray, and Avalon had simply told her she wasn't comfortable that far from the ground and wished the mattresses to be removed. Several were taken away. She lay there now, thinking through the things she'd learned from Prince Golan that afternoon. Her mind traveled all the way back to his story of the supposed giant who owned the old throne, when she realized Golan had said *brothers*. But Joran was the only other prince she knew of.

Golan had asked her to join him again tomorrow and promised he'd bring books that might have information about her jewel. He seemed so kind. Was he too kind? She'd never been so suspicious in her life as she'd become over the last week.

Is Golan hiding secrets too? Should I have trusted him with all of mine?

CHAPTER 13

Whisper of Spring

Golan leaned against the wide door frame, waiting for Avalon. He hoped she would meet him there like he had asked. He had brought the books he had told her about and set them on a table inside. He had enjoyed yesterday's conversation.

He didn't go gallivanting like Joran did, and his parents were too smothered under their own secrets and struggles, most of which they didn't share with their sons, to be present, so he was often bored during the summer. He wasn't young enough to pester the servants or have a nursemaid anymore, or play games outside with his brothers like he used to do.

He missed Benrid. He had slipped yesterday when talking to Avalon, but she hadn't seemed to notice. He studied his boot for a minute. She had told him her story and trusted him with her secrets, even though she barely knew him. He hated that he couldn't do the same, but he had given an oath not to mention his oldest brother.

He thought about the first time he had seen Avalon, the night of her surprise arrival. She had stepped into the tearoom, looking elegant in a simple blue gown with no adornments. He had seen the servants wear dresses as nice on certain occasions when they accompanied his mother as ladies-in-waiting at a grand event, and he thought it might have come from one of them. She had looked so alone, so slender and fragile in that moment as she hesitated for a second on the threshold, and his heart jumped up in her favor, especially when she raised her eyes and he had seen the courage shining inside.

His heart had leapt again when she had appeared up here yesterday, not as much from surprise as from excitement that bounded up before he managed to capture it. He'd all but begged her to stay and tried to put her at ease, though his attempts had been fumbling. It wasn't every day that he got to talk to a girl unchaperoned, one with an interesting story, and a lovely face. He longed for a friend, and he wanted to know her–the real her—without the protocols and stiff proper manners that their statuses forced them into. She had seemed wary at first, but then she'd seemed to melt, as though she had been waiting for that moment her whole life. And she had told him her story.

He thought back to the tears filling her eyes, seeming to surprise her when they fell, and the way she had pulled herself back together. The sight hurt him. He felt sick watching her pain, and then watching her bottle it up inside again. He had known at that moment that he would make it his mission to right her world again. He wasn't Joran. He didn't have wiry good looks or easy manners to make girls swoon, but he cared. It may not be enough for most girls. It may not be enough for Avalon, but it was all of him, all he could give.

She approached, dressed in the same blue dress she had worn the first night, and he tried not to let her see how it drew his eyes to her willowy form, the way it was hemmed under her bosom, and gathered at her small ankles, flowing around her long legs like air. Instead he smiled, brushing the image of her stockinged legs bared while she straddled the horse, out of his thoughts.

"Good afternoon, Your Highness. I've brought the books I told you about. I am hoping they might help us discover something about your pea. We can search them together."

He led her to a set of chairs facing each other over a small tea table. They looked to be set up for an intense private conversation, and he hoped it wasn't more than she was comfortable with, but she sat primly, her hands in gloves, just as proper as the day before. He didn't mind, of course, as long as she spoke what she was truly thinking, not just what she was supposed to say, as they had both been taught to do.

She was silent at first as they thumbed through the old volumes. Then she asked quietly, "Did you used to have another brother?"

Golan looked at her in surprise. She was still bent over the book, but her eyes were raised to meet his, and they were brimming with compassion. "That is, yesterday you said your brothers used to tease you. I thought maybe he..."

Golan sighed and ran a hand through his hair. He hated breaking an oath, but outright lying, especially to her, would be worse.

"He's not dead. His name is Benrid, and he's the eldest son. He couldn't come with us this summer because he isn't...well. We're not supposed to talk about it, really. Or about him at all."

"I see."

"I'm sorry."

"Don't be. I understand. Well, sort of. Thank you for telling me," she finished softly.

Golan smiled at her, and their eyes locked again.

Finally, he blinked and looked back to the book before him. His was on the history of the magical realm. There were others on enchanted objects, and one on known gems and crystals of the world. Avalon spent a long time in that one, turning each page and scanning it for something similar to her own gem. There were illustrations of many of the gems, which made them easy to rule out. Finally, she closed the book and stretched.

Golan sent a furtive glance up at her from where his head was bent over the book on the table, suffocating a grin at her unladylike expanse as she raised her arms and pushed her elbows back. Then she yawned, though this time she tried to hide it.

"Are you tired, Your Highness?" he asked, trying not to laugh.

"I'm Avalon in this room," she corrected, and the happiness that danced through his chest surprised him. "And, yes, I am tired, though I apologize for showing it like that. It could be all the squinting at the small writing in these shadows."

"I'll ring for some lamps," he offered, but she shook her head.

"No, that's all right. To be honest, I didn't sleep well again last night."

His eyes were instantly on her face. "What was wrong?"

"I was just...uncomfortable. I shouldn't be complaining."

She didn't want to admit how afraid she felt at night alone in the wing of suites.

"It's fine. I am honored that you would bear your honest complaints to me." Golan tried to sound light, but he couldn't keep the earnestness out of his voice or in the way he involuntarily leaned toward her. Why did he always have to be so straightforward? He could never pass through a situation with an easy demeanor like Joran could, no matter his actual feelings on the matter. His face was too honest, Joran said. Benrid would agree, though his oldest brother told him candidness was better than hypocrisy. As a prince, though, Golan knew it wasn't the best gift. Now Avalon would see right inside him, the way he wanted to drink in her every movement, and how eager he was to be her friend. Her protector. She would laugh at him.

He looked back down at his book quickly.

"What in the Kingdom! Avalon, look!" Even in his eagerness, he didn't miss the pleasure of saying her name.

He pointed to the paragraph his eyes had fallen on a few seconds before. He scooted the book over so they could both tilt their heads and read it together.

It has been said that the Magister of the Beginning of Kerrynth was given a gift from The One. He then held the secret to all power in his hands, a magical crystal that could trump any potion or spell and control all people. In his wisdom, The Great Magister of the Beginning foresaw the trouble such power could bring. He saw that man's heart was greedy for control and recognition and riches and fame, things that would destroy his motives and make such power in his hands work many evils in the world. It is said that The Magister of the Beginning took the crystal and split it among his three sons, warning them never to unite the pieces again.

His first son hid his safely, and when he passed away, his secret may have died with him. The second son gave his to the woman he loved because it was true love, and he did not want any secrets between them. The third son also lost his to his wife, who wheedled the secret out of him for her own selfish intentions.

While this information is in the Ancient Chronicles of the Maker, the actuality of this legend has never been proven. It is said that the puzzle consisted of only three pieces, and that they were small. Each one was a gem the size of a pea. Each pea held power on its own, but if brought together again, they would forge back into a whole, and their power would be unstoppable.

The Magister of the Beginning hoped they would be used for good individually, while preventing disaster by making their reunion impossible. Very few of the first people even knew of the puzzle, except those who read it in the Ancient Chronicles, and eventually, every gem disappeared. If any have survived the past few centuries, they are well hidden today, and the legend is very little known, and even less believed.

Golan felt a chill shudder through his body as he realized the impact of what he had read. His own incredulous eyes met Avalon's across the book. She was blinking at him.

"What is this book? Where did you get it?" She grabbed it and began searching its cover as though it could reveal all secrets.

"I found it in the library. Most of the books in this castle are old and fragile, or just outdated. They are good for a collection, but no one uses them for study or information anymore. I just picked out the ones I found that seemed like they could help us. I never read any of these, and I doubt my father has either. This one is called *Histories and Stories from the Ancient Kingdom to the Present One, a look at the origins of the Pillar Kingdoms and the Magical Realm.* I have never heard of the writer, but the date is from sixty years ago."

"Author."

Golan furrowed his brows. "What?"

"The word is author." Avalon said it absent-mindedly.

At first Golan was taken-aback. Being corrected like that, especially by a young woman, was something he had never experienced. But this one looked so innocent while doing it, her upturned nose sitting adorably on her face, her wide hazel eyes drawn pensively as she stared into space, musing, that he sat back and breathed out a small snort. He wanted to pull her close and tweak that nose, and make her look up at him, and then...He shook his head. He was getting distracted.

"Author then." He grinned. "His name was Kinsley, B.H. Kinsley. I have never heard of him, and he is likely no longer alive, but perhaps he wrote other books which will help us decipher who he was and whether his writings are credible."

"I want to see the Ancient Chronicles. I want to see the part that talks about the pea crystals." She looked at him, determination in her eyes.

"That might be impossible right now, Avalon," he said apologetically. "There is a copy of the Ancient Chronicles at home at the castle in Lilt, as I'm sure there is in every kingdom, but they are extensive. Thirty volumes long, and I wouldn't know exactly where to look."

Avalon nodded, but she was biting her lip, and she looked defeated. Golan knew he had to try.

"My Father usually makes a few journeys back during our summer respite here, just for matters that cannot wait until our return. It's only a twelve hour carriage ride, which can be done in a day if you have the stamina, but it's shorter on horseback. He may let me return by myself, if I have a good enough reason. I don't know when he plans to go again himself, otherwise maybe I could just ask to accompany him. We have only about three weeks left of our stay here," he added hopefully.

"I won't be here for three more weeks," Avalon said quietly.

He rubbed his face and considered. "I'll go now then," he said.

She looked up sharply. "What?"

"Yes. I will go now and return immediately. I could be back by tomorrow evening," he decided. "No one even needs to know that I've gone."

Hope brightened Avalon's eyes, but she shook her head. "You can't make that kind of journey just for me."

Golan smiled. "That's exactly why I'm going to do it. For you. I meant it when I said I want to help you."

CHAPTER 14

All I know is Winter

Mava strained her ears from her spot just outside the doors of the mezzanine parlor. The Queen had told her to keep her eye on Avalon and gather any information she could. Although the Queen seemed to have figured out something about the girl, she still wanted to know all she could while she made a plan.

Mava had seen Avalon leave her chamber that afternoon and followed her discreetly, leaving a wide distance between them. She had disappeared near the parlor, and when Mava caught voices drifting from there, she knew she must be inside. Mava couldn't risk leaning around the doors to see anything, but she lingered in the hall, trying not to breathe too loudly as she listened for clues. Obviously there was someone with her, and, at first, she couldn't make out who, but then she heard the Prince's voice clearly, "Here is a hopeful one. Why don't you see what you can find?"

Then all had been quiet for a long time. Every so often she heard a rustle, and her mind began to run wild with indecent images. Why were they hiding in there together? Were there murmurings she just couldn't hear? She burned with the desire to just peek into the room and see what they were doing, but she was half afraid that she would see something she couldn't unsee.

She hadn't disliked the strange princess at first, but now that Mava and the Queen had accidentally discovered the gem she'd brought with her, Queen Lilian's plan was only growing. The girl's small gem was quite similar to the Queen's own, and Queen Lilian had done nothing but evil with her own. Who knew what she'd be capable of with two magic gems? Avalon's treasure had been given to the Queen by Mava herself that first morning, and Lilian had kept it, unconcerned that she was stealing. Then they'd scoured the room and found the original gem still safely under the mattress tower where Mava had concealed it for the queen. The glow was faint, but it was alight, indicating that it had sensed magic. That was all the Queen had needed to know to start plotting. And now she had both powerful crystals. It was all terrible news for Mava, but what could she do now?

She'd love to stop the Queen's plans if she could, but she could not risk disobedience, and the Queen had ordered her to stalk the girl for information. However, Mava had never held Prince Golan responsible for any of the secrets of his mother or the competition of the elder princes - his real brother, Joran, and Benrid, the one who was actually Mava's nephew. Golan was the most honest and sensitive and kind of all of them, even Benrid. He wasn't as naturally regal as her nephew was, but he was *good*.

Now as she waited, her thoughts toward Avalon were growing anything but kind. The girl may not have planned it, but she'd wiggled into their castle and unwittingly brought the answer to Queen Lilian's dastardly plan. Was she now going to seduce the pure prince? Just as Mava's thoughts convinced her to march into the room and put a stop to the roguery, she heard their voices again. Golan's voice rose in excitement, allowing her to hear every word. Apparently they had found what they sought, and it appeared they had merely been in study, not stolen romance, much to her relief.

Her eyes widened as she realized the nature of the information she was hearing until she heard Avalon's resolute statement about not being at Blackstone for three weeks. If Queen Lilian had anything to do with it, Avalon might never leave again, Mava knew. She really couldn't hold it against the girl for being Gifted. Surely Avalon didn't know she was exactly the kind of person Queen Lilian had been searching for. She was practically trapped here now. Unless...Mava weighed her options. She could tell the Queen what she had overheard–she would have to, but maybe she could help Avalon escape her just the same. Maybe she could find a way to do it without endangering herself or her nephew, Benrid.

She walked away softly, her mind heavy with ideas and fear.

Avalon joined the family in the dining room that night. It was the first time they had dined together since she had met them the first night. Apparently, the rest they were supposed to enjoy here was busier than they thought. Only Golan's seat remained empty. He was already well on his way back to Lilt. He'd left right after their conversation. Besides Avalon, he had told only his personal guards and two servants. He took one of his guards with him. The other stayed stationed at his door, as though the prince were in his chambers. His servant delivered the message that Golan wasn't up to dining with them tonight. Avalon smiled to herself as the man discreetly gave their Majesties the message, grateful that the Prince had been able to slip away unnoticed.

Queen Lilian gave Avalon a disarming smile. "Dear Princess, we are honored to have you join us. I apologize for the busyness of the last few days and our absence at meals. I hope we may make it up to you now."

Prince Joran gave his mother a wary sideways glance, but the King nodded along with his wife. "Quite right. In fact, dear, I have news from the scouts. They were unable to locate a traveling convoy from Cleft. We still await a missive from Haven. Perhaps the lack of news means only good things," he said hopefully.

Avalon's appetite plummeted at his words. He had spoken nonchalantly, as though foretelling the weather for the following day, nothing more. This was her family's lives he was talking about! Her home. Her future. She blinked, trying to gather herself while dismay made her head swim.

Her eyes locked with Joran's, and his gaze did nothing to calm her. He was sitting more jauntily than before, and his interest seemed to be suddenly renewed. His looks her way were open and appraising, and she noticed his eyes kept slipping down her form, but she was too preoccupied to care.

She managed to choke down the food and continue her polite smiles to the Queen whose mood had taken a talkative turn. "We will commission a seamstress right away, Princess, as it seems you will be staying here for a while. You must certainly be missing the finer gowns and variety to which you are used. Again, my apologies for not doing it sooner, but my headaches have kept me often in bed this week." She held the back of her hand to her forehead to acknowledge the affliction.

"But I need to get back to Haven as soon as I can," Avalon persisted.

"Only once we know it's safe. We must wait for a message," the Queen reminded her. Avalon met her eyes, which were so alive and bright that the green of her irises almost glowed. The Queen went on as though she'd merely brushed aside a fly. "And then, for entertainment while you await word. Joran is a splendid rider. I'm sure he would love to accompany you into the village tomorrow and show you around. Doesn't that sound like a plan, son?"

Avalon shot a look of surprise at Joran, but he just quirked an eyebrow and agreed. "Of course. May I have the pleasure to escort you tomorrow, then, Your Highness?"

Avalon blinked and half nodded, strangely unable to comprehend the question or remember what she should say. The Queen beamed.

Avalon could not get to her chambers fast enough after the meal concluded. She had kept up her calm facade and polite conversation the whole evening, which had seemed to drag on forever, but inside, her heart was trembling with despair. As soon as she reached the long hall, the weary fog that had hovered in her mind during the meal evaporated, leaving stark anguish to overtake her.

"Why?" she moaned out loud. "Why did I run? I meant to help my sisters, but I've lost them. I would have had more of a chance if I had stayed near them. They don't even know what happened to me!" She ground her palm against her forehead, as the heated whispers filled the air around her, echoing back into her ears after she'd said them.

She sank down onto her bed. Her gown would be crumpled, but she didn't care. She didn't care about going riding with Joran, and she didn't care about getting new dresses made. Spirits! How long did the Queen expect her to be here? She had been planning to make a decision as soon as she had gotten word from the patrol who had tried to follow the Cleftans, or from home, whichever came first. But now that the Cleftan marauders had disappeared, and she had no way to follow them, she must return to Haven.

No matter the state of her kingdom, she needed to be there. If her parents were alive, they would need her to return. They needed to know *she* was alive, and the information she had could help them rescue Raine and Amelie. And, if they weren't alive...a wave of nausea immersed her at the thought. If they weren't, she needed to be there too. For Haven. For her people. And for her sisters.

Determined, she stood up. She picked up the white dress she had been wearing the night she arrived. Although it had been laundered, her trip in the wagons and then through the woods in the downpour had rendered it less than acceptable. There were light stains around the hem, which must have been from the mud. The marks had been soaked and scrubbed, she could tell, but they couldn't be erased completely. A few tears had been neatly stitched, but parts of the beadwork had been torn off. However, it belonged to her, and the other clothes here didn't. She would look more like the bedraggled girl who had stumbled in during the storm than a true princess, but it couldn't be helped.

As she began to change, her earlier determination faltered. She didn't have a horse. She would have to ask one from the castle, and she was sure the King and Queen would not let her leave alone–and at night, even though darkness had a safety that daylight did not. She could simply demand a horse from Steward, but her authority didn't really extend here. Maybe Alice would help. Or, better yet, Golan. She felt a pang when she thought of him. He'd been kind. Wise. And he was secretly dashing to Lilt right now, just for her sake.

If nothing else happened from her refuge at Blackstone Castle, she would be thankful for the friendship she had received from Alice and Prince Golan. They were the most sincere friendships she had ever experienced, besides her bond with her sisters, even if they lasted all of a few days.

I can't leave yet, not while he's helping me find answers. There was more involved here now than finding her sisters.

Her fingers suddenly went cold as she thought about the pea — the one she'd lost. She did not know exactly what it meant to her mother, or if her mother knew of the legend of the peas. Perhaps the legend wasn't even true. But if her mother had rescued it before anything else when they had been under attack, it must be remarkable indeed. How could she leave without it?

Besides, she realized, *I don't even know the way home.* She hadn't even been able to see the roads while she had traveled this way. So she would need a map and directions, and the map would be unusable in the darkness. What if she encountered Cleftans left to watch the roads for her?

Avalon bit her bottom lip hard and scrunched her eyes shut. She'd never felt so helpless.

I need to talk to Golan, she reminded herself.

She would wait until he returned. But then she needed to make a move.

CHAPTER 15

A Garden of Plans

Avalon left her room and headed to the mezzanine parlor the next evening. Most of the castle was dark, and she walked softly. Golan had returned. He had missed dinner again tonight, but his guard had handed her a note just after she left the dining room to let her know he had returned. She had waited for a few hours, hoping he was getting some rest. His message had said he would see her in the morning, but now she didn't think she could wait another day. She had declined the invitation to go riding with Joran that afternoon, knowing Golan could arrive at any moment, if everything had gone according to schedule. But that meant she had passed most of the day by herself, anxious and bored.

She rang for a servant at a bell in the hall, and when a woman appeared, she asked her to deliver a message to Prince Golan immediately. "Please tell him that the Princess has urgent matters to discuss. She will meet him at the usual place."

Her face burned as she realized how risque her request might sound, so she added, "This is confidential. No one else must be present when you relay the message."

Her shoulders sagged when the woman turned on her heel and headed up the stairs to the royal suites. That hadn't sounded any better. Oh, well. The servant's face had remained impassive, so either she was well-trained, or she was tired and disinterested in the rendezvous of the young members of the house.

Golan appeared just a short time later. Avalon had taken the candle from her room to light her way up the dark stairs and used it to light a lamp in the parlor. The rest of the room remained dark, and Avalon felt unnerved for no reason, so she jumped when Golan appeared, relief and surprise hitting her at the same time.

He looked worried. He was dressed, so he probably hadn't been in bed yet, considering how quickly he'd made it here.

Still, Avalon felt the need to apologize. "I'm sorry for disturbing you, Golan. You must be exhausted after that trip." He must have hardly taken a break since he left. Had he slept at all?

He waved her apology away. "What is it?" His whisper was intense.

All at once, she felt sheepish and lost. "I just got confused and worked up. I'm so worried. I thought if I talked to you, it would help." She sounded plaintive in the quiet room, but his face softened, a gentle pleasure settling in his eyes, and he took a step closer.

"Shall we sit, then?"

Avalon swallowed, then began pouring out her thoughts.

"I don't know what to do, Golan. I need to leave. I need to be at home right now, but I don't know if I can get there by myself. And I don't want to leave without the pea," she finished. "I waited until you got back because I wanted to learn what you found, and I need your help, but I just can't wait anymore. When I'm alone in my room, the things at stake are all I can think about, and I panic."

Golan's elbow rested on the arm of his chair, his thumb under his chin, the rest of his fingers resting at the bridge of his nose. He closed his eyes for a moment to think. "I found the Chronicles and the part about the pea. I copied the article, but it was not much longer than the one we read. It gave a few more details, though." He pulled a folded paper from his pocket and handed it to her, pointing to the third paragraph.

The first pea had the power of pleasure. It could mask any disturbances happening around someone by making them feel happy and peaceful. It could also erase memories if used for long periods of time. The second pea could break any curse or cause pain. The third pea could sense any magic. It could find anyone Gifted and could extend their Gift to another while in use. Its power was called possession. The peas would cause formidable pain if ever brought too close together. The pain would come from the power of them trying to merge back into the original crystal, and the Magister hoped that would make certain the peas were never reunited. He instituted another measure of protection by making sure that the peas could only be activated and used by certain people, usually the Gifted, unless the pea was given as a gift, in which the power to control the pea was given along with the gift.

Avalon's eyes were round. "And this is true?"

"Apparently. It's from the Chronicles."

"Golan, I need that pea, but I don't know where to look. I don't want to go home without it, because my mother trusted me to keep it safe, but I can't stay here any longer. Your Father told me last night, after you had left, that his guards had come back without news of the Cleftan soldiers. My sisters are lost, and I have to get home to help."

Golan rested a hand on her arm. "I have already promised to help you, and I will. If you need a map, or a guide, or a horse, I will get you those things. I'll go with you myself, if I need to. And I will keep my eyes and ears open for what happened to your pea. I will write if I find anything. But I think you should at least wait until morning." He gave a wan smile.

"You'll really help?"

"Of course."

"Why? I mean, I feel like your parents don't place any importance on me or my story. I don't understand why you've been so kind to me."

Golan seemed to hold his breath for a moment before he sighed. "I guess I care about you. You're beautiful and fascinating, but even more than that, you've trusted me. I've never had someone care about what I think or need me. How could I not help you? Real friends are not given often in life, but I think you are one."

Avalon was tempted to reach out and squeeze his hand, but she refrained, murmuring a thank you instead.

"Now, go get some rest. I will be ready at sunup, and I'll grab you something to eat from the kitchen. Meet me there as soon as you're ready to go. I'll have everything."

"Thank you," she said again, more clearly this time.

Relief wrapped around her like a blanket. She stood. He got to his feet as well, and they stood there for a minute in the dark, inches away from each other. Neither spoke. Finally, Avalon reached out and brushed his arm. She meant it in gratitude, but it was awkward, and she let out a nervous laugh, quickly turning away.

"Your candle, Your Highness?" he whispered behind her.

She retrieved the candle, which was slightly more than a stub now, and relit it from the lamp, which he then extinguished. The small flicker gave off even less light, and Avalon stepped carefully as her eyes adjusted to the dark.

They paused at the bottom of the staircases which rose in different directions. Avalon wished she could make the moment last. She dreaded being alone again in her big, eerie room, dreaded leaving the safety of Golan's calmness.

Golan was thankful for the dark, so she wouldn't see the blush rising furiously up his face as she reached out to him. Sudden desire rose inside him too, and a vision of pulling her closer to him played before his eyes, but he blinked, forcing it to end. He couldn't think like this. He had to let her go. She had a life she belonged to, and probably someone she was promised to, and she needed to get back. *Wanted* to get back. And he had to help her.

He walked with her back to the bottom of the stairs leading to the west and east wings of suites.

"Good night," he said softly, and ascended the staircase to his chambers, forcing himself not to look back at her.

You could have kept her talking, just to spend a little more time with her, his thoughts accused him. *Tomorrow she will leave. You'll likely never see her again.*

"Which is all the more reason *not* to prolong this," he said under his breath, though he couldn't shake the sadness he felt gathering in his core.

His head was down as he rounded the corner at the top, so he had to stifle a yelp when he bumped into something. Someone. It was Mava.

She had been watching him ascend, apparently. Watching them, maybe.

"Excuse me," Golan muttered, but she didn't move.

Her eyes were glassy and hard. "Where were you?" she asked in a low voice.

Golan cast a quick glance down the stairs. Avalon was gone. How much had Mava seen? Why did it matter to her? "I was talking to the Princess," he said truthfully.

She might go tell his mother, but all they had done was talk. It was obvious the Queen was pushing Joran at Avalon, which meant she had a reason. Joran went to rendezvous with ladies all the time and never got in trouble for it, but no one he'd ever been truly interested in had met his mother's standards. It worried Golan, mostly for Avalon's sake, although he had to admit, he wasn't fond of the thought of Joran with her for his own sake either.

"About what?" Mava's stare was frigid, but he saw desperation gleaming behind her eyes.

"She's lonely, Mava," he said. "She is worried about her home and family. She just needed a listening ear so she could settle down and sleep."

"She needs to leave," Mava whispered back. "She needs to leave as soon as possible."

Surprise made him blink. "Mava? What's going on?" The usually soft-spoken maid seemed troubled and harsh.

"She's trouble. I've seen things in her room. I can't tell the Queen without endangering her, but you seem to care, so I'm telling you. I think she's a witch. You must convince her to leave as soon as you can. Don't tell the Queen, it will only raise suspicions, and, who knows, even bring the curse back because of the proximity of magic. You know, with the Black Forest and all," she said in a rush.

Golan tried to keep up, but she wasn't making sense. "You think Avalon is a witch?" he asked, more loudly than he should have.

Mava looked terrified. "Hush, boy," she said, and Golan let the disrespect slide as he tried to decipher her message.

"Why haven't you told the Queen?"

"Because of the laws. Who knows what the Queen will do to her? They may suspect her of ambush, perhaps leading a rebellion from the Forest, or something. I think she's young, and maybe misled, but I don't want to see her hurt, do you?"

Golan shook his head slowly.

"And the Queen is trying to push her and your brother together, can't you tell? If she is a witch or has any dealings with magic, who knows what she will bring upon the future kingdom! Make her leave, quickly," she repeated.

"All right. I'll help her go in the morning," he agreed, his decision already made before he'd spoken to Mava.

Mava finally stood aside and unblocked his path, but as Golan headed to his room, he was still confused. Mava was hiding something.

When he neared his room, he heard voices in the chamber next door, his brother's room. His mother's tone caught his ear, and he paused before entering his own chambers, advancing instead toward the slightly cracked door ahead. It was late. Why was his mother up?

The voices were low, but once he was just outside the door, he could make them out if he strained.

"Please, Joran, as your mother, you know I wish only the best for you."

A mumble in reply.

"I know you aren't ready to settle into a marriage yet, but I have information that this girl could be good for our kingdom. She has skills that could help you. Help you take the throne, don't you see?" It was a hiss. Then, "At least give her a chance, and I won't push anything. But you will help me keep her here a little while longer. It won't hurt you or your pride, seeing as how you like to woo the ladies, and it will only help our family. I'll explain as soon as I can, my son. Trust me?"

She was trying to extract a promise, Golan knew. His mother was nothing if not calculating. He knew better than to trust her, and he thought Joran did too. But, take the throne? Is that what she had planned for Joran? She could be tried for treason for such a statement. He gaped at his brother's face in his mind's eye. Joran went along with her so often...was it because *Joran wanted the throne?*

His mother was shrewd, and she was always on the lookout to promote their family, their kingdom, and, he suspected, inevitably herself. Joran was obviously her favorite, but Golan had never felt jealous. It just made sense. Joran was wordly and confident and handsome. *I'm serious and private and not as tall as my brothers.* She could showcase Joran. She couldn't find Golan half the time, even if she wanted to display him.

But there was Benrid. Golan's heart clenched as he thought of his eldest brother. The smart one, the one who had a quick temper, who was destined to kingship, until the accident. He'd thought of Benrid constantly this summer. They had been closer than he and Joran were, and this summer wasn't the same without him at Blackstone. But mostly he ached for Benrid himself, locked in darkness as he was with the blindness that had caged his world. He must be so lonely with the enforced solitude. Purposeless and empty.

Golan wanted to be there to distract him, but even if he had been at home, the shame of Benrid's state, and the curious nature of what had happened, had made his parents lock him away secretly. Only two trusted servants who had been sworn to secrecy could attend him. The Queen visited him, and the King had too, a few times, but even his brothers were banned. Golan had still sneaked in once or twice.

He felt his throat growing tight as he remembered the misery of those visits. Benrid had been so angry the first time, beside himself, and then, a few days later, he was just empty. He sat at his desk, staring at nothing, seeing nothing, for hours. Golan had tried to talk to him, comfort him, coax him to interact, but other than a small shake of his head once, and then a sigh, he hadn't responded at all. Golan hadn't been sure if those feelings were natural in such a circumstance, but the invisible weight his brother seemed to carry as he slouched on his chair seemed to smother the life from his bones.

Benrid seemed too exhausted to get his voice out, to gather his thoughts, or even move. His blindness was crushing him, and Golan was worried. It was one of the most strained hours he had endured, as he cowered in front of his brother-turned-stranger and tried to elicit some semblance of the boy he used to know.

A dull pounding was starting at the base of his neck now, and Golan massaged the spot, trying to ward off the headache. He was tired, but he needed to stay awake longer. He needed to think clearly. He headed to his room and sat down. There was something going on, he could sense it, but there must be something he was missing.

Avalon, the mysterious Princess, who had entered their lives a week ago was beginning to fill a space in his heart. She was fighting her own battles, and he had vowed to help her, but so far nothing he had discovered had really solved anything for her, and tomorrow she was leaving. How could he help then? Then there was Mava's strange warning, and now his mother's...plan, was the only word he could think of. She was pushing Joran toward Avalon, that was clear, though her motive for their union was unclear.

He went over what he knew so far. His mother was planning for Joran to be king, although he was the spare. She wanted him to marry Avalon, which was strange, seeing as how she had barely been civil to the princess at first. Golan bolted upright as an idea snapped into place. Avalon's pea that held so much power. Could that have anything to do with it? Perhaps even why she was abducted in the first place? He considered his mother's sudden change of heart toward the princess, her determination to keep Avalon here, and Mava's unfounded fear. It didn't all make sense, but it must be connected.

Chapter 16

Carry Me Home

Unconcerned with propriety, Golan hurried down the dim hall, and into the next wing to Avalon's room. He waved aside the guard who was standing there, and knocked, breathing heavily from his haste. Nothing. He knocked again, more loudly, and there was some movement, and then a timid, "Yes?"

"I'm sorry, Avalon, it's me. Golan." He hadn't meant to frighten her. "I need to talk to you."

Avalon cracked the big door open, only one hazel eye peeking through. There was fear on her face, but she met his gaze steadily, and her bravery again warmed his heart.

"Please give me a moment," she said, shutting the door.

When she opened it again, she was dressed, though her hair was loose. She stepped into the hall and looked at him questioningly.

"What is it?" She glanced around warily.

"You can go," Golan told the guard, and Avalon nodded to him when he looked to her for permission.

The long hall was empty now. It was barely lit, but he knew no one would be up here at night. Unless summoned, the servants would all be in bed now.

"When I left you, I met Mava at the top of the stairs. She spoke to me fiercely, told me to get you out of here as soon as possible. I could not figure out why, even though she babbled something about your being a witch and having magic–" he paused as Avalon gasped, but plunged back into his story.

"I told her you wanted to leave anyway, so I would help you. Immediately after that, I overheard my mother in Joran's room, telling him you were very special and you had the power to help our kingdom. She told him to entertain you and keep you here and 'give you a chance'. And I think she wants him to fall in love with you." His tone softened on the last line.

Avalon just blinked at him. "I don't understand. I don't understand any of that. I don't have any power, good or evil, and I can't help this kingdom–right now I cannot even help my own!"

"Neither do I, completely. But I think they found your pea. Mava must think it is evil, and my mother must know something or suspect something of its power. I needed to let you know before the morning in case you wanted to stay until you got it back, now that you know where it is."

"But I still don't know where it is." Avalon shook her head.

"I'm pretty sure my mother and Mava found it. Surely they still have it. I could just ask them."

"No." Her eyebrows furrowed. "No, if that is not the case, I do not want them to know about it."

"Right. I will search, then, if I have to."

"Okay." Her voice sounded small in the long hall. The shadows under her eyes were pronounced, and her features were strained. He could almost feel the exhaustion emanating from her, and it matched his own.

"Go back to bed, Avalon. We can still meet in the morning, and you can let me know then if you want to search for the pea or leave as planned," he said gently.

She nodded, staring into space behind him and biting her bottom lip.

She looked much too slender to be standing there like that, weighed down by trauma and grief and the responsibility of a kingdom and a powerful jewel. His hand reached out shakily and brushed her hair. Then he rested it on her shoulder and squeezed softly. He was about to turn to go, when she finally drew her golden eyes up to meet his.

"Golan, I'm scared," she whispered, and his heart twisted.

"I've been afraid almost every night. I feel so alone over here, and yet, I hear noises. And there were those strange pains the first night, and then my pea disappeared, and I can't lock this door."

She stopped. She was looking down, but her lashes didn't hide the tears that slipped down her cheeks.

"I don't want you to leave. I'm tired, but I'm too afraid to sleep. Especially now." Her chin trembled, and Golan instinctively drew her to him.

"I won't leave. I'll stay right here. All night. I promise."

"Wh-what?"

"I'll sleep here, Avalon. In the hall. You'll be safe. I promise," he said again, barely able to look down at her upturned face, the wet cheeks and the huge shimmery golden puddles in her eyes, for fear his throbbing heart would beat out of his chest.

A few minutes later, bedded down on one of her mattresses—she assured him she still had plenty, Golan lay back in his clothes. He had removed his boots, but, true to his word, he hadn't left, even to ready for bed. Avalon had receded into her bedroom, looking much more at ease.

"Thank you so much, Golan," she had whispered before shutting the large door safely between them. Even in the uncomfortable position on the floor, Golan felt a weary peace stealing over him, and he closed his eyes, reliving the feel of her cradled against his stocky figure, and the honey color of her trusting eyes as she looked up at him. Then he fell asleep.

Avalon slid into bed, strangely calm, knowing that her friend was outside her door. For the first time since she had been here, she dropped into a deep sleep.

The sun had already risen when she awoke, though the light was still thin, and it was early. She wanted nothing more than to drift back into the sweet rest she had been enjoying, but Golan was expecting an answer from her this morning, and, in fact, she hadn't even decided on her plan yet.

Her eyes strayed to the door, and a smile tickled her lips. He was so kind, sleeping out there like a devoted guard. She got up and dressed, washed her face and teeth in the basin, and brushed her long hair. Slipping on her shoes, she stepped lightly to the door.

She would stay. She would tell him she would stay another day or two. They could try to find the pea together, and maybe the messengers would bring an answer from Haven.

She pulled hard at the door, but her arm jerked as the door refused to budge.

She was locked in.

CHAPTER 17

Look for the Sky in the Ceiling

At first, confusion furrowed her brow as she tried the door again. It really was locked. Mava had said they couldn't find the key. But someone had found it, obviously. Anger began seeping in as she called out. "Hello! Is anyone out there? Can you let me out?"

Her voice only bounced off the walls of her room, still bare, even with the armchair and rug Queen Lilian had added. There were no sounds on the other side of the door. She put her ear to the crack to hear better, but all was still.

"Golan?"

Nothing.

The keyhole was empty, but she could see nothing on the other side except the dim shadow of the wall across the hall, even straining as she did to get a better angle.

Golan.

If the key was missing, maybe he took it. Maybe he has had it all along.

Her trusting feelings of the night before vanished in doubt. Not only did she feel foolish for trusting him, she felt angry for the hurt she felt around her heart. How could she have leaned on him like that last night, let her tears fall in front of him? She had told him everything–everything! How dare he do this!

Because if he hadn't done it, who had? He had been out there.

She paced for a while, expecting someone to come. Mava, with breakfast, at least. Or even Golan himself. Deep in her heart, she hoped Golan wasn't at fault. Maybe it was Mava's doing, considering what Golan had said last night. But he had been sleeping outside to watch out for her. What had happened? She didn't want to hate him. But as an hour passed, and then another, the sun high in the sky and her stomach growling with hunger, small sparks of panic twitched through her.

She banged on the door and yelled in a very un-princesslike way, but only silence answered her. She bit back the climbing fear, and went again to the window, peering down at the yard below. It was too far to reach safely. Even with a rope, she wasn't sure she was brave enough to climb from this height. She had never attempted something like that before. She scanned the space below her, hoping to see someone to whom she could call out, but no one appeared within view.

Curse this room with no servant's bell! What kind of guest chamber was this?

In exasperation, she pulled the chair over to the window and plopped down. All she could do was wait.

A key clinked in the door, and Avalon flew toward the sound. A servant Avalon had never seen before pushed a tray of food through the crack, trying to pull the door shut after her, but Avalon clung to the doorknob and pushed her foot in the way.

"What are you doing? Who locked this door? Let me out!"

She struggled with the woman for a moment as they each pulled on the door. Then the maid pushed something against her face, and her vision clouded. The smell was strong, and the world spun in a dizzying circle. Her grasp on the door loosened as she tried to keep her balance, but her knees suddenly buckled, and she crashed down, succumbing to blackness.

Afternoon sunlight slanted through the window before anyone else approached the room. Avalon had been unconscious for a while, but she wasn't sure how long. The breakfast tray on the floor beside her looked fresh enough that she assumed it hadn't been a long time. She gazed at the food from her spot on the floor, a surge of hunger and then of nausea crashing into each other. She grimaced and turned her face away.

She felt sick. Her head spun, and she tried to take shallow breaths to keep from retching. Things settled after a while, but she stayed still for a long time, afraid to move. She tried to recall what had happened. Although the last woozy moment was unclear, she remembered the servant who had tried to deliver her breakfast without letting her leave the room. The woman had put the cloth against her face and overwhelmed her with the strong, stinging scent. It must have been a sleeping potion of some sort.

Finally she sat up. She was groggy but unhurt, and this time her stomach didn't rebel. She was hungry, but after what had happened, she was afraid to eat.

I'm a prisoner. I was drugged. I wouldn't put it past anyone if this food were poisoned too.

This was all part of a nightmare. It must be. It had started with the attack from Cleft, and now it continued here in Ethereal, with mysterious people who pretended to be kind, but then took her prisoner.

Avalon felt worse than ever. Why did people want to capture her? She stood, swaying just a little, but feeling nothing but hot indignation. She bent down and scooped up the breakfast tray. She squeezed her frustration into it, and in a sudden surge of anger, flung the whole thing toward the door. She had never thrown anything in anger before, but it felt good to watch the juice and food splatter against the door, the dishes shatter and the whole mess pool on the floor.

When she heard a tentative knock on the door, hours later, she jumped up. There was a key in the keyhole, and then the door opened slightly. Queen Lilian eased herself through the crack. She surveyed the mess at her feet, one eyebrow arching just slightly.

"My dear, you must be so frightened," she cooed, ignoring the broken things and facing Avalon. "I am so sorry to treat you in this way. Believe me, it is not at all what I would want for you or for any guest of ours, but, with everything going on, we had to ensure your safety."

"By locking me inside my room like a prisoner?" Avalon choked on the words.

"I know that is how it must seem, but that is not what we meant. That is not how we want you to feel. There was no time to explain this morning, and I wasn't able to get back here until now. Please accept my apology and try to understand."

But Avalon was angrier than she had ever been. She had always been able to bite her tongue and coat her answer in graciousness before, but this morning had pushed her past that. Whatever this woman in front of her was trying to say just wasn't good enough. It sounded as nondescript as any greeting royal families sent to nobles in their kingdom. "We hope you are faring well; our condolences for your loss; our congratulations on your addition; our dearest hope for your well-being." She would not be deterred by those cliches.

"I do *not* understand," she said levelly. "I have not been told anything that is going on, and my time here has been nothing but guessing and worrying. I do not care what the reason for locking me up was, there is no reason you cannot tell me everything in full right now. Though, in fact, I don't believe you or anything you say. I believe you locked me in here because you want to use me for some reason, and you're afraid I'm going to run away."

"Don't get worked up, *Princess*. Of course you are feeling upset."

The way Queen Lilian said her title condescendingly wasn't lost on Avalon. In fact, "Princess" was the barest acceptable term of respect she could use, and she made even that sound sarcastic.

"As I said, circumstances just hindered me from letting you know. There were soldiers looking for you this morning, and I sent Mava up to warn you lest you wander downstairs while they were here. As you were still asleep, she merely locked the door. It was only to protect you. Then, with their search, and the arrival of some visitors, things simply got out of hand."

"That is what you have servants for," Avalon practically growled. "You could have sent someone up here to explain. But instead, you sent a woman with breakfast several hours too late, who suffocated me with a sleeping potion when I tried to find out what was going on."

"It was merely a calming smelling salt in case you were frantic. No sleeping involved, unless she used too much, which I would not doubt her to do. She's not the brightest girl we have. For that, my double apology."

"Let me out." Avalon's voice was deadly quiet.

She approached the Queen, expecting her to step in front of her to block her path or perhaps shove another cloth against her nose, but Queen Lilian raised her open palm to the door.

"Of course, my dear. Joran is expecting to ride with you shortly. He was disappointed yesterday. Now that the danger is past, of course you may leave. I'm sure the fresh air will raise your spirits."

Avalon bristled at the sickly sweet tone of voice, but she was still surprised at the sudden change of predicament. She did not want to go riding. She wanted to find Golan and find out what had happened. Why hadn't he at least warned her or come to explain what was going on? Maybe he had already awoken and was gone before Mava locked the door. Maybe he had not really stayed there through the night at all. Or, maybe, he was helping the Queen.

She brushed a hand over her forehead, pushing her messy hair back. Maybe she should go riding. Maybe she should get to know Joran after all. And one way or another, she was determined to get her pea back.

CHAPTER 18

Silence is an Answer

Joran was raffish in his brown high-waisted breeches, spotless boots, and gray riding shirt. The casual outfit suited his wiry figure. Someone had brought a green riding habit to Avalon's room shortly after the Queen had left her standing there with the door wide open.

She had put it on, reveling in the soft velvet fabric, which was welcome against her skin after so many days without her usual rich fabrics. This gorgeous outfit fit perfectly. She turned this way and that, gazing down at her figure, highlighted by the gold trim, and feeling pleased with the fit. She went to the servant's bell in the hall and summoned two girls to plait her hair around her head. They were skilled, and within a few minutes, she was ready.

Although she told herself she wasn't looking for Golan, she couldn't help scouring the halls as she made her way outside and down to the stables. She didn't see him anywhere, so she clenched her jaw and made up her mind to enjoy Joran's company instead. She was too upset to try to talk herself into giving Golan the benefit of the doubt for what had happened this morning.

She entered the stables without an escort. If she needed one, Joran could certainly assign her someone, but, as she guessed, other than the perpetual guard who followed at a distance, he meant for them to go alone. Fine, if that was the way it would be, she would stop worrying about it. Just because something was proper in Haven didn't mean it was proper in Ethereal.

She mounted her horse sidesaddle this time, like a princess instead of a wild woman, and arranged her soft skirts perfectly about her legs. Joran mounted his horse, a huge powerful stallion, with an easy fluid motion, then grinned at her.

"Shall we be off, Your Highness?" His right eyebrow was raised in a smirk, the look that he often wore, as though snickering at a secret joke, the one that perhaps he realized was charming.

She nodded, and they spurred their horses forward.

The ride went much better than she was expecting. Although her conversation with Joran was the normal, simple polite conversation she'd practiced for years, nothing like the raw communication she had with Golan, Joran was eager to please, always looking out for her needs and her comfort. She enjoyed the attention, even if the efforts didn't touch her heart. The breeze was refreshing, and the steady trot of the horses made her feel like she could outrun her worries and leave them all behind. She and Jordan didn't discuss anything worrying or even important, and for a while she let her mind rest from the endless questions and decisions that had been burdening her for the past week. She did not even tell him about being locked in her room or ask him about the Cleftan soldiers who had come after her. She was afraid he would brush her off, and she didn't have the energy to face that, so she kept quiet, willing just to enjoy what she had in the moment without inviting any more hurt.

The day was balmy, with enough of a breeze to keep perspiration at bay, and they were gone for several hours. The village was modest, but quaint, and the townspeople inclined their heads or bowed slightly when they passed, but they didn't gape, and Avalon assumed they were used to seeing the Prince in their town.

"Small place, but big enough to get into trouble," Joran said with a wink. Avalon didn't ask what he meant. They stopped for lunch at a pleasant tavern. Joran ordered ale with his meal and laughed when Avalon asked for water.

"What's this? Her Highness doesn't partake?"

"No, I - I don't. I haven't," she stumbled.

He just laughed. "You're missing out then. Or maybe I'm the one who's missing out."

He waggled his eyebrows and leaned forward. His hand stole over hers. "They say strong drink loosens a person's lips. Maybe a glass of ale, and you'd even give me a kiss," he teased.

Avalon flushed. Joran's long, straight nose and full lips hovered too close to her face, and she knew all she had to do was lean in, and for a moment she wanted to, just to see what it felt like. Just to forget her other burdens for a moment. Her eyes fluttered closed, but then Golan's green eyes flashed through her mind.

She slumped back, suddenly feeling weary. "Let's go back after this," she said.

Golan was not at supper that night, and Avalon felt a twinge of worry when she saw his place empty. Maybe she had jumped to the wrong conclusions too quickly. She tried not to sigh. *I just don't know what to believe about him.*

The Queen asked her about the afternoon, and she answered politely, but didn't go into details.

Queen Lilian gave Joran a sideways glance. "And you, son, did you also have a pleasant ride?" she asked as she cut into her roast.

Joran stared at her with slightly narrowed eyes for a moment before smiling widely and winking at Avalon. "Just lovely, Mother."

Avalon blushed at the unexpected wink, and the King chuckled. He began chatting mildly, saying nothing of the apparent disruption this morning. Avalon wondered if it had really been all that invasive, the visit from the soldiers. Either he was good at hiding relevant information, or the Queen was not entirely truthful.

When there was a lull in the conversation, Avalon spoke up, "Is Prince Golan unwell?"

The Queen's eyes met hers sharply, suspicion darting through her gaze, but her voice was light as she replied, "Hardly. He's on a journey for a few days. He and Lady Hahly have been growing affectionate recently, and I believe he's missed her with all this solitude here at Blackstone. He left early this morning and probably won't be back for a week at least." She waved her fork dismissively and changed the subject, but Avalon felt her stomach drop.

Avalon did not go to her chambers after dinner. She wandered outside, the evening freshly fallen, and the air still warm. She bit her lip as she rounded the grounds to the gardens, trying not to think about Golan's departure. Why was she feeling this despondent? He had every right to leave any time he wanted, and no reason to tell her.

Except that he had said he would meet her this morning and help her. Of course, she hadn't shown up, and he might have assumed she had changed her mind, at least about letting him help.

No wonder he left without a warning. He'd been so kind, but Avalon had been reluctant in her own feelings toward him, and she had probably seemed much colder than she intended. She remembered the way she had shut the bedroom door primly last night, when all he had done was give up a good night's rest right before a journey. *A journey he didn't tell me about.* But, then again, she was supposed to have left by then herself.

The rose bushes climbed the trellis partitions, creating floral walls that concealed her from view of anyone on the property or behind the windows of the castle. She sank down on a bench near one such rose bush, the faint perfume of the petals wafting to her on the air. The flowers were almost all closed for the night. The way they hung their heads in slumber was dejected and mournful, and suddenly Avalon felt tears rushing down her cheeks. She had been trying to keep them back all week, every time she was frightened or confused or overwhelmed, choking them back when they pooled up, but she couldn't stop them this time. She was too tired to try.

She let them fall, running down her neck and splashing down her front. Her voice came out in hiccuping sobs as she cried for her family, the terrible twilight of not knowing whether they were dead or alive. She cried for her sisters, and for the pea, which she had lost, and all the weight she had been carrying, trying to solve everything herself, and constantly being disappointed in her saviors, the Rearevgards of Blackstone. She cried for the pain and fear that pervaded her room every night, and she cried for Golan.

She had liked his strength and calm, the way he listened to her timid speeches, and the way he had pulled her into him last night. Surely he could not have been behind the plot to lock her up this morning. She didn't want to make any more decisions without him, and although she needed to go home, she did not want to leave without seeing him again.

Although that is what he did to me.

She cried harder. She couldn't even bear to think of his gentle eyes focused on this Lady Hahly, listening to her without judgment, the earnest adoration in his gaze as he leaned toward her, his sturdy arm draped around her. The thought hurt, but she knew it shouldn't. She had no right to feel that way. He didn't belong to her. And for some reason, that hurt the most.

Avalon woke the next morning feeling groggy and deflated. She had spent hours in the garden, letting her grief water the ground the night before. When she'd returned to her chamber, it was late, but she had requested a bath, and the maids had complied. She'd asked them to leave while she soaked in the warm water until it cooled and she felt chilly. Though the sticky tears had been washed from her face and neck, her eyes had stayed red and her nose stuffy from crying, and the bath hadn't cured her grief.

A knock at the door brought her fully awake now. She sat up in bed, waiting for the breakfast to be brought in, but the knock sounded again.

"Who is it?" she called.

"Alice, Your Highness."

Avalon rushed to open the door, rubbing the sleep from her eyes in the process. Alice smiled at her when the door opened, but it was a sad smile, not her typical slice-of-melon look.

"Avalon, how are you?" She reached her hand out and squeezed Avalon's arm. Avalon just shook her head, unable to put any of her feelings into words.

"Listen, I have news that I think you should know. I was talking to the men yesterday afternoon, and I mentioned the missive that had been sent to Haven. I thought I could help glean some information for you. I asked them who had gone to deliver it. They told me that no one has left since you've been here. Then I asked about the patrol who was supposed to go in search of your captors and your sisters, but they told me again that no one has left—no guards, no messengers, no one." She looked pained, and Avalon felt lightheaded.

Alice paused for a moment. "I wanted to tell you last night, but I couldn't find you. I'm so sorry."

Avalon's pain was reflected in Alice's bright blue ones, and her empathy steadied Avalon just a little.

"What do you mean? Was it all a lie?" she whispered.

Alice nodded slowly. "Yes, it appears so. I suppose the King thought it too dangerous or unnecessary, but he didn't want you to be upset. Maybe he is still planning something — something even bigger that he can't tell anyone about— an attack or something, I don't know. I just don't like dishonesty, whatever the reason. If I were you, I would want to know."

No one had left. No patrol, no messenger, no missive. The King and Queen had done nothing the whole time she had been here. They hadn't pursued her sisters or tried to get news from home. Did they still not believe her, or was there another reason they hadn't made a single effort?

Anger tried to surge up, but she hushed it, trying to think of a good reason for all of this. Both the King and the Queen had *said* the scouts had returned without information. Why the lie? Surely she was missing something.

Alice was still talking. "There is something else. Trouble. Someone was locked in the prison tower last night. I know because I left my window open, and I heard someone calling out. When I got up, I realized it was coming from the tower, but, of course, the entrance is always locked, and, besides, I wouldn't go up there myself to investigate. I would have gone back to bed, thinking it was a prisoner maybe caught stealing or something, awaiting judgment from the King in the morning, but then I heard your name. The person was calling you. I'm sure of it. I asked the other girls, but they didn't hear it and said I was probably dreaming. I've tried to keep watch this morning, but I haven't seen anyone ascend the tower or come down either."

"Calling my name?" Avalon wasn't sure she believed her either. "Should I try to find out who is up there?" Shivers ran up her arms as she thought of going up the tower stairs to the holding cells at the top by herself. Who would be calling her name from the prison?

"I'll go with you, if you want," Alice offered, giving her a fortifying smile. "Martha can handle breakfast without me."

CHAPTER 19

Show Me the Path

Together the girls crept outside to the tower which stood apart from the castle, near the east corner. The thick wooden door was locked securely, and even Alice seemed nervous near the prison. They rounded to the far side, which would be invisible from the castle, and Avalon called hesitantly, "Hello. Is anyone up there?"

She was afraid to be louder, lest someone in the castle hear her, but she wasn't sure even the person in the tower could hear her at that volume. There was no movement or answer, so she called again more loudly, but finally, they gave up and left.

"Maybe you did just imagine it," Avalon suggested.

Alice shook her head. "I know I didn't, but maybe whoever it was is gone now. I will keep my eyes and ears open for anything you should know."

Avalon didn't have Golan to help her secure a horse or a map or provisions now, but she still needed to get home. Blackstone was starting to feel more and more like a trap. She decided to ask Alice for help that evening.

She declined supper, too seething to be polite to the King and Queen, and requested a tray instead. She ate in her room, waiting till twilight when she could catch Alice finishing up in the kitchen. She sat by her big window, enjoying the breeze and the sunset over the hills beyond the forest.

The sky was brilliant, and she watched the blinding orange fade to an amber glow, and then, too soon, to the deep blue of new night. *One,* she whispered, *do you hear me? Do You care that I need help?* She was about to stir from her reverie and head to the kitchen, when she spotted something in the darkness. She looked back quickly, her pulse increasing, though she wasn't sure why.

Then she saw it again. The lights from the forest. She hadn't seen any movement, human or other, beyond those trees since she had been here, and as much time as she had spent in this bedroom, she had gazed often enough through her window which faced the forest wall. She shivered a little in both excitement and fear. Those lights had led her here, and things at Blackstone certainly hadn't turned out well. Except she hadn't lost her life or been recaptured. And she had met Golan and Alice. She didn't want to trust the lights, but as she watched, she could see them summoning her, falling over each other to wave her over, and curiosity and a pull of something she couldn't name made her walk down the large stairs, and ease out the castle's back door.

There were guards at the gate–of course. She grit her teeth, annoyed at herself. She wanted to get out, but there was no way to do that without alerting someone, even if it was just the sentries. She couldn't face the disappointment of giving up, though, so she walked straight down the pathway with purpose, her head held high.

The lanterns on the gate were lit, making the surrounding space appear especially dark. She cleared her throat as she entered the circle of light, and surprise crossed both men's faces.

"Please open the gate," she demanded.

They glanced at each other, as if deciding. Then the taller one said, "We can't do that, miss. We're under orders by the King not to open the gates after nightfall."

She resisted biting her lip, which she knew would make her seem less confident, and said in as haughty a voice as she could muster, "That's 'highness' to you."

The guards fumbled for a second before bowing uncertainly.

"I'm the visiting Princess of Haven," she said, as though explaining to children. She disliked using her status as a stage for condescension, but she needed the guards to be intimidated.

"I completely agree with the King's orders, but, of course, he meant do not open them to allow anyone *in* after dark. I'm just going out for a bit."

The soldiers eyed her suspiciously, and she wished she had a good reason to be "going out for a bit" after dark, unaccompanied, and toward the Black Forest, but she didn't, so she just stood her ground, trying to look expectant. After a bit of shuffling, the men reluctantly eased the bar away from the gate, then opened it just enough for her to pass through.

Once the gate shut behind her, she felt at once free and frightened. She considered heading east, trying to make her way back toward home right now, but she had no provisions for such a trip.

Her mind focused again on her reason for being out here. The lights. They'd shown up the last time she'd prayed, and now that she'd prayed again. She drew a breath and reminded herself that Alice had said to trust them. And she trusted Alice.

The forest loomed invisible to Avalon's left, a wall of black that she could hardly differentiate from the blackness of the rest of the night. She was terrified, yet compelled to go closer. She took a few cautious steps, shortening the few yards between her and the Forest, hoping the lights would appear again.

And they did. More than a dozen at once danced in a frenzied cloud, almost as if they were dancing for joy. A tentative smile lifted the corners of her mouth. Then they flew closer, surrounding her, and coaxing her toward the Forest wall. They encircled her, moving as she moved. She sensed no threat from the little creatures, whatever they were. She entered the trees, her feelings of fear still under the surface, but not overwhelming.

She glanced down, Alice's story about tripping in a rabbit hole coming back to her, but it was too dark to make out the ground, so she would just have to trust the lights, as she had when they had brought her here. She walked for a long time, her eyes slowly adjusting to the darkness, and she could make out the shapes of trees. The further into the forest they went, the more twisted the trees became, much less like real trees and more like the misshapen gnarled stuff of dreams. The stories she'd already heard about this place trickled through her thoughts. What was she doing, heading straight into this evil cauldron of magic? But she was desperate, and something about these lights and the way they guided her didn't feel evil at all. *Alice said she knows people here. She called them friends,* she reminded herself again.

Finally, the lights stopped and landed at the base of an especially large tree. Avalon bent, trying to get a closer look. The long arrow-shaped lights dimmed. A sudden breath issued from them, a *whoosh* that was a mix between a whistle and a sigh, and she drew back a little. The tree trunk began to glimmer, as though a light had been switched on inside, and she could see a door. It opened from the inside, and someone ducked out.

Avalon stood rooted to her spot and found herself gazing into wizened eyes, which shone from inside a deep hood. The little lights flickered on, and they all bowed toward the man before her.

He pushed his hood back, revealing white hair growing thick on his aged head. He was regal, handsome even in old age, and his eyes were a pale bright blue. Lines in his skin outlined his eyes and his strong cheekbones, which tightened when he smiled slowly.

"You have brought her."

Avalon's gaze flew between the old man and the lights, and she stuttered. "Who, who are you? What–" but he held up his hand and cut her off.

"Come inside, Princess Avalon. We will talk. There is much to discuss."

She had no choice but to duck into the tree behind him. To her surprise, the tree was merely a facade front, and the room opened up behind it, apparently under a hill. There was a soft light glowing from the fire, making everything bright and cozy, in stark contrast to the blackness outside. In the light, she could see the man better. He had a strong square forehead that looked untouched by wrinkles and gave him the bearing of a king, and, indeed, he wore a band on his head. It wasn't exactly a crown, just a simple ring, but it glowed a dim purple under the light.

The lights crowded in the door after them, and Avalon was surprised to see they were tiny winged creatures, with long tails extending from them, not unlike a dragonfly. "Fairies?" she said, hardly believing that such things existed.

The old man smiled. "Sparks. They do my bidding. Summoning people, keeping watch, and delivering my messages."

He turned to the Sparks. "You are devoted. I am grateful. Thank you for bringing the Princess. You may go until it is time for her to return."

The tiny lights flew toward the door and blinked on their lights as they entered the darkness. The man turned to his small round table, pulling out a chair for Avalon, and then seating himself across from her.

"Ah, a good bunch, the Sparks. They truly are helpful. They have keen senses, if not feelings like we do. They're my creations, you know. "

She didn't know, but he didn't wait for her to answer. He looked into her eyes, studying them. "So, you are the Princess with the Pea."

She gave a tiny gasp.

He smiled again. He reminded her a bit of King Henry with the jovial crinkles and the kindness around his mouth, but unlike the King's eyes, which roamed absently, seemingly unconcerned with anything, this man's eyes were intense and focused.

"I am Erlich, the Great Magister of the kingdoms of Kerrynth, as you may have already figured out. I am sure you are wondering now how I know you, and why I summoned you here tonight."

She nodded.

"First, some tea? The kettle just whistled." He got up with an agile grace that belied his age, and plucked the kettle from its hook over the fire, pouring the water over the tea leaves and filtering it through a cloth into wooden mugs. "Every problem is easier to bear over tea."

Avalon took the cup gratefully, and he sat down again. This time she ventured a question first. "How long have you been hiding here?"

"This has been my home since the banishment of magic nearly a quarter of a century ago. The Great Magister Ferin was my father, and he instructed me in magic as I grew. By the time it was banished, I had taken over the duties of Great Magister, but I took him with me, of course, for protection. He didn't survive very long here, though. He was too aged, and it took a while to eke out a life of any sort in the Forest. The living conditions took a toll on him, and less than a year after we took cover, he fell asleep for the last time."

Silence took over. Magister Erlich gazed at the fire, lost in the past, and Avalon took in her surroundings, while trying to absorb the facts she had been told. If the man in front of her was the Great Magister, he was the ruler of magic in all of Kerrynth. Even Haven had magisters, though, without magic to keep, they simply performed ceremonies and religion. She had known that the Great Magister had disappeared years ago, but, as his disappearance had little effect on Haven, it was nothing more than a trivial fact there. But now she was meeting him, not just a magister of magic, but *The* Magister of all, hidden in the Black Forest.

Finally Magister Erlich looked at her again.

"The Sparks noticed you as soon as you drew near to the Forest last week," he said. "You had the pea. It's potent, you know, and its magic could not be hidden from creatures as sensitive as they. They told me about you immediately, but we didn't know who you were or if we could trust you, so they led you to the castle yonder. We've kept watch on you. Now we've asked you to come back so that we may explain everything and hopefully engage your help."

Avalon swallowed the hot tea, enjoying the tangy flavor. She hoped desperately that Magister Erlich had the answers she needed. She nodded him on.

"My Ancestor, the Great Magister of the Beginning, passed down his stories and his magic, and every generation has learned them. One legend, or such it has become, is that of the peas. To be honest, it's not a well-known legend these days, but there are still those who cling to it. And it's entirely true. If brought together, the three peas would give unlimited power to the ones who could activate them."

He shook his head. "Of course, the temptation of such power corrupted men, and when the Great Magister saw the danger, he distributed the peas, so that they could be used individually, but never together."

The man paused to see if she was following, and she nodded quickly. "We read as much in an old history," she offered.

"We?"

"The Prince and I, Prince Golan. He was trying to help me because...my pea disappeared," she tried to explain.

"We know where it is, do not fear, Avalon. But, back to the history lesson. Once the peas were scattered, the Great Magister hoped they would be used for good, or even lost, preventing their ever being brought back together. Of course, the knowledge of the peas was common in that generation, and many searched for them, but after a few generations, none had been reunited, and most people lost interest. The holders of the peas have changed often. They have used the power–and sometimes just the allusion to power–to lure partners to a marriage, a kingdom into alliance, and enemies to war. The gems have been stolen, traded, and bestowed as great gifts. Through it all, we Magisters have kept track of them, keeping records as they moved. We have always been able to feel the power emanating from them, if we are close enough. I created the Sparks to help me with that, among other things. Other Magisters before me have had their ways as well. My Sparks travel to the relative location of the peas, and if they ever sense the power dim, we know the crystal has moved. Just after you appeared in our Forest, the Sparks who guarded the pea at Haven arrived to tell me the power had faded there. Conveniently, we already knew where it had gone, thanks to your arrival. In fact, the magic peas have been busy moving quite a lot these past weeks, keeping my Sparks just as busy tracking them."

He smiled at her, and she warmed to the kindness crinkled in his face. Her apprehension was fading as she sat here in the simple, cozy underground home, warmed by the fire and the tea and lulled by Erlich's low voice.

"If you know where the pea is–where they all are–why do you need me? And why do you need to track the peas, if they aren't meant to be together?"

"They aren't meant to be together in the hands of humans any longer. However, we Gifted ones have always needed extra protection. Many people fear those who are different. They are afraid of our power and try to harm us to preserve themselves. It is sad, because in all my years and in all the history I've learned, I have never known a Gifted person to be wicked.

Except for us Magisters, who choose magic, all the Gifted are born with it innocently. They do not choose it, and they cannot change it, and with the gift comes a humility which causes them to use it responsibly."

"Except for the disease of evil which spread and caused the banishment, right?" Avalon asked, her brow furrowed.

Erlich simply shook his head as he looked down at the raw boards of the table. "Dear Princess, many times those who most want the power seek to destroy it the most."

"I don't understand."

"If someone can control the magic, they can own it. They can monopolize it. There was no disease of evil, at least not among the Gifted. Only in the heart of an evil human in Aspenia who tried to infect the magic. We were able to break the infected vein of magic before it spread to other kingdoms. Queen Lilian, however, turned the story against us instead, perpetuating the idea that *we* were harmful."

So, the whole history Golan was taught about magic needing to be banished because of an infection was untrue. And my own mother is from Aspenia. Maybe the reason Haven is silent on the whole subject of magic is because she's afraid of what nearly happened.

"But—" the Magister sighed—"the hour is late. There is much history to learn, but first I must reveal why we need you, Avalon."

No sooner had Erlich spoken than the door was flung open. Avalon's heart stuttered.

Golan stood in the doorway, his curls wild and his eyes wilder.

CHAPTER 20

Lost my Faith in the Blue

Avalon awoke in her chambers in the middle of the next day. Confusion threatened to suffocate her as she scrambled to remember where she was and what had happened. She felt dizzy like she had the first time she was given the sleeping potion, and she vaguely wondered if she had been poisoned again. Then she drifted down once more.

Even later, when the afternoon shadows were growing long against her wall, she woke again. This time she sat up. Events came flooding back from the night before. Her long quest through the Black Forest, the Great Magister's house, and then Golan rushing in. He'd been yelling, and he'd grabbed her roughly. She rubbed her arms where he had squeezed her.

Erlich had stood, trying to reach out and calm the prince, though Golan jerked away. "We can't do much with him right now, Princess," the old man called out, as Golan took hold of Avalon and moved her toward the door. "Your Gift..." The Magister's words faded as Avalon wrenched against Golan's grip, her mind whirling.

Golan had pulled and pushed her through the woods with him, overpowering her when she tried to struggle free. He didn't answer her questions.

She remembered no more.

Days passed, and she was still locked in her room. Food and drink were delivered in a timely manner, and her chamber pot emptied. Even a bath was drawn once, but her door was always blocked by guards when the maid entered or left, leaving no way to escape. She could tell from the regularly timed movements that there were always guards stationed there in shifts. She was a prisoner.

She gave up trying to call out or demand answers from the maids or guards. They barely looked at her. She begged them to give a message to Golan, Queen Lilian–anyone–but no one agreed. Other than those attendants, no one came to see her, not even Alice. She spent the days fuming.

She hated Blackstone Castle. She hated the Cleftans. She hated the Great Magister who seemed so kind but had let her get stolen again and now locked up. If he knew so much and had so much power available, he could have helped her. She was beginning to believe that it had all been a trap after all.

Most of all she hated Golan. She might have been able to forgive him for leaving her to be locked in her room the first time and for going off to see his Lady Hahly without telling her, but physically dragging her away from the Magister? He hadn't tried to assure that he was protecting her. He had barely talked to her at all, just grunted and shoved her. She couldn't forgive that. It hurt.

She wasn't prepared when a key clicked and her door was pushed open without a warning knock. The Queen entered the room and closed the door behind her. She approached Avalon, who was lying on her bed, with a mix of curiosity and fright, like she was examining a stray kitten who might suddenly hiss and unleash its little claws.

"Well, Princess, it seems you are always determined to do your own thing—try to solve everything yourself. You've failed. I made sure of that. It makes me furious when my plans don't go the way I want, but I'm willing to forgive you in exchange for a favor."

Avalon stared at her numbly. She hated Queen Lilian and her fake tones.

"I was told when you headed into the Black Forest the other night. It's illegal to go there. I had to send Golan after you to rescue you. You could be executed for breaking the law, but I've decided to overlook your mistake if you do what I say. We're having a ceremony tomorrow. I need you to attend. The maids will attend you and dress you. You must appear exactly as they dress you, and promptly. There will be many in attendance, and I will not have disappointed crowds. If you do well, you will be free of this room. If not, I'll keep you locked here as long as I need to, even if it's forever."

She spun on her heel and left before Avalon could say a word.

CHAPTER 21

A Wall of Fog

T rue to the Queen's word, maids bustled into Avalon's room before breakfast the next morning. They fed, bathed, and dressed her in the finest gown she had ever worn, even at home. The square neckline dipped dangerously low, and she was self-conscious to see the shadow between her breasts bared to the world. The shimmery skirts were long and full, and the overlay was entirely lace. The girls smiled and congratulated her figure when she twisted and turned to see all of herself in the mirror.

Then they sat her down and began on her face, rubbing cream under her eyes, and rouge on her lips. Her hair took the longest, and her back ached from sitting on the stool for so long, but when they were done, she couldn't help but smile. They had braided her long tresses in dozens of tiny braids which were coiled around her head, creating a crown, and looped under and around each other in beautiful detail on the back. They finished with gold jewelry at her throat, on her ears, and even on her arms.

"What is going on this evening? What kind of ceremony?" Avalon pressed the friendly girls, but they looked at each other warily.

"It's a celebration for Prince Joran," the tallest girl, a pretty brunette, finally offered.

Finally, Avalon was ready. Although she felt heavier than she had in a long time with all the extra undergarments and jewels she was wearing, the excitement of dressing up had cheered her up, despite herself. Perhaps the Queen wanted to parade her around as Joran's beloved or some such thing, but if her compliance really meant the Queen would be satisfied and let her go, it would be worth playing the part for one party. Besides, even if she couldn't rely on the Queen's words, at least this was a chance to leave her room. Maybe she could sneak away and find her pea. Or even run from the castle.

Though she had to work to keep her head high with her heavy hair and pins piled on top, she felt elegant as she descended the stairs. At the bottom, a guard waited to escort her. When she reached him, he turned, and she was surprised to see Golan's face.

Annoyance rushed up her neck, heating it.

"What are you doing dressed as a guard?" Her whisper was harsh.

Sadness muted his mossy eyes. He offered his arm.

She hesitated, not wanting to take it, but finally she relented, barely resting her fingertips on his elbow. She stared straight ahead, her features hard, and her lighter mood quickly plummeting.

"You lied to me," she hissed.

He pulled his elbow close to his side, squeezing her hand softly. "Avalon, please listen to me. I don't know what all happened, but it wasn't me. Not the real me."

He kept his eyes carefully in front of him. He hardly moved his lips, and she could barely make out the words as he breathed them out.

"You're a better liar than the rest of your family, pretending to be all kind and caring, and then treating me like a ruffian." Hurt coated her words. "You let me be locked in my room, and, and..." Emotion tightened her throat, tangling her words.

They were getting close to the ballroom, and Golan slowed his pace. Ahead, people were bustling through the doors, and servers passed them in the hall, heading to the kitchen to refill trays.

"Avalon, we're being watched. I can't explain right now. I am sorry for what happened, but you have to believe it wasn't really me. I was under a spell of sorts. Now, listen, tonight my mother is going to trap you."

"She said—"

"Shh," he hissed, squeezing again in warning. "I don't have time to explain this, but whatever you do, do not look directly at the Queen. That's how she transfers her power. That's what she did to me the other night. Erlich and I will distract everyone here. When we do, that's your signal. You must go through the side door the servants use. Alice will be there. Follow her. She will take you somewhere safe until I come for you. If you don't, Avalon, the Queen will use her power on you too and make you do things you don't want to do."

He pressed his lips together as they got to the main doors, bowing low as Avalon was announced, his brown curls hidden under his helmet. He backed away then, blending back into the shadows.

Emotions poured through her. Anger and hurt toward Golan still bubbled near the surface, but confusion, and dread, and a terrible wish to trust him followed behind.

The King stood there, waiting for her entrance. He extended his hand, grasped hers, and smiled. But she didn't trust his kind smile anymore. She did not trust anyone.

"Your Majesty, is it the Crown Prince's birthday?" she ventured.

King Henry's smile faltered, and he looked confused. "Benrid?" he whispered, and Avalon recalled another secret this family had, the ill older prince. The king blinked at Avalon blankly. "An engagement. This is an engagement."

Icy dread washed through Avalon all the way to her toes.

She looked around for Golan, but couldn't see him. The King was escorting her down an aisle created by people crowded on either side. She noticed the silk runner on the floor that her feet were carrying her over and then saw the platform in the front. Joran stood there, and the dread that had begun with the King's strange sentence deepened as realization dawned.

I'm the intended!

Music trumpeted, billowing around her, but the roaring in her ears drowned it out. Her breath constricted. She pulled back, tugging at the King's arm to stop.

"No," she tried to get the word out, but it was a wheeze. She began shaking her head.

The King merely smiled gently at her again and nodded. He patted her hand reassuringly and kept walking. Avalon stumbled, a step behind him. Her vision blurred as panicked tears pricked her eyes.

"N-n-no," she said again, her stutter coming out strangely loudly.

Then she saw the Queen, there on the front row, turned toward her. Queen Lilian's stare was hard, and Avalon noticed her eyes glowing green.

Golan had said—but she was confused, as if she had just woken and couldn't remember where she was.

She tripped again, her wet eyes and whirling mind rendering her half blind, and someone from the side caught at her hand.

"Now, Avalon," she heard him whisper, and she knew it was Golan.

She turned to him, but he was pushing through the crowd, away from her. She whimpered. What was she supposed to do? She didn't remember.

A cry went up from the back of the crowd, and someone screamed. She heard the word fire as if it were spoken in slow-motion, and by the time it reached her, the King had already released her arm. Everyone ran in blurred colors around her, and she didn't recognize anyone.

She felt her feet move forward–down the aisle–even as her heart rebelled, but she could no longer resist. Her voice was stuck, her mind full of fog. What had Golan wanted?

Someone tugged at her arm, and she tugged back. Then Alice's face focused. The girl looked terrified, and she dug her fingers into Avalon's arm. "Hurry, please. Come with me," she urged, but Avalon shook her head.

"Alice, stop pulling on me. I am going to meet my betrothed. Let the others run if they must, but this was meant to be. I will not leave this room until we are engaged!" The words sounded surreal as they came out, and again her heart screamed inside, but she couldn't release the pain.

Fat tears rolled down Alice's cheeks.

"She's got you. I'm so sorry, she's already got you." Her face crumpled, but Avalon shook her off and kept moving forward, though the room was getting smoky.

Then she was at the front of the room, but no one was there. It was hard to breathe. She choked and looked around in desperation. "Joran!"

But it was Golan who materialized from the smoke. Avalon began coughing. Her eyes stung and watered. She felt faint and let Golan scoop her up. He ran awkwardly with her in his arms, her heavy dress billowing up around them. She put her head down on his shoulder and succumbed as everything went black.

CHAPTER 22

The World is Shifting

When she awoke, Avalon was first surprised to see she was in only her chemise and underclothes. She stared down at herself, wondering why she had gone to sleep half-dressed. But she was on the floor. She sat up gingerly. The stone floor was strewn with bits of straw, but it was still hard and cold against her skin, which was barely protected by the thin undergarments she wore.

Her shoes were still on. She looked around. She was in a cell. It was dark and bare, except for the straw on the floor, and more piled on a stone slab in the corner. A window high above her head let in thin sunlight. She stared at the window, trying to remember why she was here. She couldn't.

It was the strangest thing. She remembered a crowd of strange people. She could picture Alice's face crumpling into frantic tears, but she could not recall anything else. She tried to think back earlier and calmed a little as she relived the preparations of the morning before. She remembered her lovely dress, and the upcoming birthday party the Queen had threatened her to attend. And then she remembered Golan, dressed as a guard, whispering his warnings and instructions to her as he escorted her down the hall. He'd said the Queen had controlled him the night he dragged her out of the Magister's cottage, and that she was planning to use her control on Avalon too. It must have worked. The rest of the evening felt like looking through a blurry window.

And now she was in the prison tower.

Golan did not look up at his mother. He knew what could happen if he met her gaze when she held the power.

His mind wandered back over the past few days. He had not understood his mother's power, though he'd suspected something strange for a long time. He had often wondered about the meaningless things his father did, but she had not used the power on Golan until recently. It had taken him a few times before he realized it was eye contact that allowed her to overpower him. She had put him in the prison the night she had found him sleeping outside Avalon's room because he would not look at her, and her inability to control him made her afraid. He'd made the mistake of looking up at her later when she surprised him in his cell, and then found himself racing off on horseback away from the castle just moments later, though he had no recollection of the reason for the journey. Whatever destination she had put in his mind had faded once her power did.

The Great Magister had intercepted him that morning. Magister Erlich had been looking for Avalon, and had felt power hovering around Golan. He had stopped the horse, and even though Golan had fought to continue on, the old man had apparently used a scent to calm him. Golan remembered when his focus had come back several hours later. He had been lying on the Magister's rough wooden bed, the pine boughs no match for the softness of the royal mattresses.

He hadn't been asleep, just absent. He had stared up at the ceiling, his mind out of focus, his thoughts hard to reach. Erlich had waited patiently while his mother's magic had worn off, and his own calming effects had faded, and Golan had suddenly sat up, demanding answers faster than the old man could give them.

Erlich had shushed him. "Young Prince, there are many questions I can answer, many questions I *need* to answer, and I will. But first I must ask you one. Do you know the girl, Avalon?"

Golan's eyes had jerked to the man's, suspicion creeping into his features. "What do you want with her? What are you going to do to her?"

Erlich put his hands out. "No harm, no harm, certainly. But now, what would you do to protect her?" he pushed further.

Golan had drawn himself up. His broad chest rose and fell deeply. He narrowed his eyes at the man. "I would give my life to protect her," he vowed, the certainty of his own words surprising him. *I think I love her.*

Erlich had smiled so grandly, his widely spaced teeth showed through his whiskers. He nodded happily. "Then, Prince and Protector, I need you too."

Magister Erlich had gone to explain who he was. He'd confirmed the things Golan and Avalon had discovered about the peas. He'd even helped Golan understand why his mother was so obsessed with Avalon.

"Ancient laws restrict your mother from ever ruling Ethereal, do they not?"

Golan thought about it. He did seem to remember something about kingdom reign passing only to men. He nodded.

"She cannot change that law perhaps, but it seems she's intent on having power. Perhaps through the King for now, but you know he's quite a bit older than her, so that won't last forever. Now, think. If her son became king – and you tell me you suspect she's trying to get Prince Joran into that position – she could rule through him in a way. Imagine if he were bonded in marriage to someone Gifted. She could literally use their power as her very own. I suspect the girl, Avalon, is Gifted. I must bring her here to meet me and let my perception ring discover her Gift," he mused, touching his fingertips to the purple band around his head.

Golan had soon trusted the Magister, and he knew better than to trust his mother, who was ranting as she paced in front of him now. The hour was late, but even after the ruined engagement ceremony and the feast that followed, she'd not forgotten to corner him.

"Golan, you are my son. You know I do not want to hurt you, but you keep interfering with my plans!"

"You put me in the spirits-blasted prison last week, Mother–"

"I had to keep you from yourself! Protect you. You didn't know what you were dealing with."

"I was helping a friend. That's all," he ground out.

"Then let's get one thing clear. You are not the Crown Prince. You'll never sit on the throne. No matter what kind of friendship you think you have with that girl, do not mistake it for love. She must marry Joran, for he will be the next king. In order to help our family, she must marry Joran!"

He didn't look up, but considered stalking out.

"Look at me!" she hissed, grabbing him by the shoulder and shaking him. He jerked his face away from hers.

"No, mother! No, I know what you do. Father may not know that you control him more than half the time, but I've figured it out. I will not look at you. I won't even listen to this!"

He stood, but felt a sudden pain rip up his back. He flinched, shock causing him to spin around. Out of the corner of his eyes, he saw the glowing of his mother's eyes. He had his mother's eyes, big and soft and green, but this green wasn't the muted tint of an afternoon sea. It was bright and sickening and alive. He closed his own eyes, ignoring the pain, and breaking into a run.

"Do not interfere, again, Golan. Think about what happened to Benrid," she called, as he fled down the hall.

He fell onto the couch in his chambers after locking the door. His body shook until the burning pain finally dulled. His spine was stiffening where the ripping pain had hit him. There was no blood, no opening in the flesh. He hadn't seen a weapon. It must be part of her power. He shuddered.

What had she said? Think about what happened to Benrid? He thought of his frustrated brother, the picture of health and handsomeness and success, suddenly blind. Horror ballooned in his chest. Had mother...?

A mother would not do that to her son, he argued to himself. She *couldn't.* But...

He needed to find Avalon, but he did not know what had happened to her after she had been taken from him earlier that evening. Several hours had passed since he had pulled her out of the smoky ballroom, his fire diversion merely a pot of wet brush that smoked more than anything else and had been contained.

She had passed out on his shoulder, and he'd staggered under her dead weight, cumbered by the long dress she wore. It swirled around both of them, tangling his legs and catching on things.

Once in the hall, he'd laid her down as gently as possible, then tore at the skirts of the dress, trying to remove the heavy fabric. The skirt had finally given way, and he and Alice and Steward had thrown the extra clothes to the side before he'd picked her up again and hurried down the hall and out the servant's entrance.

It was nearly dark then, and he meant to hide her in the stables for a bit until she woke up. He was planning to take her on horseback to Erlich's cottage to hide and so the Magister could finish telling her what he knew. But he wasn't certain he could manage a safe journey with her unconscious. Steward would make sure she was safe until he could get her away.

Then the guards appeared. Apparently the Queen had commanded them to bring the girl to her, and though Golan could not tell if they were just following orders or if they were under her controlling power, they had halted him. Two had held him back, while another took Avalon from his arms. A guttural cry had risen from his throat, and he'd pushed the guards off, but there were more, and even though he was strong, he couldn't over-power six men. He watched in agony as his plan failed and Avalon was carried back inside the Castle, her head tilted back unnaturally far over the guard's elbow, her throat bared to the sky. Her dozens of braids were coming loose from their design and hung down like golden ropes to the ground.

He sat forward now, his elbows on his knees, and rubbed his hand over his face. He needed to find her. At least he had kept her from committing to Joran. He hadn't seen his brother since the ceremony and wondered if he knew he'd been under a spell the whole time. His mother had used her power on them more and more this past year, and though they hadn't realized it at first, he was pretty sure Joran was also aware of it now.

His parents had appeared after the ruined announcement, ever gracious and elegant, apologizing to the guests for the scare, regretting that the Princess had fallen ill due to the shock, and hosting the feast as though nothing truly terrible had happened.

Golan hadn't attended the feast. He'd found Steward instead, and they had tried searching for Avalon, but she wasn't in her chambers. Her door wasn't even locked. Alice was far too busy in the kitchen, with the feast being needed earlier than any of the staff had expected, to join them in the search.

He had even wandered to his mother's chamber, hoping to discover Avalon there perchance, or to find the pea, or the source of Queen Lilian's secret power, but it was all locked up tightly. He shoved the tight handle in frustration. Of course, anyone with secrets would need to use locks. He felt sure she had Avalon's pea, but she had been using her power long before Avalon arrived, so there had to be something else, too.

It was late now, and most of the guests had gone, some to their encampments around the castle grounds, some to their homes, others to lodges in the village, and the more distinguished guests had been given rooms in the castle. He had no desire to entertain visitors or hear their gossip about the terribly orchestrated engagement with the confused Princess who fainted on the scene. Having such a sudden betrothal would be reason enough for gossip, but Joran was a known rogue, so they wouldn't be surprised.

His intention to marry couldn't have been announced more than a few days ago. In fact, Golan was surprised so many had come on such short notice. Those days locked in her room would not have felt short to Avalon, though. While everyone in the kingdom had been traveling to Blackstone, she had been treated like a prisoner with no news or contact. He hadn't even been able to see her. She was heavily guarded. He had tried to give her a message at least, but the guards denied it, on orders from the Queen.

People had started arriving at the Castle two days ago, but it wasn't until the morning of the ceremony that Golan had finally caught wind of what was happening. He'd rushed to the Magister as quickly as he could manage. He'd been there twice before, but both times he'd been under the spell, so his memory of the way was foggy. Together they had thrown together a plan. A plan that had failed.

I need to find Mava, he decided now, shoving away his exhaustion. If anyone had information, it would be her, and he needed information before he rescued Avalon. Then he'd find her and take her to the Magister. The old man had helped with the initial flames of the diversion, which were tall and hot enough to grab everyone's attention, but ended harmlessly in clouds of smoke. He had disappeared after that, most likely back into the safety of the Forest, until it was time to reveal himself.

CHAPTER 23

Sometimes a Flower Dies

M ava was not surprised when Golan cornered her. She had been with the Queen at the ceremony and had seen him pull Avalon into his arms before hurrying through the side door with her. She had hoped deep inside that they'd escape, that Avalon would be gone and it would all be over, but then Queen Lilian had demanded an answer from her, and she'd hung her head and told the truth, pointing in the direction they'd gone.

The Queen had gotten her way, as usual. She had captured Avalon again, and dealt with Golan, and Mava had not stood up for them, her yearning to defy the Queen caught as always between the fear of hurting her sister or losing her nephew.

"Mava, my mother trusts you, but she uses you," Golan began.

He had been that way since he was little—blunt and truthful. He hadn't made trouble often, but when he did, he could never hide it. His eyes were too honest, his face too earnest, and he never hid behind fanfare. He was looking at her now, willing her to disagree with his eyes hard on hers.

She looked away.

"I know it, and so do you," he continued, pausing to let his words sink in. "We need your help. I need to know where Avalon is, and, mostly, I need to know why my mother needs her so badly. You called the girl a witch just a few nights ago, and I was confused then, but I think now that you were trying to protect her. You thought I'd fear her—or for her—and help her leave. You have some compassion in you, Mava, I know it. Please help us."

Mava sighed. "I was just trying to protect myself, Prince," she said sadly.

He questioned her with his eyes. She met his gaze, feeling sorry for this young half-brother of her nephew. He'd always been close to Benrid. Kind to him. The constant competition between Benrid and Joran didn't exist with their little brother, Golan. Even after Benrid's blindness, Golan had tried to bring him back from the darkness in his mind, even though he could not cure the darkness over his eyes. He'd grieved for him. When everyone else pushed Benrid away, Golan had tried to pull him closer.

Mava glanced around, then whispered, "Come with me. Stay quiet."

She led him around the Castle, upstairs and down and through the halls, going nowhere on purpose for most of the journey, just in case anyone tracked them, but finally, she centered on her destination. They entered the Queen's rooms. Mava unlocked the door easily, as was habit, because that room always remained locked. Her hands trembled as she turned the key, every small sound twisting her nerves a little tighter. She was doing this. She was betraying the Queen. And she was terrified.

She knew Lilian wasn't in her chambers. She was out with two lady friends who had been there for the wedding. They had arranged for a luncheon at a tearoom in the village before the ladies traveled on.

Mava had been asked to stay and keep watch over the valuables instead of attending the Queen, who took a lady's maid instead. Mava was supposed to make sure the pea stayed safe, her sister stayed concealed, Avalon stayed in the prison tower, and no one knew about any of it.

The Queen rarely left her stakes at risk like that, especially in the hands of one who could see it as an opportunity. But Mava had been nothing but faithful her whole life, and Golan was right. The Queen trusted her.

Still, her heart was beating loudly when she stepped into the room, furtively glancing around just to be sure, as though Lilian could materialize from the walls and pounce on her. She yanked Golan in behind her and locked the door again. She led him through the rooms–the large sitting room, the bedroom, the dressing room, and beyond that, a small alcove, which ended at another door. This door led to another bedroom. It was also kept locked, and the Queen was the only one who had a key to this room, but Mava needed Golan to at least hear for himself one of the secrets.

She stopped at the unassuming door, hidden in shadows and almost obscured by trunks and hat boxes stored in the alcove, then turned and faced him.

"My sister lives in this room." She knocked on the door softly, the long-short pattern they used to identify themselves, then called out softly, barely above a whisper. "Dera, it's me, Mava. I don't have the key. The Queen is out for the morning, so I cannot open the door, but I must speak to you."

Golan's brows furrowed deeply as he listened, trying to understand. But he stayed quiet, waiting patiently, and Mava was glad. A few minutes passed before she heard her sister's voice at the keyhole.

"Mava. Are you well?"

Her older sister always asked her, but being trapped by Queen Lilian and keeping her secrets was never *well*, not for either of them.

"I'm well," she lied, ignoring the sweat on her palms and the pounding of her heart. "The youngest prince is here with me, Prince Golan. He needs to know the truth, Dera. There is a princess he is trying to save from the devices of the Queen. He needs to know everything."

She didn't wait for her sister's answer. In fact, she didn't even want to be around to hear the story. Her stomach was churning so much she thought she might be sick.

She needed to keep watch for the Queen's return, and she needed to pray for mercy from The One. Benrid needed His protection now, as He was the only one who could grant it. She had just annihilated her only means to protect Benrid herself. And it broke her heart.

She positioned herself by a window looking out toward the road so she could see the Queen approaching from afar and have enough time to get herself and Golan far out of the chambers before they were caught. She let the Adrenaline subside, leaving her shaken. And she grieved for the little boy she had given her whole life to protect, the one who had still been ruined by the Queen's evil, who suffered alone back in Lilt, who would be destroyed completely if the Queen ever suspected what Mava had just done.

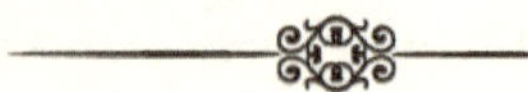

Golan peered anxiously after Mava as she disappeared, mumbling about keeping watch. He glanced back at the door. It felt awkward to speak to the wood and to the mysterious woman's voice behind it, but the fact that his mother was concealing someone in her own chambers was upsetting. Terrifying, really. He had to figure this out.

He leaned his forehead against the door. "Woman, who are you?"

A brushing sound, then a hoarse, "Who are *you*?"

"I'm Prince Golan. Mava tells me you can help answer my questions, but you must do so before the Queen returns."

"Well then, we must start at the beginning. My name is Dera. I was a noble lady many years ago, daughter of Lord Easton and Lady Joce of the Sayche line, but they passed away during the spread of the fever one summer when I was but eighteen. I knew your father." Her voice trembled as she spoke, as though it hadn't been used for a long time and needed to be oiled.

It was rough, but soft, and Golan had to press his ear against the door to hear her as she continued.

"I loved him, in fact. I didn't care about the throne, I only cared about the man. But true love is zealous, and zealousness can be mistaken for selfishness. There were those who suspected I was only trying to become queen, so they warned him. He didn't listen, and he came to me anyway. He found me every night, and we'd go walking together and loving each other. He promised me we would wed. But then the council warned his parents who believed them and decided to protect him from himself. They arranged his marriage to Lilian. It was announced before his permission was sought, trapping him. If he refused, he would shame her and severely undermine his authority and bearing as a ruler. In fact, his parents threatened to remove the crown from him if he revolted. That would have left his brother to reign, and the man spent more time drunk than he did sober. He was not fit to rule Ethereal, and Henry knew it. He fumed and cried, and lashed out, but in the end, he brokenly told me he would have to break his promise to me. I cried, of course. Oh, how I cried. Life was so unfair. Because I loved him, and not the throne, I would be refused both, and even though Lilian only sought the position for herself, she would be given everything." A beat of silence. "Are you still there, Prince?"

Golan swallowed, nodding. "Y-yes," he stammered quietly.

"Within the month, the ceremony had taken place, the kingdom rejoiced, and Henry had taken Lilian to be his Queen. I wanted to die. Every day I lived was torture, torture to hear her name and see them together, torture to be completely ignored by the one I had loved. I made myself sick, Or, at least, that's what I thought. But the sickness wouldn't go away, even when my heart was distracted by it, and then I realized it wasn't my heart that made me ill, it was the life being created in me. I was with child.

"I rejoiced because I still loved him, although I hated him too, and now he had become part of me. We, together, had become another. It was sweet, agonizingly sweet. I would always have a part of him with me, proof that I had not just imagined our love. And I wept because this son, the firstborn of King Henry, would never be heir to the throne. In fact, he'd probably never be acknowledged, at least not beyond being an illegitimate. And, yet, my noble blood and the King's made him royal. He deserved to be acknowledged by the throne. He deserved more, so much more, than a lonely, forsaken mother, and no father to raise him. I rejoiced, and I wept, and I planned.

"By the time I was three months along, the announcement that the Queen was carrying a child spread through the Kingdom. Everyone marveled at the speed at which she had conceived, and they praised The One for such posterity! I was angry and hurt. He had planted his seed in her barely a month after he'd planted it within me, and now we would give birth to his children just weeks apart.

"As I grew with the baby inside, I hid in my home. I had only one servant attend me, and through her, I commanded the rest of the house to carry on the duties as normal. My excuses were well-received whenever I had to be absent from something. Eventually, I sent a message to the King, asking him to meet me where we used to wander in the woods after dark. I did not tell him why, and I feared he would not come.

"I hadn't been out much since I had started showing, but in the first month or two of my pregnancy and his marriage, he would not look my way, let alone address me when we were in the same room. But he came that night. Alone, as I'd requested, though I saw his guard hovering near the tree line, as though he was wary of foul play, and my heart burned in indignation.

"He came toward me, and I opened my arms wide, unraveling the cloak around me. My stomach protruded ahead of me, much like his wife's did, though I was more petite. I had worn my tightest gown, one that barely fit, and it stretched around his child, and pulled tight against my hips and backside. He gaped at me for a moment and stopped walking. I can still hear his words, every one of them.

" 'What is *this*, Dera?'

" 'This is your son,' I told him. And he shook his head. Can you believe it? He shook his head, as if to deny it. I seethed.

" 'Yes, Henry, this is to be your firstborn son. What, do you suspect me of being with another man? I'm unmarried, and you're the only man I was with, especially seven months ago, when this child was put here. This is your child, and I want him to be claimed. You broke your promise to me, and I can live with that, but do not ignore our child!

"I was so vehement, I felt as though steam were rising from my words, but he didn't seem to hear me. He came up to me and put his hand on my stomach, and I felt the baby move deeper inside me, as if he feared his father's touch. Henry brushed his fingers over the babe, then over my cheek, and I felt the fire of anger in my heart melting into warmth, into forgiveness.

"Until he said, 'I cannot, Dera. I am sorry. I will make sure you are looked after, but Lilian is carrying my heir, and I cannot acknowledge this baby.'

"Then he turned his back on me and left. I will never forget that night. Agony plummeted through me, and brought me to my knees. I screamed his name, but he did not turn around, and I groveled on the ground, unable to sink any lower, my sobs and tears bleeding into the dirt, and I couldn't see beyond the blackness. I thought the night would never end, that I would never be able to stop crying, that my heart would never recover."

Her voice shook even more, and Golan could hear the wetness beneath it, the tears that came back with her memories, even now, more than twenty years later.

"But the sun rose, and I lived. Life went on, the child in me grew. I went into labor and struggled for hours to have the babe. He was finally born, and I lingered on the verge of exhaustion, falling in and out of sleep and nursing the baby in between, with only the servants to aid me. Then, on the second day after the birth, the crier heralded the news. The Queen was giving birth.'

"I flew out of bed, dressed, trying to hide my face as much as possible, and grabbed my son. I wrapped him in a simple cloth, leaving out any garments that could identify him with me, let him suckle just for a few minutes, then headed to the castle on foot. I was sore and depleted, but determined. I slipped inside the servant's entrance and made my way up to the Queen's chambers. There was a flurry of excitement up there, young maids running to and fro for supplies, and some just hovering to hear the first cries. No one noticed me. I marched into the chambers and demanded that the Queen accept my son as the firstborn heir, telling her the whole story. The truth.

"Her face was twisted in pain and weariness, but instead of fearing me or feeling sorrow at her husband's first love, she smirked.

" 'I would never accept your son,' she said, breathing hard between contractions. 'Be gone.'

"I burned hot with fury. I beckoned the midwife, nearly pulling her with me. We reached a secluded place in the hall. And then I used a power I had never used. I was Gifted, but my Gift had not manifested until I was sixteen. In fact, I was afraid of my power, but desperation made me brave. I would use it for my son. I called on my power, feeling no remorse, as I looked straight at her and let my will overtake her. I handed her my son, who rested angelically against her chest, unaware of the slicing of my heart when I pulled him away from me. I longed to kiss his soft forehead once more, but I had no time. I could not trust myself, so I simply commanded her to present him to the King as the newborn Prince. And she did."

Golan felt ice in his veins. "Who are you?" he asked hoarsely.

"I am Benrid's mother."

"That's not possible."

"But it's true. The midwife presented my son to the King as his firstborn, and he didn't know Lilian hadn't birthed him. Not long after, Lilian delivered her son, who was also presented to the King as the younger twin. I disappeared, making it back home to grieve and exult. The Queen was livid, as you can imagine. It wasn't her fault. It was all Henry's, really, but we were both caught in his trap. She'd been caught with the lure of power, and I'd fallen for love. We were both disappointed. But I thought I'd outsmarted everyone, that I had the final triumph, that my son would be King. Then her guard came and arrested me. It was the middle of the night. I was unprepared. She did it secretly.

"She couldn't go to the King and tell him about me—she didn't know he'd already refused my son. She feared if he learned Benrid belonged to me, he would acknowledge both the boy and me. At least this way she could claim all rights to the heirs she had supposedly given him. But she hated me. Hated Benrid. I hadn't even named him. The King did that. She found me; apparently she threatened the midwife enough to realize that she had been under some kind of spell. She wanted my power as much as she wanted me destroyed. She asked around for the gossip of who the King had courted before her. My name came up. Our romance had been known, and once she knew who I was, and that I hadn't lied, she found me easily.

"I had already faded from the public as a noblewoman, and though I never showed up in public again, few missed me. My servants both died soon after, accidentally, it seemed, though it was mysterious enough for me to know the hand behind it. Darla, my personal maid, the woman who played midwife for me, drowned in the river, apparently having slipped and hit her head while gathering water for laundry. Heden, my only manservant, guard, and driver, ate bad meat and died of food illness, or so it was said.

"The only one left in my family was my younger sister. I had sent her away to protect her and myself when I knew I was pregnant. She had just come back from our cousin's when the Queen's men abducted me. She followed them and offered the Queen our pea in exchange for my life. The pea is a gem that has been in our family for generations. We passed it down and cherished it as a keepsake, though some said it held magic powers. Neither of us had ever known those stories to be true."

Dera stopped talking for a minute. When she spoke again, her voice was tired. "I've been at Lilt mostly since the arrest. Lilian has brought me here occasionally, but keeping me secret while traveling is more difficult. She has been getting bolder with the power and using it much more than ever these days, so she needed me with her this summer. Would you believe Henry has never seen my face since my abduction, even though it's his own wife who conceals me?"

There was silence on both ends for a few minutes, Golan still too speechless even to ask more about the power Dera mentioned.

"Lilian was brutal," Dera's voice continued. "She brought my baby to me once I was locked up. I had given him away only three weeks before, but he was so much bigger. My heart broke all over again. My breasts, which had finally stopped leaking, throbbed with pain, and milk soaked my dress. She kept him there all day, just feet away from me, but out of reach. I was locked behind bars. He cried, and I couldn't comfort him. I couldn't touch him, couldn't feed him. I've never felt such pain. Every part of me ached and throbbed with misery and yearning, and I sobbed. I had thought there was nothing left of my heart to break, but it broke afresh, tearing me from the inside out. Her torture lasted hours, and I would have done anything to help my Benrid. Anything. Given my life. So, of course I gave in when she needled me about my power. I didn't care about power. I didn't care about life, just my son.'

"Mava had given her the pea in exchange for me, but of course the Queen didn't let me go. Instead, she took us both. I gave her my secret easily when faced with my exhausted, starving baby, and she finally took the baby to his other nurse, though milk poured from me like a spring. She was cruel. She has kept me ever since."

"Why?" Golan's voice sounded as tortured as he felt.

"She needs me to activate the pea for her and give her my power through it. The pea can sense the magic in Gifted people, and if it's activated, it can transfer their abilities to whoever holds the pea. I have the gift of mind and will control, and once

I activate the pea, she can use my power herself while she holds the pea. And I do it. Because I do it all for him. I have no morals anymore, no hope in life, just hope for him."

"How do you activate the pea?"

Mava rounded the corner before Dera could answer.

"She's approaching," she hissed. "Dera, the Queen is returning, we need to go." She paused for a moment. Then, "Thank you, sister."

Golan didn't say goodbye as he hurried out of the chambers behind Mava. His mind was dizzy with what he had just learned.

CHAPTER 24

The Stars Align

Benrid was not Queen Lilian's son, though Lilian was the only one who knew that, except for the sisters she had manipulated into silence. Golan felt the weight of the knowledge settle heavily on him. Benrid needed to know. Now that Golan knew, it was his responsibility to tell his brother.

My half-brother.

No wonder his mother had encouraged so much rivalry between Joran and Benrid. No wonder she was desperate to secure Joran's place on the throne. But had she really blinded Benrid?

If she could enslave two women, kill their servants, and lie to her husband, then surely she could. In fact, he was surprised she hadn't figured out a way to kill Benrid yet to make sure he really was out of the way. Unless that is where this was headed. Perhaps blindness was only the first symptom. Maybe she had something planned for this summer when they were all away and she could never be traced. His skin prickled.

Then again, she needed Dera's mind control abilities, and surely the woman would refuse to help her if anything happened to Benrid.

If Joran became king and Avalon became his queen, Lilian would have supreme power. She had two peas now, if she did indeed have Avalon's. By keeping Avalon close so the peas would react to her and produce their magic, Lilian could control them both by holding on to the peas herself. Magister Erlich was right. The kingdom would practically be hers.

That brought his mind back to Avalon. Avalon was Gifted. She had magic, and she didn't even know it yet. The Magister had figured it out, but he hadn't had time to tell her. Apparently, Queen Lilian had figured it out as well. Dera had said her pea could detect anyone Gifted. The pea must have revealed Avalon's power to the Queen.

Avalon sat on the stone floor, searching her mind for answers. She recalled what Erlich had said. "Those who want the power the most sometimes seek to destroy it."

She forced herself to think. Who wanted power? Queen Lilian, obviously. Had she been the one to banish magic? That made little sense.

Except in a way it did. If she fought against magic so adamantly, no one would suspect her of dallying in it herself, and, once it was gone, there would be no power to compete with her. No one left who could reveal her and give her secret away. If she made the rules, she could live above them.

She had destroyed the lives of hundreds of people, including Magister Ferin, who had died from the rough living conditions in the Forest. She had no regard for her husband, her sons, or the other kingdoms, apparently, judging by how she'd treated Avalon. Her selfishness was such a force, that she would stop at nothing. She would destroy Ethereal, and Avalon doubted she would be content to stop there. If she could take Ethereal, why not take all of Kerrynth?

Realization dawned heavily. Lilian's own family hadn't even fully realized what she was doing. If she were to be stopped, Avalon would have to stop her. The prison walls towered around her, as strong as ever, but a new resolve settled in her heart, burning steadily like hot coals in a fire. For the first time in weeks, her thoughts settled, and she felt a calmness descend on her. She would find a way out of here, and she would get to Magister Erlich. He had said they needed her, and she suspected he already had a plan. She was more than willing to help him. He didn't frighten her the way Queen Lilian did. Perhaps he was right; magic itself wasn't evil. Only some people were.

She would eat the meager food that was brought this evening, sleep for a few hours to gather her strength, and then she would make her move.

CHAPTER 25

Into the Woods

Night was falling, and Golan paced impatiently after his talk with Mava and Dera, willing the shadows to come faster. He needed to see Erlich, let him know all he'd discovered, and enlist his help in rescuing Avalon. He wanted to wait until darkness shielded his exit, but the hours that had passed made him itch with impatience.

Finally, he stole his way into the Black Forest toward Erlich's house.

Golan rattled the door in the tree loudly. There was shuffling inside, then the Great Magister cracked the door open, the apprehension on his face draining when he saw the Prince.

The door was barely open before Golan had pushed himself inside. He was not under the daze of the Queen's controlling influence this time, but he was desperate, and that made him almost as rough.

"Erlich, she's gone. I don't know what the Queen did to her, or where to find her. I need your help."

Erlich's old eyes met Golan's, which burned with passion and desperation, and he nodded slowly.

"Come, Prince, have a seat. Things are dire. We need to make our plan and move."

"Tonight!" Golan agreed.

He sat down at the table, his back tense, and finally noticed Alice already sitting. He sent her a questioning look, surprised to see her in the Magister's hidden home.

She gave an encouraging smile. "It's good that you're here too, Prince Golan. Together, we can come up with something."

"Why are you here?" he asked.

"Alice has visited us several times before," Erlich spoke for her. "Her Gift isn't magical, but a heartfelt one, that of loving people. We welcomed her here a year ago, and she welcomed us into her heart. Since then she has been part of our resistance, gaining information and persuading loyalties to our side."

Alice's eyes were wet, like she'd been crying, but a corner of her radiant smile broke through. "I've missed visiting this summer, but I've been promoted at the castle, and it's not easy to get away to trip in rabbit holes anymore." She turned to Golan. "I had to come tonight, though. I wasn't sure I'd even remember the way, but you and Princess Avalon need help, and The Great Magister is the only one I can truly trust."

"Yes, Prince Golan, she's already told me how the Queen's guards caught you the night of the wedding and took Avalon away, though none of you know where. I am glad you came here instead of trying to do something rash on your own. Perhaps we underestimated how difficult that rescue would be. I also wasn't expecting Queen Lilian's power to be so strong over Avalon, seeing as how the princess herself is Gifted. Maybe because her pea is gone, and she's never used her powers herself, they didn't act as the usual deterrent."

The old man stared thoughtfully into the distance. "It seems we need to move sooner than expected. We've been planning a revolt for years now. We need our freedom back, and Ethereal needs the balance of power between magic and ordinary in order to thrive. We are almost ready. We'd planned to ask Avalon to use her power and her access to the castle when we did this, but if she's in danger, we cannot wait any longer. We must do this for her, as much as for ourselves. This time we won't fail. Prince Golan has my trust, and, of course I count you as one of us, Alice. "

Alice's lips trembled a little, but she nodded. "I am devoted to any cause which would put an end to the darkness at Blackstone and Lilt. The Queen hurt Princess Avalon, and she ruined Benrid, and that's ruining me. I will fight against anyone who caused him to suffer," she whispered.

Golan caught Erlich's expression of surprise, which quickly softened to something sadder. Golan considered Alice, in all her winsome big-heartedness, still just a young girl with the servant's kitchen uniform. She looked vulnerable as she admitted her truth, her blue eyes big and serious. Had Erlich's face clouded because of her inevitable heartbreak? Benrid was the Crown Prince, for, blind or not, the title had not been removed, and Golan worried along with Erlich that she, who had so much love to give, was giving it to one who would never return it.

The Great Magister stroked his beard, then reached out a hand and placed it over hers. "Few people could ever deserve the heart of Alice. I am honored to have you with us," he murmured to her. Then he looked at Golan. "Now, tell us what you know."

CHAPTER 26

Shield Me from Cold

Avalon tried to sleep, but found it hard to relax. Not only was the straw over the stone uncomfortable, but her mind was buzzing with alertness. She had no weapons. In fact, she barely had clothes, but she did have one desperate idea.

The guard changed at midnight, and last night, the new guard had checked things over quickly before assuming his post. If she could just get him close enough, she might have a chance. Her heart raced with Adrenaline, even though it was probably still two hours until midnight. She was terrified. She had never had defensive training. She was a princess, and her guards had always been enough.

Until they weren't. She shut out Jem's pale face.

Now she was here, trapped in a prison in a strange kingdom with a conniving queen. And she was alone. She had to do this because no one else could rescue her. As far as she knew, no one else would even try. Her own family had no inclination where she was, and she wasn't sure she had any allies here at Blackstone. She squeezed her eyes shut, refusing to let her mind wander there. She didn't have the strength to relive the pain King Henry and Queen Lilian had caused her, or Golan's betrayal that night in the woods. He'd tried to warn her the night of the engagement, but she still wasn't sure which of his actions to believe.

Finally, she heard the new guard come in. The noise was distant and muted, but she strained to make out every small sound. She heard the outer door and the indistinct murmurs the two men exchanged. Every nerve buzzed, even while she feigned sleep, willing herself to keep her eyes shut and her breathing even. Keys jangled as they were passed from one hand to the next. Then the door shut again, and Avalon knew the first guard had left. She could hear his footsteps descending the stairs, fading into nothing.

The new guard shuffled a bit, then began his slow gait around the prison. He was predictable, at least. Avalon wished she'd been more careful to study his habits before this. She could tell he obeyed routines, since he paused to check all the cells, even though she was the only prisoner, as far as she could tell. Her cell was last.

When he reached hers, she coughed and moaned. Then she pulled her eyes open, looking dazed as she tried to focus on the room. She let her eyes settle on him. He was turning away when she croaked, "Guard, I'm ill. I think–I think I'm dying. Please, can you give this to my family?"

She raised her fist slightly, and then let it drop limply, as though she couldn't hold it up. His eyes narrowed suspiciously, and her heart picked up speed, though she couldn't show it.

Spirits, I've never had to act before, she worried. *Will he believe me?*

She coughed again, and, against her will, allowed her eyes to drift close and her head to roll. The guard took a step away, and she opened her eyes again, willing it to look difficult.

"Please. It's valuable. No one must know," she whispered. She was almost surprised at how truly sick and dying she sounded, as though she could barely get coherent words out. She let her eyes glaze and roll.

"My gem," she ended weakly, praying the guard would open the cell and come closer.

He hesitated, and Avalon's breath stopped, hope and despair crashing into each other for one torturous second before he blew out his breath and fit the key into the lock. He kept his eye on her, she could feel it, so she carried on her show of being disoriented and weak, and made no indication that she even knew what was happening.

He was still cautious as he eased the gate open, but when she did nothing but let her eyelids languish, he seemed convinced enough. He closed the gate behind him, though he didn't lock it. His approach seemed nervous, but Avalon knew he wasn't afraid of her, probably just of her illness. Still, she needed him closer.

Please, oh One, help me.

She mumbled a whisper, and the guard bent down, quite close.

Faster than she'd ever moved, Avalon had her strip of cloth, torn from the hem of her chemise, around his neck. She pulled as tight as she could, doubting her strength for a millisecond, before the realization that if she lost, she would face punishment, perhaps even death, gave her resolve and strength she didn't know she had. She jerked her knee up hard, catching the guard between his legs. His hands, which had grabbed at her arms, loosened as he keened in pain.

She didn't expect him to sink to his knees, facing her. It slackened her grip. Quickly, she pulled tighter, and kicked him again, this time in the stomach, to regain power. By his grunt, she assumed she'd hurt him, but it wasn't enough to stop him from grabbing her elbows. Although his eyes were bulging and he choked, he was still much stronger than her, and she could feel him pulling her arms apart.

She would not let him win. She could not afford it.

If she didn't get out now, she knew she would never have another chance. In a frenzy, she went wild, using her knees to drive into his chest and thrust up into his chin. His head cracked back, and for a second she thought she was free, but then he grabbed her waist and shoved her. The blow was unexpected, and she lost her balance, stumbling back. She caught herself with the cloth strip, which she still gripped, and the guard gagged as it tightened around his throat again. He managed to get to his feet, although his legs were still trembling in pain.

He pulled back his arm and landed his fist in Avalon's head. Pain exploded through her, sparks blinding her vision, and she thought she fell. Anger surged through her, right behind the pain, and she began clawing at the man before her, desperation fueling every rabid move. Her vision was still clearing, so she felt it before she saw it. He'd drawn a knife, and he held it at her throat.

Instantly, Avalon stilled, her pulse pounding in her head.

"Stupid girl," the guard muttered hoarsely. "Foolish. Get back on the bed."

She hesitated. If he moved the knife, she'd only attack again. Surely he knew that, and she wondered briefly if she still held the upper hand.

But he had a *knife*. Clearly, it was he who held the upper hand. He pressed the blade harder, and she could feel the sharp tip, then a spark of pain as he pierced the thin layer of skin on her neck. She gasped and pulled back sharply.

"On the bed," he ordered, louder than before.

Tears rushed into her eyes as she moved toward the bed. He stayed with her, the knife just as close, until she sat. She had no intention of trying to fight him again. Already the side of her face ached, and the pain seemed to settle deeper every minute. Her jaw was tight and beginning to swell, and the cut on her throat burned. She could feel the blood as it dripped down her neck, too warm at first, then cold as the air dried it.

The guard took a step back, the knife still extended toward her. She didn't look at him, but she could see him peripherally. He didn't leave, just stood there considering her, and when his eye took on a gleam, she felt a new shudder rush down her back. He wasn't old, probably not yet forty. He had a short brown beard and a square head, and spite in his gaze.

Avalon suddenly felt sick.

The man threw a look toward the main entrance down the hall, but they both knew no one would be coming at this time of night. The next guard relieved him at six in the morning. They had hours together alone, and Avalon had never regretted anything more.

One? She cried, almost accusing. Why had she done this? Did she really think she, a seventeen-year-old princess, could outwit and overpower a prison guard with years of experience and training? She had been asking for help from The One since this nightmare had started, but things had only kept getting worse.

"Seems you need a lesson," the man smirked. "And I have one that will teach you well."

The air was charged with danger, and Avalon could feel the hairs on her arms lifting. The man stepped closer again.

"Don't struggle," he reminded her. His voice was soft, but there was menace in his eyes. He waved the knife a little. "You don't want any more marks on your beautiful face, do you?"

Her instincts screamed. "I'll tell," she squeaked.

He was bending over her now, and all she could see were the bruises forming around his throat. She'd hurt him. She had taken him by surprise and taken him to his knees. Despite her fear, she felt proud of her small triumph. The thought made her brave.

"I'm the Princess of Haven, and I'm an important prisoner." She actually had no real idea why the Queen had imprisoned her or exactly how valuable she was to the Queen, but she pressed on. "If I'm hurt–in any way–you'll pay. And I won't keep silent about this."

He merely tipped his head and smiled slowly. "Unless you're dead. You were very ill, just tonight, remember?"

Her stomach dropped. He eased himself over her, pushing her back, and holding her down with his body. She tried to squirm, but he was crushing her, and she wheezed for air. He picked up the discarded makeshift garrote and grabbed her arms, holding them firmly together. His grip was as strong as iron. She couldn't even budge as he bound her wrists together. She winced as he ground her bones into each other. The feeling in her hands vanished almost immediately.

Once her arms were secure, he tied the extra length to the chain hook near the bed.

"Who knew you should have been chained?" he murmured.

"Please don't," she begged, but he cut off her words with his mouth on hers. She spluttered and turned her head, and he laughed.

"I was almost sorry about this at first," he admitted, "But we're going to have fun." The crazed gleam in his eyes made her sick.

Avalon whimpered and thrashed, unwilling to give up, but with her arms tied above her head, and his body holding hers down, she was trapped. Fear clawed her as his fingers brushed her skin, and she screamed.

He slapped her cheek. "Quiet, or I'll have to gag you as well. But you'll like the way I play with these lips," and his thumb brushed her lips. She bit at him, and he pulled back, chuckling.

"No, no, no. Oh, One, please help me," she cried out loud.

There was noise on the stairwell. Neither of them heard it at first, but when the door rattled loudly, and a voice called out, the guard cursed. Panic blanched his face for a second, then he pulled Avalon up from her shoulders, and slammed her head back down against the hard stone. She heard the crack, but the pain didn't even register before everything went black.

CHAPTER 27

Not all Treasure is Gold

G olan put on his best authoritative voice, letting the all-too-real impatience filter into his tone as he knocked again and called for the guard. There was an answering "Aye," and footsteps hurrying toward them before the window flap was unfastened and the guard looked through the small bars at them.

Golan thrust the papers toward him, hoping this guard wasn't keen on extensive inspections, as these hurriedly drawn up orders were not even near official.

"Orders from the King. My guard and I are to escort the prisoner to a new location."

The guard glanced nervously at him and Erlich, who stood on the step below, dressed in a guard's uniform that Alice had retrieved from the laundry. Golan prayed the prison guard didn't grow suspicious about Erlich's age, or the awkward fit of the uniform. Alice had found three, and this had been the best fit, but the Magister's tall, gaunt frame was still too long, and the pants rose above his ankles.

The man's eyes blinked a few times as he took in Golan's embroidered jacket, recognition dawning in his face, followed quickly by horror. He seemed to choke the reaction back, cleared his throat, and nodded smartly. The door latch snicked, and a moment later Golan was inside, running around the curving corridor and calling Avalon's name.

"Excuse me, Your Highness," the guard spoke up from his station. "I was under strict orders not to allow the prisoner any visitors, nor was I told about any movements tonight. May I look over the papers? You understand, of course."

Golan's heart sank. He turned back and handed over the false papers, catching the hardness in the man's eyes. The man glanced down at the papers in his hand, and Golan did not hesitate. He landed a blow to the man's skull that resounded through the prison. The man crumpled at his feet.

"I'm sorry," Golan muttered. Erlich sidled up from behind him and bent to retrieve the keys, and they hurried along in their search.

Avalon was in the farthest cell, sleeping through the disturbance.

"Avalon," Golan called gently while he tried the keys.

Stark silence met him, and he jerked his head up. She wasn't moving. Was she breathing? His lungs tightened around his own breath. He grabbed the bars, shaking the door.

"Avalon. Avalon!" *No, no, no, no!*

Erlich took the keys from him and quietly opened the lock. Golan pushed into the room and flew to Avalon's stone bed.

She was breathing, but it was shallow. The ice inside him shattered with relief to see the rise and fall of her chest. He sat beside her and gently took her hands. They were cold, and she didn't respond. He felt panic rising again.

The Magister bent over her too. "She's unconscious." He turned her head carefully, and Golan gasped when he saw the swollen bruise on her jaw. Erlich pointed to her throat, an inch-long slice still visible, though the blood had been swiped away. It was a fresh wound, still shiny and wet.

Golan looked up into the old man's face.

"We cannot move her. We need to know if she has any serious injuries," Erlich said gravely.

"Can't you perform some magic?" Golan's voice was strained, and he felt just like the little boy he sounded like.

Erlich furrowed his brow. "I will try," he promised.

Golan gave up his seat to the Magister, pacing and praying while the man performed his service. The band around his head glowed brighter. Finally, he looked up.

"I am not a healer, Prince. As a Magister, I can only infuse healing with certain crystals. But I've chanted a prayer of peace for her, so she can awaken without fear, and lent her some strength so she can come with us and begin healing on her own more quickly. Now we wait, and pray that she will wake up soon."

Golan just nodded, not trusting himself to speak. Hatred burned in his chest. Had his mother condemned her to this? Tortured her? Had her beaten? The knowledge made him sick, and he swiped his hand over his mouth, trying to keep the bile down.

Erlich stood. "I should go see to the guard out there. We've given away our pretense. If he awakens, he will surely summon help."

Golan felt torn, his eyes drawn to Avalon, even as he stepped forward to help Erlich. The old man must have sensed his struggle, because he shook his head. "I'll tie him up. I can manage. Stay with her."

Golan sat by Avalon. The stone was hard and cold. He knew firsthand how hard it was to sleep on the stone. Just a few days ago, he'd been here for a night, before his mother had caught him unexpectedly, and he'd accidentally looked at her. Then she'd sent him off on a journey he couldn't even remember, the morning Magister Erlich had stopped him. Then, when Avalon had been spotted going into the forest a few nights later, Queen Lilian had infiltrated Golan's mind for the second time in days, this time sending him right into the Forest after her to drag her back. He still hadn't been able to explain to her what had happened that night. He worked his jaw, thinking about that being one of her last memories of him.

Avalon was still dressed only in the undergarments she'd had on after he'd ripped the cumbersome skirts from her dress two nights ago.

Stillness filled the room, their breaths barely breaking the quiet. He gazed at her, noticed the tear streaks down the sides of her face. The bruise looked shiny and painful, and his gut clenched just looking at it. Tenderly he reached out, brushing her other cheek, running his thumb down her jaw, and around her lips. There was a fluttering in his stomach, a yearning that hurt, and he let his hand drop.

Erlich entered the cell softly. Avalon's eyelids twitched and finally blinked open. Her eyes met Golan's. She stared at him for a long minute, her face blank. The soft golden brown of her eyes stole his breath.

Then she glanced at Erlich. A small smile ghosted her lips. "You came. You both came for me."

"Can you sit up, Princess?" Erlich pressed.

She nodded, then winced. Her face twisted in pain. "I don't know. Everything hurts." Her hand went to her cheek. "My head." She trailed off. "I think he hit me."

"Who? What happened?" Golan was livid. Erlich pressed a warning hand on his arm.

Golan breathed out heavily. "I'll help you. Let's try to get you up," he said instead.

"Okay," she agreed feebly, reaching out to the arm he extended. He put his other arm under her, easing her up slowly.

It took a minute for everything to come back. Although even as Avalon remembered, she still wasn't sure she remembered everything because she couldn't explain the calm she felt right now. She remembered the guard, remembered accosting him in an attempt to get out, and she remembered he was going to hurt her, but the fear and humiliation she had felt when that happened had given way to a deep tranquility. Erlich was here. And Golan. Somehow they had found her, and they were rescuing her.

She remembered the guard's panic, but everything after that was blank. She must have been unconscious. She wasn't sure how long she had been out, but she was pretty sure it was still the middle of the night. She wondered how much these men had seen. Did they know what had happened? She wasn't worried about it, though. A sweet peace warmed her from inside, and for some bizarre reason, everything felt right with the world. She smiled, though her swollen jaw hurt when she did.

She touched it gingerly, pain pulsing through her at the slightest touch. The back of her head hurt too. Immensely.

Then Golan was trying to help her sit up. She used his arm to brace herself, aware of his strength beneath his jacket. He reached his other arm around her, supporting her weight as he drew her up into a sitting position. Her breath hitched, and it wasn't just from the pain.

Her face was pressed near his chest, and beneath his open jacket, she could see the muscle ripple through his shirt, and she caught his scent, pine and mint. Her head swam, and she closed her eyes. She could feel the flush on her face, and she hoped he would assume it was from the exertion.

"Are you all right?" Golan asked softly. His breath tickled her ear.

"Yes, I think so. A little dizzy. Just give me a minute." She couldn't move her head without the ache racing through it, but the world slowly steadied.

"When you are ready, Princess, we need to leave," Erlich said. "The guard was going to cause trouble, so the Prince had to render him unconscious as well, but it would be best to leave before he awakes. We should try to get back to my place before anyone realizes that you're gone. Are there any more injuries that we should know about at this moment?"

"No."

He sighed and reached into his pocket. "And this?" He held up the strip of cloth. "It was hanging out of the guard's pocket. Is there anything we should know about it?"

Avalon's face infused with heat, for more reasons than one. She didn't look at Golan.

"I tried to strangle him," she admitted.

Golan's eyes had flown to her bare leg, where the fabric had been ripped away, but now they jumped back to her face. "You what?"

"I was trying to get free. All I got was this." She touched the back of her head. She was embarrassed, but not enough to hide the truth, although she left the rest of the story out.

Golan opened his mouth like he wanted to ask more, but Erlich waved him off and reached out a hand to Avalon. "We must go," he reminded them.

Avalon took his leathery hand and stood. The world rushed around her again, but once she got her balance, she tried to ignore the throbbing in her head and followed them from the cell.

CHAPTER 28

A Glimpse of Sky

They had taken too long to reach the Magister's cabin, Golan thought, but the man still insisted they rest and recover before addressing anything else. Avalon seemed on the verge of passing out by the time they got to the hidden house. Golan was sure he never would have seen the place, even if he'd been looking, if Erlich had not brought him here himself the time Golan was under his mother's spell. Alice had been here before too, he knew, but he didn't know how she had first found it either. She seemed to have a history here–and with Benrid–that he still hadn't learned.

Avalon had begun swaying an hour before they arrived, and Golan had been half carrying her, whispering to her about how brave and strong she was, promising to take care of her and keep her safe. She'd smiled gratefully at him, but he wasn't sure how many of his fervent comments had registered in her weakened state of shock. She'd taken only a few sips of tea before gratefully sinking into oblivion on the only bed.

Golan slid to the floor in the corner, his back against the wall. He had no intention of sleeping, though Erlich was insisting.

"Things will be in uproar once the new shift comes at dawn and discovers the prisoner is missing. And that guard last night knew I was the prince. My mother will be notified, and she will come after us. She sent me into the Forest after Avalon once already. She knows something is in here. We have to be ready."

"None of us are ready to face a battle in this condition, let alone formulate our plan. And my house is well hidden. You forget I've lived here safely for twenty years, Prince. No one dares enter these woods, as you well know, and a host of Gifted people live nearby. Although we rarely need to use defense, I'll have a few of my friends watching and prepared to stop anyone who enters. I think we can risk the few hours of rest."

Golan wanted to protest, but the discussion was obviously done because the Magister promptly lay down on his bench and turned his back to the room. Golan sighed and slouched lower. He was surprised how weary he felt inside. Worrying could do that to you, he guessed. He focused on Avalon, watching her back expand with each breath she took until sleep blinded his eyes.

Avalon felt much better after sleeping for a few hours and after eating. Although her head was still sore, she felt focused again.

She'd woken to Magister Erlich moving about the kitchen. "Thank you," she said, approaching him and laying a hand on his arm. "You saved me."

He patted her shoulder. "Thank the Prince, Avalon. He saved you."

Golan was asleep in the corner, propped against the wall with his head on his chest. She bit her lip. "I was angry with him. I didn't trust him, not after he took me away from here that first night. He tried to save me at the engagement ceremony, but the Queen confused my mind, and I couldn't listen to him. He didn't make any sense. When I woke up in the prison, I wasn't sure what had really happened. I thought maybe he had been part of her plan all along."

Erlich had turned back to the pot over the fire, but she heard his steady voice. "You can trust him with your life *and* your heart."

She tilted her head at Golan, considering him, recalling the things his voice had breathed in her ear last night, though it felt more like a dream. Had he really said she was brave, that he admired her strength? That he'd always be there for her? He opened his eyes suddenly and saw her staring.

"You're awake." He scrambled up and strode toward her like he was about to embrace her, but he stopped before her instead, rubbing his hand through his hair. "Are you feeling better?"

His voice was thick. Heat crept up her neck as she recalled the way she'd clung to him in the woods last night. Her skin, barely covered by her underthings, pressed up against his warmth and strength. He'd held her up most of the way. She wouldn't have been able to stay on her feet so long without him.

"I'm fine," she said quietly. "Thank you, Golan. For coming for me, I mean. And for helping me make it here. I'm sorry I didn't listen to you the other night. I thought..." She couldn't explain.

But when she lifted her eyes to his, he was staring at her, his own green eyes shimmering with—tears? "I was so scared, Avalon. I thought I'd lost you." The huskiness in his voice gave away his emotion.

Erlich cleared his throat. "Eat, my friends. The Sparks have already gone to summon others. It is time to get ready for war."

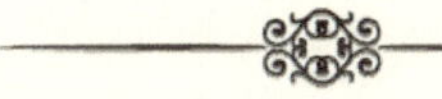

The house was full of Erlich's friends, a tangible anticipation humming in the air. Avalon was surprised that almost everyone there looked as human as her. When the old man had spoken of Gifted people, she had pictured fairies and strange beings, but these were ordinary-looking humans. Did they all have magical powers? She gazed curiously around, and was met by curious stares as well.

"Thank you, band, for coming," Erlich addressed the crowd. "As many of you know, we have been blessed with a powerfully Gifted person on the outside who is aware of our situation. We've now gotten her safely here with. My friends, this is the Gifted, Princess Avalon!" He gestured to her, and the room echoed with cheers.

Avalon smiled at them, but bewilderment furrowed her brows. Perhaps the injury to her head was more serious than she realized. *Gifted?*

But the Magister was still speaking. "And our friend, the trustworthy and determined, Prince Golan, youngest of the Rearevgard family. He is also our ally!"

The cheers continued for Golan. The people stared unabashedly at him, and they looked hopeful, but no one bowed. Golan's eyes met hers and she saw the ghost of a smile touch his lips, and a steadiness in his eyes that reassured her.

CHAPTER 29

A Rose in Bloom

Everything was in place. Magister Erlich had been right. No one from the castle had ventured into the Black Forest, so nothing had come of the search for Avalon and Golan. The Sparks blinked a coded message to the Magister, assuring him there *had* been a search. Things were in upheaval at Blackstone with Avalon and Golan's disappearance. Surely Queen Lilian would soon surmise they had fled into the Forest. Golan felt sure she'd breach the law to follow them, even if she had to use her mind control to convince the guards to do it.

The Sparks had also reported that a group of soldiers had left the castle in the morning, and they hadn't returned yet. It was a good time to move, while the security forces were somewhat lessened with the soldiers gone. And who knew if they'd gone for backup? Lilt was at least a day's journey south, so they had time to take control of the castle before then.

Golan had asked Avalon not to join their forces, but she'd just shaken her head. "I have to do this, Golan." She stretched out her hands and looked at them. "I'm–I'm Gifted." She peered up at him like she barely believed the words. "Erlich said the Sparks sensed my power when they were watching the pea. I've never even known. But these are people like me, who have had to live here in the shadows for longer than I've been alive just because they were given magical blood. Erlich would fight for me, and I will fight for him. Once the balance has been restored in Ethereal, I'll be able to learn how to use my powers. I will be able to help my family."

Her eyes glistened, and Golan breathed in deeply. He knew why she had to be there. She'd lost too much, and she would lose more if this didn't work.

But if he lost her, he'd lose everything. She'd become everything to him.

"Just stay close to me," he urged.

She bit her lip, but nodded. Together, they followed the others in their group into the darkness.

The air was warm and thick, and even though the sun had long gone to bed, sweat gathered at Avalon's temples. The swelling on her face had gone down, but the bruise was still an ugly black, and she favored the knot on the back of her head. Still, she was thankful she was well enough to join this revolt. The danger didn't scare her, maybe because she knew she was doing something right, but magic still made her nervous. When Erlich had taken her aside earlier to apologize for not having the chance to tell her his discovery earlier, repeating the words that she was Gifted, dread had washed through her in a cold wave. *Magic is dangerous!* Her mind screamed in defiance. *I don't want anything to do with it.* But Erlich was looking at her with his kind, wise eyes, and she couldn't call him evil. He had come to her rescue more than once, and he cared about all the people who hid away and lived secret lives in this Forest. She glanced around at them, the plain, simple clothes they wore, the hard work of staying alive etched into lines on their faces, and she realized she couldn't call them dangerous either.

Erlich had quickly told her more. "You're Gifted—and not in the simple way that many of the others are, with one certain gift they can employ." This morning she'd met men who could change into the likeness of animals, or throw fire with their hands. Some women could heal wounds with a touch, or grow plants before her eyes. She could do none of that on her own, but Erlich said her Gift was greater. She had the power to control crystals, the common ones *and* the powerful peas. Her natural magic was at the level only magisters attained. "We need you, Princess Avalon," he'd said. And she'd made her decision then and there, regardless of the consequences.

Since no magic had been practiced in Haven for so long, Avalon's power had never manifested. She wouldn't have dreamed she herself was one of the things she most feared. If anything, she would have fought against the Gift, fought to stay clear of anything to do with magic before she'd met the Black Forest band. She couldn't imagine that her mother had known Avalon was Gifted, *although she did give me the pea.*

The Sparks had sensed Avalon's power when she held the pea, though they had thought it was all in the pea itself. Then, when Queen Lilian took the pea to her own chambers, and they scoped it out, they still felt the power radiating from Avalon. They'd brought her back to the Forest, and Erlich himself had tested her with his perception ring while they talked that night. If not for her capture and then her escape into Ethereal, she may never have realized her own Gift. Every magical crystal that existed would activate for her and bend to her power. That meant that with the right crystals, she could perform any supernatural gift that existed.

"Why can't the Sparks rescue the peas from the Queen's room and bring them back here?" she'd asked. Stripping the Queen of her power was half the battle.

"They're delicate. The power in those peas is much too dangerous for their sensitivities, I'm afraid. They'd die if they got too close," Erlich explained.

Avalon looked down at her hands through the darkness. They were steady. If this was who she was, she was ready to embrace it. Even if that meant she was a princess who was sneaking through the woods in the dark, preparing to attack a castle. Her poor mother, if she was alive, would be devastated at the unruliness of this. She'd probably also be disappointed that Avalon was not only helping those with magic, but that she had a Gift herself. *Oh well.* Avalon couldn't dwell on that right now. Her mother was a wonderful woman, but her life was so determined by protocol that any action not in adherence to those rules frightened her. Avalon suspected that fear was part of the reason her mother had never told her about the pea. The past two weeks had taught Avalon that sometimes the right thing to do wasn't written in the rules at all.

Avalon clutched a protective hand around the pouch at her waist. Erlich had given her the crystals he thought would be useful tonight. He also carried some. Because they were the only ones in the group who could use crystal magic, he wanted them both armed, though he'd assured her he'd do most of the power wielding. He'd wanted to give her more training before they waged their war, but time had run out, so her lessons had been brief. She prayed she would remember what to do and have the presence of mind to control the power when the time was needed.

For now, she was content to creep along beside Golan, his strong frame a refuge in the darkness. They were quiet, and her mind returned to more of the information she'd taken in today, all the secrets Golan had discovered. Mava's involvement with the queen, the concealed woman, Dera, Benrid and his suspicious blindness. Even the reason she'd felt the pain on her first night at Blackstone finally made sense. Both peas had been under her mattress, unbeknownst to either her or Mava. The proximity of the crystals as she had shifted had put them in danger of merging, resulting in the pain the first Great Magister had decreed as a safeguard against such a combination.

All those mattresses, designed to conceal the pea of perception and gauge the strength of her magic by seeing if it would glow even through the barriers had probably absorbed a lot of the ensuing pain. Perhaps The One had been taking care of her all along, even in ways she didn't recognize as His.

No one talked, and they tread carefully in the shadows, with only moonlight to illuminate their way. Avalon wondered again about the holes she had been told were here. She had traveled in the Forest several times now, but never encountered anything like that. Of course, all the sinister rumors were mostly untrue, she realized now. Those who had disappeared mysteriously had been terrified citizens seeking refuge and understanding as they discovered they had a Gift that was illegal. She wondered how many more still lived in the kingdom, trying to hide their magical Gift, and living in fear. Her heart went out to them. She knew what it was like to bury herself beneath duty and what other people expected, not truly allowed to be herself.

She was fighting for them.

She felt something warm brush her fingers, and she tensed, but then his fingers found their place between hers. Golan was holding her hand. The warmth traveled all the way up her arm and swelled inside her heart. She squeezed his hand, and he exhaled a shaky laugh, giving her a sideways sheepish glance. He was nervous.

And that was...adorable.

CHAPTER 30

Take Me With You

Golan studied Erlich in the dark, making out his mouth moving, perhaps in silent prayer, as he picked his way through the trees. The Great Magister had been planning this for a long time. He and his band of fugitives had made weapons and practiced with them, spied on the castle and grounds, and amassed their group, but he'd admitted he wanted this to go quickly. He didn't want bloodshed. He didn't want a war. Just justice for the oppressed.

"My bones are old now, and I'm not up to being a soldier, but I'd never let my band go alone. These are my people, and I am their leader. A kingdom of misfits who deserve a place in the world, the right to live with those they love, a right to be themselves in every glorious way," he'd told Golan privately.

But was it right to risk Avalon? Golan knew Erlich had struggled with the question as much as he had. The poor girl had been through so much in such a short time, and he worried Erlich was putting too much pressure on her by asking her to use a power she'd just found out she had, but Erlich assured him Avalon was determined to help if she could. And then there was Alice's life. Turned out the servant girl was much more aware of the secrets of the Black Forest and Blackstone Castle than Golan had ever realized. Even now, she was waiting for them at the castle. The world needed her pure soul.

Both of the girls had *wanted* to be here. They had chosen to join this fight, and he didn't have the right to stop them, even if he was worried. So Golan kept the fears at bay by following Erlich in praying to The One to give them favor. He prayed He would spare those the world needed the most.

Golan approached the gates alone. Everyone else stayed hidden behind the perimeter of the Forest. Strangely, the Forest seemed close to the back gates when he wanted to avoid it, but now that he had to cover the distance alone, it seemed to be miles. He breathed deeply, trying to keep his heart steady. He wasn't afraid for himself. Neither side would be keen on harming the Prince, but even in an accident, he was thinking only of Avalon. He needed to be there to protect her. He would never let his mother use her again. His hand was still warm from Avalon's clutch, and that grounded him. He strode up to the gates and knocked.

The guards recognized him quickly and opened the gates without hesitation.

"May I have a torch?" Golan asked as he strode in confidently. They handed him one, but as they turned to close the gates, he drew his dagger and held it to the first guard's back. "Leave the gates open," he instructed.

Avalon and a woman named Isha should be approaching to get in range to use the first magic. The plan was to shed no blood unless absolutely necessary to save the lives of their small army. The guard stiffened, and Golan pressed the dagger harder, making him feel the seriousness of the threat. The other guard made a move toward him, but Golan held the torch out like a scepter.

"Stop!"

The guard hesitated, glancing at the other man's face.

"Stop or I'll kill him," Golan warned again.

The man with the dagger at his back nodded imperceptibly. The other guard swung on his heel with a shout. He was trying to alert others to help them, but he hadn't gone a step further when Golan tossed the torch at his head.

He howled when it hit, and though it fell to the ground a second later, the fire had caught his collar. He cursed as the flames scurried around his neck, clawing at his uniform to get it off. Golan had twisted his fist around the first guard's collar and moved the dagger to his neck. He held him there while the others poured through the gates.

Golan was searching only for Avalon. She was supposed to be first, along with Isha, the only other Gifted with sleeping power, to help clear the way, but he didn't see her. His tension put pressure on the dagger, which he wasn't aware of until the guard flinched.

Then he spotted her beside Erlich. She had her head bowed, and her hands cupped, and Erlich was whispering to her. Probably instructions. Her hands shook slightly, but when she raised her eyes to the guard, her stare was completely level. Isha, more sure of her power, moved forward quickly, but Golan couldn't take his eyes off Avalon. The flames from the sconces danced around her face, and her honeyed eyes glowed with a light of their own. Her hair flowed around her in diaphanous waves, and she looked otherworldly.

His legs weakened as he gaped, but she was focused and did not spare him a glance. She held out her fists, her gaze fierce, and a purple light poured between the spaces of her fingers. Immediately, the guard slumped. His dropped weight pulled Golan off balance, and he nearly stumbled over the man as he fell.

Avalon gasped, pulling back quickly, and Golan's reflexes shot him back before he even realized that he'd almost put himself in the path of her power. But it hadn't touched him. He looked at her to reassure her, but her eyes had grown huge. The light was gone, and she looked terrified.

Erlich took her arm. "It's okay, Princess. He's fine. You did well. The guard will sleep for hours. Now, let's see who else we can put to sleep."

Avalon bit her lip hard, but she followed Erlich anyway. Golan was proud of her for staying determined despite her fear. The second guard was being held by four Forest men. One had disarmed him, and the burns on his neck weakened him enough that he had stopped struggling. Erlich encouraged Avalon gently and Golan watched from behind as she put that man to sleep, too.

Other guards had come running when they heard the shouts, but Avalon, Erlich, and Isha faced them bravely, and they had all fallen into a heap before they even reached the gate, sleeping soundly. The Forest Band was organized, and everything was going according to plan. No one had died, and they were already getting into the castle. Golan breathed a prayer of thanks and hurried to his place beside Avalon. She looked relieved to see him.

"You are amazing," he said quietly.

"She is very brave," Erlich agreed. "It's an incredible responsibility to wield power. Besides, using magic creates a vacuum inside you that feels uncontrollable. It is a very uncomfortable experience, terrifying, if you're not used to it. And then you almost fell into her path of force, which gave her a real scare." He looked at Golan sideways, his brows fierce, but a twinkle in his eyes.

"I don't think sleeping would be the worst punishment," Golan tried to reassure them.

"But I need you here," Avalon protested.

His heart grew tight in his chest. "You could wake me with a kiss, though, couldn't you?" He ventured, pleased when a blush infused her cheeks. So, he did know how to flirt.

Erlich actually chuckled.

As far as Golan could tell, they had gotten through most of the guards. He wasn't sure how much of the disturbance had been heard from inside the castle. The hour was late, and his family and the servants should all be sleeping. And there hadn't been any real fighting–just a few struggles, but Avalon and Isha had put everyone to sleep easily, and now snoring was the loudest thing they could hear.

Then he noticed a light from one of the rooms. The Queen's room? His heart skipped a beat. They needed to hurry. They needed to get the peas away from her before she realized what was happening and used her power against them.

Alice met them at the entrance to the servant's hall. One of their quadrants went with her to surround the servants and keep them in their quarters.

"No fire," Erlich reminded his Gifted troops who followed her. "We don't need to burn the castle."

Alice had wanted to recruit the servants to their side, but Erlich had told her it was too risky. It would be hard to know who to trust and who would stay loyal to the King and Queen. The Sparks had been back and forth all day with messages between Alice and the Black Forest Band.

Erlich watched apprehensively as Alice faded out of his sight, but she knew Blackstone Castle. No one else in the group did, except for Golan, and he had to guide Erlich to his parent's chambers. Avalon would stay with them too. She wasn't accustomed to magic use, so her energy drain would be significant. Magister Erlich had already reclaimed the purple sleeping crystal from her to use himself if needed, but while she was drained, her power would be nonexistent. Neither Golan nor the Magister wanted her out of their sight.

CHAPTER 31

A Petal Falls

They crept up the stairs. The hall was dim and quiet, but the green light emanating from the Queen's chambers drew their eyes immediately as it flooded out from under her door. Golan hissed a curse. She was prepared. Somehow she had found out they were coming, and her power was ready.

"Your Father?" Erlich questioned.

Golan pointed further down the hall.

"We must put him to sleep."

Magister Erlich already had the purple crystal shards in this hand, and he held them toward the guards stationed at the chambers. The men dropped mid-stride, thudding on the floor.

Golan winced as one guard's skull cracked against the stone floor.

Then he swiveled around to see Joran's room. Where was his brother's guard? There was the possibility he'd followed Joran out on some nighttime rendezvous, but a warning in Golan's gut told him something else was happening.

Then things all happened at once. The Queen's door flew open, the sickening green glow glaring into the hall. Erlich shoved Avalon's arms down. He'd warned her that the power of the peas was stronger than the other crystals, especially if the Queen used both of them. Not only that, but they'd create a negative reaction if used against each other, which could hurt her.

Golan jumped in front of Avalon, blocking her from Queen Lilian, who was holding the peas in her hands, fully visible on her upturned palms. She was laughing. It was the oddest sound. Golan had never heard his mother laugh, and the noise sent chills down his neck.

"I have been waiting for you," she said.

The three others who were with their group stood still, unable to use their powers in the face of the peas. Golan heard one of them shout a warning, but it was too late. Avalon thudded into him from behind, throwing him forward. He twisted as he fell, just in time to see Joran's guard behind her.

Golan roared and lunged to his feet, but the guard caught his shoulders before he had time to draw his weapon. Joran stood behind the man, sneering.

"Little brother?" he asked, mildly surprised when he recognized Golan.

Three other men came out of Joran's room, rushing the Magister and the other three Gifted. The battle was short-lived. Although they struggled, they were no match for trained soldiers, not when they couldn't use their magic. Golan threw a look behind him, only to see his friends being bound. All of them. His stomach dropped, but he couldn't lose focus.

The guard restraining him hadn't drawn a weapon, which still gave Golan an advantage. He dropped his weight unexpectedly, pulling the man off-balance, then twisted and rammed his elbow into the man's gut. The guard wheezed, but didn't fall. The room was too crowded for swords, so Golan tightened his fist around his dagger.

But Joran had recovered his surprise and lunged at Golan's legs as he was getting in position to strike out at the guard. Golan felt himself airborne for a second when his legs shot out from under him, then he hit the floor hard. The guard was on top of him in a flash. Golan swiped his dagger at the man's hands as they reached for him, and the man hissed as his the flesh on his palms tore open. He drew back involuntarily, but the others were joining him, now that everyone else had been subdued, and they pinned Golan's arms to the ground.

Golan twisted his head around, desperate to see Avalon. The Queen's glowing eyes were in his periphery, and he slammed his eyelids shut, refusing to succumb to her power. Instead, he looked back up at Joran, who stood over him.

"I didn't expect you to help me, Joran," Queen Lilian purred. "Though you are certainly efficient."

Joran didn't spare her a glance as he flicked his wrist at someone behind Golan, nodding with his head toward the stairs. Joran was also avoiding the Queen's gaze. Queen Lilian was kneeling, the peas in her palms still alight. She was just out of reach of her sons. She spoke calmly, prodding them, trying to get them to look up. But they all knew that she could only wield the power if they made eye contact with her. Erlich had explained that, unlike Avalon, whose gift allowed her to propel the force of the magic forward, Queen Lilian could only transmit it through eye contact. She could not project what was not hers. The force entered her, and could only travel through metaphysical connection with someone else.

The Queen stood and took a step toward Joran. He turned his head away, but addressed her. "I'm not helping you. I don't know what your plan is, Mother. And I don't really care. I don't even care what you do to me, but you won't get the girl. You took my girl from me, so I've taken yours from you."

Then he turned and stomped away, his guards following him down the stairs.

Golan rolled to a sitting position, barely noticing the tight ropes that held his wrists and ankles. Joran's words had filled him with dread.

Avalon.

Erlich sat with his head bowed, dignified, but bound. The tall girl and the two men from the Forest were also tied up. One of the men was still stretched across the floor, and Golan thought he was unconscious. He hoped it was only that.

But where was Avalon?

NO! His mind screamed at him first, but then he was roaring. "*Where is she?*"

Queen Lilian heaved a frustrated sigh, then hurried down the stairs after Joran and the others.

"Where is she?" Golan demanded again. But everyone was silent. The King had not appeared. Surely the rest of their band would come to help them any minute.

"Mava!"

Nothing.

He twisted toward the others. "Look, we can untie each other," he said, his voice cracking. "Help me. The rest of our band is still fighting. We're not done."

Erlich was wordless, but he turned around, scooting closer to Golan until his hands could reach Golan's. Golan grit his teeth as the old man struggled. Every heartbeat was a second longer that Avalon was in danger. Finally, he felt the knot loosen.

Impatient, he pulled with all his strength, but Erlich grunted. "Be still."

A few more eternal minutes passed before Golan was able to pull his hands free. He was frantic. He hurried with Erlich's hands, then unwound his own feet, and lunged toward the stairs, leaving Erlich to help the others.

Chapter 32

All I Can Feel is the Winter

E rlich was stunned. He'd been hit on the head, and every thing was out of focus. He untied Chet's hands, who, in turn, helped Ethan and Lucia. Erlich's fingers were sore from straining at the tight knots, and his vision was blurry. He wasn't sure what to do next. He bowed his head again and prayed. Chet, Ethan, and Lucia scrambled up once they were free.

Chet asked, "We haven't seen the King. Should we seek him out or follow Golan?"

A muffled sound from the Queen's chambers froze them. Lucia cocked her head after a moment. "Is someone saying 'help'?" she whispered.

Ethan and Chet crept to the door, unsure what trap might await them. Lucia threw a worried look at Erlich and knelt beside him, putting her arm around the old man.

Someone in the Queen's chambers was struggling to call out. From the sound of the voice, they had been gagged. The door opened without resistance. Erlich looked up as the men pushed it open. He could see there had been a struggle in the room. Things were toppled everywhere, and on the floor lay a lady's maid, gagged and bound.

Tears were pouring from her eyes. She was shaking. Erlich's mind suddenly burned clear. Mava. Golan had told him everything he had learned from her, but they hadn't warned her of their attack, hadn't asked her to join them. There hadn't really been time, but his heart sank just the same.

There was a gash on her temple, but it wasn't deep. She sat up and pressed her fist against her mouth, the sobs still racking her.

Lucia moved toward her and spoke gently. "Will you tell us what happened? We are here to help you." She used gentle fingers to unwind the cloth over Mava's mouth while Ethan pried the knots loose from her wrists. She'd been tied with a sheet, not a rope.

Mava gulped air. Her thin hair was frizzy all around her face, her cheeks soaked and her eyes swollen. "The Queen. She suspected that Avalon and the Prince had escaped to the Forest because no one could find them. She knew you all would be coming. She had my sister up all night keeping the peas activated for her."

She drew another stuttering breath as tears tried to overtake her again. "Lilian killed her. After a while, my sister refused to give her any more power, so the Queen attacked me. She has never hurt me before, so I was caught off guard." Tears dripped off her chin, and she motioned to the disarray around the room.

"My sister was afraid for me then, so she did what the Queen asked. Lilian tied me up, and I couldn't do anything to stop her. Then a guard came to report you all had gotten through the gates. Lilian was locking Dera up again, but Dera knew Avalon was here, and she fought back. Sh–she..." Mava's words caught on a sob. "She tried to use her Gift to overpower the Queen. But the Queen's magic was already too strong. There was a terrible noise and a flash. It was only for a second, but Dera screamed. And she fell. And she didn't move anymore." Mava sobbed the last word, and melted into a heap on the floor, unable to continue.

"Where is your sister?" Chet pressed.

Mava lifted a finger toward the bedchamber, but didn't get up.

He and Lucia hurried to the bedchamber. Erlich knew the Queen would be more desperate than ever to get Avalon if Dera were dead. He had to find her and Golan first.

"Find out what you can," he said to Ethan. "Get reinforcements and locate the King. I am going downstairs."

"The servants will help you," Mava offered, her face still pressed into the floor. "I told them to."

Erlich's heart cracked for the woman's agony, and he was touched by her courage. She had tried to help. She and her sister, after years of living under the Queen's dictation, had finally rebelled.

Golan was raging. If anything happened to Avalon, he'd make Joran pay. He wouldn't think twice. She had collapsed, but Joran had rushed her out of there, which he hoped meant she was still alive.

He raced down the halls. He was surprised to see most of the Forest army fighting the servants out on the grounds. Except they weren't fighting each other. He paused, trying to see into the darkness. They were fighting the King and his guards. Together. They definitely had the upper hand, just by sheer numbers.

He couldn't stop to help. He had to find Avalon. He ran through the Castle, throwing open doors and calling her name. He called Joran's name too, but was met by nothing.

Think. I have to think.

He needed help. Surely someone had seen Joran and his guards. He wondered where his own guards were. He'd often trusted them with guarding his life, but he didn't trust them tonight. They were ordered only by the King, and who knew what his father had instructed them. Or, his mother, really.

He ran up to the growing crowd outside and pulled aside the first two people he saw. An older woman and man.

"Did you see Prince Joran or a group of guards recently? They have Avalon."

The couple shook their heads, but the woman's eyes widened suddenly, and she pointed. Golan swiveled in time to see Joran's horse appear through the back gates, which were neglected in lieu of the larger struggle in the yard. His brother was in the saddle. Golan sprinted toward him. Joran's three guards rode up behind him, but Golan didn't stop. He grabbed the reins and hoisted himself on the horse's back before Joran could respond. He shoved at his brother, and they both lost their balance, tumbling to the ground, rolling together away from the prancing hooves.

The guards jerked their own horses out of the way, dismounting and rushing toward Golan. He stood, backing away from Joran before he did something stupid. "Where is she? What did you do?"

Joran stood and dusted himself off. He smirked at Golan, but his eyelashes were wet. The sign of recent tears caught Golan off guard.

"Where is she?" Golan asked again, more quietly. Joran's guards surrounded him. No one touched him, but they were tense, ready for his any move.

Joran tilted his head, and understanding filled his blue eyes. "Oh. You loved her."

Golan's lungs clenched. He couldn't take in air.

"Now you'll understand how I feel," Joran said flatly. "She's dead."

He turned away. Golan threw himself at Joran. The guards locked him in their grip before he reached his brother.

Joran looked at him. "She's in the woods," he said, swiping a hand over his face. He motioned to his guards. "Let him go."

They did, hesitantly. Golan wanted to kill Joran right then, but the guards would only restrain him. And he needed to go to Avalon.

He spun away from them. "I need a healer!" he shouted. "A healer!"

A man from the Forest band shook his head. Others stared at him. Then a boy turned toward him. He was skinny and young–so young he should have stayed in the forest with the children. "I can help."

The boy looked too frail to help anyone, but Golan didn't have a choice.

He took off for the stables, the boy panting behind him. He took the first horse he saw, not bothering with a saddle. He pulled the boy up behind him.

"Secure the back gates," he yelled into the fray and took off at a gallop toward the Black Forest.

CHAPTER 33

Something that Lasts Forever

Golan saw Avalon almost immediately. She was on the ground just before the trees, her blonde hair a bright contrast against the darkness of the woods. She wasn't far from the back entrance of the castle, where they had started just a few hours earlier, and the sconces flooded her with light.

No,no, no,no! Those were the only words he heard pounding inside his mind.

He dropped from the horse before it had even stopped. He'd just been through this pain when he thought he'd lost her the night he found her in the prison, and he couldn't face it again. He could not lose her.

He wouldn't.

This war for freedom, for magic, was all useless to him if she was gone. He'd fought for magic because *she* was magic. She was magic to him.

The healer boy crouched down on his haunches beside her. Golan sank to his knees. He was trembling and couldn't hold his own weight any more. Her dress was soaked in blood, and her eyes were closed.

"What can you do?" he asked the boy hoarsely. He wanted to shake the boy, demand that he use his powers to fix this, but she was dead. Healers couldn't raise the dead, and agony made his words gentle. Deflated.

The boy furrowed his brow and put his hand over her heart. And then her eyelids lifted, and she stared at Golan.

His jaw dropped, and without thinking, he wrapped his arms around her. But her scream tore through the night, and he jumped back. Pain twisted her face, and she breathed in shallow gasps.

"I–I'm sorry," she puffed, "my side."

Golan's eyes grew in horror. Her injury. He had been so surprised, he hadn't thought. Blood plastered her torn dress to her side. She had been stabbed.

He winced and glanced at the healer, whose eyebrows were raised high on his forehead. The boy peered at the wound and nodded at Golan. Then he placed both hands over the wound and closed his eyes. His head fell back and his thin arms shook.

Golan could not take his eyes off Avalon's face, but she was staring at the boy in fascination. His unbroken concentration was palpable, charging the air with a solid feel. The pain that had flared in her eyes when the young healer first touched her wound began to dissipate. Golan's legs fell asleep as he knelt there, but he didn't shift.

Finally, the boy opened his eyes. They appeared heavy, and he seemed to be struggling to keep his head up. He squinted toward the wound. The bloody dress was still there, but the visible skin beneath the torn fabric was clean and unbroken. He gave them a wobbly smile, then lowered himself to the ground.

"I need to rest," he explained in a whisper. "But you'll be fine." Then he closed his eyes and fell asleep.

Avalon gasped, her hand fluttering to her side. "It's–it's gone. I'm better."

She was half asking, and Golan could only nod, the pool of tears in his eyes threatening to overflow. She started to sit up, pausing when she saw the young healer curled beside her. She put a hand on his brow and smoothed his hair.

"Magic takes so much out of us," she whispered, sounding so sure of her place among the Gifted. "Especially the young ones."

Her own eyes were shiny when she looked back at Golan. He pulled her into his arms and she melted into his embrace.

She spoke into his chest, "Joran said I had to pay. He said I was the only way to hurt his mother like she had hurt him. Then he started crying and saying, 'Krynn'.

"His guards held me, and I could barely move. I couldn't reach the crystals. He stabbed me, and I tried to twist away, but

I couldn't. The wound hurt too much. I stopped moving and hoped the pain would knock me unconscious or even kill me. But it didn't, so I just stopped breathing. I wanted him to think I was dead and leave. Someone kicked me, and then they all left. By then the pain was so bad, I couldn't get up. I couldn't even call out too loudly, and I was bleeding out fast. I was so weak when you got here I couldn't tell what was happening at first."

He pulled her tighter to him, letting one hand caress her hair. It was coming loose from its braid, strands fluttering everywhere, and he wanted to fist his hands in all of it.

"I'm sorry I didn't fight back," she whispered.

Golan pushed her shoulders back to look at her. "You stayed alive, Avalon," he said fiercely. "You did fight back."

They stared at each other for a long moment, the sleeping child next to them forgotten. The sounds of the night were peaceful, the struggle within the castle walls concealed from their view.

Then his lips were on hers, drawing her in like his life depended on it. She went weak in his arms.

CHAPTER 34

Tell Them I Tried

A valon shuddered as Golan's warm breath tickled her neck, leaving a trail of kisses there. She hadn't realized how much she had longed to kiss him until now. His mouth found hers again, and she closed her eyes, letting every detail imprint itself on her memory. His mouth was cool and soft, and she tasted his tears.

For several breaths she was lost in him, feeling warmth spread through her body before he finally drew back. Avalon didn't want to move. Ever. She wanted to stay like this for eternity. He leaned in close to her again, his forehead resting against hers. She reached out to rest her hand on his cheek.

"We have to return," he said, but his green eyes were shuttered, and he lowered his lips to hers again. "I love you, Avalon. Did you know that?" he murmured.

Happiness exploded inside of her, and she deepened the kiss with ferocity. She loved him, too.

But they had to go back to the castle. Golan gave her a step up to the horse, who was waiting patiently, flicking its tail. Then he lifted the scrawny boy, angling him across the horse's back. Avalon kept a hand on him. He'd stirred, but barely awoken when they moved him, and he slept on. Golan walked, guiding the horse.

"I saw Joran's guard behind you upstairs," he remembered. "Did he hit you?"

She shook her head. "I just collapsed. I'm not used to using my power, and when the drain settled in, I couldn't even stand. This young healer just gave me everything he had, including his strength. I'm fine now."

Lucia and Ethan and Chet had discovered Dera, dead indeed. A deep burn glazed across her brow where the powerful forces of magic had collided and seared through her brain. Her fight had only lasted a few seconds, but she had died courageous in the end.

They led Mava downstairs. Her chin still trembled, but she stood bravely, watching the aftermath of the skirmish unfold.

Besides Dera, one other man had lost his life during the attack on the King. One of the King's bodyguards had slashed him. The same sword had injured two others before they'd outnumbered the guard and fought him back by force. Under the influence of the Queen, the King had been preparing the soldiers who were still at the castle for an attack when the Forest band had found him, confused, but determined.

Most of the servants had joined the Black Forest army, some just out of fear, but most because Mava had warned them about what might happen and prodded them to fight with the Forest army instead of against it. And when they saw Alice there, taking her place alongside the Gifted, that sealed their decision. Many of them had been ordered by the Queen to do something against their will at some point, and seeing her overthrown was not an unwelcome thought.

The Queen had followed Joran when he and his men had stolen Avalon away, but he had ambushed her, two of his guards attacking her from behind while he got away with Avalon. Avalon had squirmed in his arms, but weakly. He had still struggled to keep hold of her, even with her arms tied, but he and Jun managed to throw her over a horse and get her out the castle gates. The back entrance was deserted, everyone's attention on the King and the soldiers surrounding him.

Joran took the princess to the Black Forest, too afraid to venture inside, but wanting to sacrifice her at the foot of all magic, all evil. He hated magic. It had corrupted his mother and ruined his life. He wasn't a killer by nature. He'd taken to fighting and hurting others to distract himself from the pain inside, but he wasn't a murderer.

But Krynn had to be avenged. His mother had to be destroyed. Avalon had to die.

He'd cried for Krynn, right there in front of Avalon and his guards, letting her memory consume him. He let himself feel all the agonizing pain he usually kept pushed down, the pain of knowing he'd never make another memory with her, never kiss her again, never be hers. The grief had given him resolve. He'd closed his eyes tightly, letting the scene of his gray, cold Krynn with a dagger lodged in her heart sear and burn him, and he buried the knife inside Avalon, catching her in the side, even though she tried to jerk away.

Tears obscured his vision, but he felt her stiffen and then go still. He swiped the bloody blade on his pants, sheathed it, and stood, swiping his misery off his cheeks with his arm. Jun nudged her with his foot, and she was limp. Joran turned away before he could regret it. She was dead or would be in a matter of minutes.

He'd expected to feel triumph, some sort of satisfaction that would ease his grief, but the grief was still there. Krynn was still in his thoughts—but only, ever in his thoughts. She was gone forever, and no revenge would bring her back. Maybe that is why he let Golan go. Maybe he hurt too much inside to do anything else.

He slipped past the frenzy on the lawn, leaving the jittery horses at the stable door and trudging toward the castle. He wasn't afraid. Whatever this ragtag bunch of peasants was doing, they were doing a spirits-blasted good job. They were inside the castle gates and rounding up his family quite successfully, it would seem.

He'd been surprised to see Golan with them. He shrugged now, his footsteps weary. He hoped this army would kill the Rearevgards off one by one. He'd done what he wanted to do to his mother. Now he wanted to die.

A thud behind him made him turn back. Jun had fallen face-down, an arrow in his back. The other two guards had spun toward the threat, jumping in front of Joran, but he pushed them apart to see. His mother stepped out of the shadows.

Her eyes were glowing green. He flung his eyes shut and took off in the other direction. He'd never be her slave again.

CHAPTER 35

Illusions Fade Away

“Prince! Princess!” Erlich greeted Golan and Avalon warmly when they got back, but there was worry in his eyes. The sleeping guards were locked in a room inside the castle. All the injured, which, thankfully, were only a few, were being attended by the healers and the castle physician.

“The King is secure in the prison until the Queen’s magic fades from his mind. We have nearly all the guards, I believe. But the Queen disappeared, and we haven’t seen her since she ran after Avalon when Joran had her upstairs.”

"His guards attacked her in the downstairs hall," Avalon said. "Joran carried me away from them, so I don't know what happened, but they joined him again just a few minutes later."

"And where is Joran now?" asked Golan. "I ran to find Avalon as soon as he admitted where she was. His three guards were still with him."

Erlich shook his head. "Stay alert. This is not over."

Golan and Avalon carried their healer into the ballroom, where the physician was tending to the hurt. The servants had produced several pallets for the wounded, and they eased him down on one.

A woman hurried up to them. "Thank you," she said. "This is my son. I was so worried, but someone told me he'd gone with you when you asked for a healer."

Tears sparkled in her gray eyes as she looked at Golan. "Thank you for bringing him back."

"He healed me," Avalon told her. "I was dying. He was just in time. He gave me everything, every last ounce of strength he had."

The women reached out to Avalon, and they embraced.

"What's his name?" asked Golan.

"Tiden," his mother whispered. "He's thirteen, and his power just manifested last year. He hasn't had much practice with it yet. He inherited it from me, and we'd suspected it since he was little, but...we're honored that he could save a life." One tear overflowed and slipped down her cheek. "He will be out for a while. He needs to replenish."

Avalon touched the lady's arm before turning to leave.

She stopped short when she saw Mava huddled in a corner. The girl, Lucia, sat with her arm around the woman. Lucia looked up, but Mava's eyes were glued to the floor as though she were frozen.

"What happened?" Avalon noticed the cut on the maid's temple and worry flared.

Lucia whispered. "Her sister died tonight, trying to stop the Queen. She's in shock."

Avalon's heart felt like lead. She pressed her lips together. How would she feel if Raine or Amelie were dead? She wanted to comfort Mava, but the woman still hadn't moved. Golan's eyes met hers and he shook his head slightly. Lucia gave them a sad smile and nodded as they backed quietly away.

Golan ran his hand through his hair, the movement catching Avalon's glance. Her eyes dropped to his lips, and goosebumps raised on her arms as she remembered how it felt to have them between her own. She looked away quickly before he could catch her blush, but his mind was clearly somewhere else.

"I don't think Mother and Joran are working together." He shook his head as if to clear it. "At first I thought they were, but she must have pushed him too far."

"We need to find them before they escape."

"And secure ourselves against the return of the troops that left yesterday–especially if they return with reinforcements."

"Do you think anyone left tonight to sound a warning or get help?"

"It's possible. If the Queen expected us, she probably sent messengers before we even got here. We must secure the gates better. The back entrance is unguarded. Then we need to capture the Queen and Joran and reassemble ourselves for the next wave of war."

He marched forward, and Avalon hurried to keep up.

Golan's steps halted abruptly, and Avalon almost walked up his heel. They were in the main hall downstairs, and they could hear Erlich just beyond the doors.

"Your crystals," Golan hissed. "Get them out. Be ready. I'm not sure what is going on out there."

Avalon immediately opened the pouch around her waist. The bag was small and colorless and hadn't caught anyone's attention, thankfully. She fumbled through the crystals, trying to decide which would be the best protection. She had sorted through sleep, shape-shifting, fire, or death—which she absolutely didn't want to use—when hands closed around her neck.

She screamed, but the noise was cut off as the fingers squeezed tightly, and she choked instead. She rammed her elbow back as hard as she could, but hit only air. Golan spun around. Avalon felt her blood shoot ice as his eyes grew in horror.

"Mother! Let go of her!"

"So you can have her? She's destined to marry a *king*, Golan. You'll never be king. She won't be wasted on you."

Avalon struggled to gasp in breath. Why didn't Golan attack the Queen? She tried to twist herself, but her vision blackened as the Queen squeezed tighter. She clawed at the hands around her throat, but a sudden searing pain hit her elbows and sent shockwaves through her body. Her knees wobbled as the pain rocked her.

"Stop!" The panic in Golan's voice made her go still with dread, even though he was talking to the Queen.

"What do you want, Mother?" Golan's voice was so tight, Avalon was surprised he'd been able to get the words out. His shoulders were rigid, the heat in his eyes burning, but even through her growing dizziness, she could see that he focused near heart-level, refusing to look the Queen in the eyes. Spirits, the magic must still be working. How much power had Queen Lilian forced Dera to use? The poor woman could have died from pure exhaustion alone, even if she hadn't tried to use her own power against the Queen's pea and caused the deadly reaction.

"You. Won't. Kill. Me," Avalon wheezed the words. Her lungs were burning for air, and unconsciousness floated around the edges of her vision. Dera was dead. Queen Lilian needed Avalon alive. She needed a person Gifted to access the power in the peas, and very few were Gifted with that.

"Maybe not yet," the Queen agreed, "But, though magic is in your blood, you bleed the same as anyone else. There are worse things than dying, Avalon."

Golan growled and closed the distance between them. The Queen jerked Avalon back.

"Be careful. I will hurt her if you move. I will hurt her permanently. It's your choice, though. Either you look at me now, and she won't be harmed. Or you refuse to help me, and I will let you walk away–for now–but the girl will not walk away. She may never walk again."

"What do you have against me?" Golan choked. "You want her to be the Queen, and you could easily make Father name me crown heir, which seems like the easiest thing to do, but you've fought so hard for Joran instead–even though he has turned against you!"

"Joran is the only son I love!" the Queen shrieked, but the sound seemed to come from far away, wavering as it reached Avalon's ears. "I never wanted you! You cost me the only true happiness I ever had!"

That was the last thing Avalon heard before she slumped.

Queen Lilian dropped Avalon when she passed out, letting her hit the floor. Golan's cry was guttural, but archers fanned out on either side of the Queen, their crossbows drawn and pointed toward him, keeping him rooted. They had nocked their arrows when he'd taken a step earlier, and he knew they'd fire if he moved again. Eight arrows embedded in his flesh would not help him save Avalon.

"Your freedom or the girl's?" The Queen asked again.

"What will you make me do?"

Golan would give up anything for Avalon. He'd live under his mother's control forever if Avalon could be free, but he didn't trust his mother. Of course she wouldn't just let Avalon walk away, and once he was under her mind control, he wouldn't be aware enough to watch over Avalon. Plus, he had a sickening feeling that whatever his mother wanted him to do, it was something so horrible she wouldn't do it herself.

"If you care about the girl, it shouldn't matter. But if you must know, I need someone to kill the Magister–someone who can get close to him without suspicion. The others won't be able to last without him. And I need Henry's life too. He's worked wonderfully for me all this time, but I think it's time for a new ruler."

The nausea in his gut increased. "No. I would never do that, no matter what spell you put me under."

The Queen smiled, though it looked like a snarl. Golan kept his eyes carefully averted from the pretty face that looked so much like his. "So you say now, but many a good person has spilled blood for me without hesitation."

Avalon stirred.

"You have five seconds to make your choice. I thought you loved this girl."

Golan's mind raced. "So you'd rather have me do your work than have Avalon? I thought you needed someone to activate the magic. Dera is dead, and you want me to kill Erlich..." He was trying to buy time, trying to understand the Queen's motives so he could get a grip on the situation.

Where was everyone? Why hadn't anyone appeared to help?

"Stop talking and make your choice." The Queen held her fists up, the peas still glowing steadily inside, and Avalon jerked and screamed. One of those peas had the power of crippling pain, and Avalon was feeling it. He'd felt a touch of it the night his mother had all but admitted to blinding Benrid.

"Fine, fine, I'll do whatever you want!" Golan clenched his eyes shut to keep from meeting the Queen's eyes too early. "But let her leave first. Once she is back with the Magister, I'll do anything."

The Queen called over her shoulder, "Someone take her outside. Leave her near the entry. Someone will find her."

One archer put away his weapon and stooped to gather Avalon in his arms. She opened her eyes when he lifted her, and Golan's blood heated at the sight of the stranger holding her against his chest.

"Golan," Avalon croaked, and his heart broke.

He didn't look at her as the man carried her past him. He couldn't. "Find Erlich, Avalon. Find him and come help me. And I'm sorry."

He finally lifted his gaze to the Queen's, wondering belatedly where she had found the archers, when he thought everyone had been put to sleep and locked in a room. He prayed she hadn't freed everyone.

Her blazing eyes were terrifying in the dimness, and Golan could feel the strength of the magic. The force hit him in the face, blurring everything but her face. There was a whirring in his ears, and then a cloud descended in his mind. Thoughts slipped by him without making sense. He couldn't focus on any of them. He wanted to strangle her, but his arms wouldn't work.

There was a shout. Golan's mind was sluggish, and he couldn't decipher what was happening, but the Queen fell to her knees. The archers around her didn't move, their arrows still trained on him. They looked in confusion to the Queen. Golan was confused as well. He wanted to do whatever the Queen wanted. He was waiting, but she was kneeling, swaying there on the floor, not saying anything. Then she fell forward.

The green haze faded, and as it did, Golan felt his mind come into focus. The guards looked at each other in surprise and then horror. The Queen was on the floor, her face contorted in agony, an arrow piercing her shoulder blade from the back, the tip visible through the front of her dress, and they were all standing around her with bows drawn. But, as they glanced at each other, they realized that everyone still held his bolt. None of them had shot the Queen.

"Guards, take the Queen to the prison," Golan ordered quickly, unsure whether they would accept his authority or not. He recognized two of them now as Joran's guards, which meant the Queen must have recruited them with her mind control. He glanced around for the assailant. Was it someone from the Black Forest who had rescued him?

"The arrow, sir?" one questioned.

"Just make sure she is in chains. The physician is in the ballroom. You can summon him to attend to her next, but only once she is locked away."

They nodded and grimaced as they lifted the Queen. The arrow was too high in her shoulder to have hit anything vital, Golan was sure. Her eyes rolled in pain, and she ground her teeth. The flow of magic had been broken from the shock, and her face was pale, her eyes a soft olive green that matched Golan's, a color he only saw in her most unguarded moments.

"Give me the gems," he ordered her, not allowing himself to flinch at her agony.

"Never," she muttered, but he grabbed the wrist of her injured arm. Her shrill scream echoed off the walls, and her palm flew open. The pea bounced away dully on the stone floor. Golan dove after it and shoved it in his pocket.

"The other one," he demanded. Queen Lilian was panting, tears welling in her eyes as she tried to breathe past the pain. She dropped it into his palm, and he nodded to the guards, dropping it into his other pocket to keep the crystals from trying to merge. He hoped he could trust the men. At least without the magic and the peas, the Queen could not control their minds any longer.

He scanned the hall again, wanting to thank the archer, but he could see no one, and he had to get to Avalon.

Then a step sounded on the staircase. He paused. The footsteps continued, and Joran emerged from the shadows. His hands were in his pockets, but he glared at his brother. Golan glared back.

Joran had tried to murder Avalon just hours ago. He *had* murdered her, for all he knew, and had Tiden not been able to save her. Emotions churned through Golan's chest, shock and despair and hatred and anger. His fists clenched. He'd never been as good with weapons as his brothers, but the wrath fueling his punches this time would give him more power than he needed. He might kill Joran before he stopped. He threw the first punch without warning, and Joran stumbled back and hissed, but he didn't raise his fists in return.

He just blinked rapidly, trying to see through the shock of pain behind his eyes, and held up his hands. Golan landed another fist in his face, the impact jarring his own arm. He embraced the pain in his knuckles. The agony felt good. But Joran stepped back again and drew his bow in a flash. He nocked an arrow and aimed it at Golan.

"Stand down," he said, his voice thick with the blood that was pouring from his nose. "Spirits, you're stupid, brother."

Golan slowed as the arrow was raised, his hands falling to his sides, but his heart racing as angrily as ever. He was breathing so hard it was ragged, and his eyes didn't leave Joran's face.

Joran lifted the bow and arrow an inch. "I did it, okay? If you love the girl, go to her. You deserve that, at least. Leave me alone."

He lowered his weapon, swiping at the blood on his face with the back of his hand. Golan had frozen.

"You?"

Joran nodded.

"You shot Mother?" Golan asked again.

"Yes. I have been her pawn my whole life. I didn't want that to happen to anyone else, even you." He paused, wiping away more blood and staring at his hand, slick with it. "Besides, killing the girl wouldn't stop her, and that's what I really want most of all."

Golan's fury vanished, and his shoulders dropped. He stared at his brother.

Joran looked up at him, his eyes growing in exasperation. His nose was already swollen and blood smeared across his cheek. "So I'm sorry, and you're welcome." He stomped past, and Golan was too surprised to respond.

CHAPTER 36

It Starts with a Seed

Avalon dashed for Erlich as soon as the guard put her down. Swallowing hurt. Her neck was sorely bruised, but she was breathing again, and she was fine. She had to help Golan. The Queen was going to use him. She had to be stopped.

Erlich was addressing the leaders of his four quadrants. They were standing in a circle. Avalon didn't bother being polite. She tugged on Erlich's arm.

"The Queen is in the hall. She has some guards, and she has Golan." She rushed away before he could even answer her.

"Avalon!" he called sharply, but she didn't stop. She felt for the crystals in her pouch. The small bag hung open, but she didn't think any had fallen out. She found the sharp orange death curse with her fingertips and drew it out. Erlich had warned her not to use these forces against the peas, but she had nothing else to fight with. He'd also warned them that killing was a last resort, but Golan's life was under the Queen's control. She had to do something, to *try*.

She pushed open the heavy door, the crystal clutched tightly in her fist, and tried to gather the concentration to ignite it, but the sound of a snarl and a fist connecting with flesh hit her first, and her eyes flew open. The gathering power inside her dissipated as her focus was torn away.

Golan was punching Joran's face. The Queen was gone.

Joran stepped back out of reach, drawing a weapon quicker than Golan could reach him, and he aimed the arrow at Golan's heart. She wanted to throw herself in front of Golan, and scream for help, but she was frozen in a silent surreal moment.

"I did it, okay? If you love the girl, go to her. You deserve that at least. Leave me alone."

Avalon's mind raced, trying to catch up. The crystal was cutting into her flesh she was so tense. She flinched and loosened her hold. There was noise outside. Erlich was coming.

"You shot Mother?" Golan asked.

Avalon's eyes grew wide. She didn't think she'd been out for that long. Wind hit her as Erlich and some other men came rushing up behind her. She simply threw out her arm, stopping them, and shook her head slightly, her eyes glued to the scene in front of them.

Joran's handsome face was a mess, but he managed to look annoyed as he said, "So I'm sorry and you're welcome."

Then he left Golan standing there, rooted to the ground.

Then everyone came alive. Golan spun around, his brow furrowed, like he wanted to ask his brother more questions. Joran spotted the group at the door, and his shoulders sagged in defeat. Erlich's men rushed to surround him. The Prince didn't even try to draw his weapon, though he had a few seconds before they reached him.

"Where does he go?" The men asked. They looked at Erlich, but the Magister looked at Golan, his head tilted.

Golan stared at his brother for a moment. "He just saved our lives," he said quietly. "Yours included," he said, his eyes darting to meet the Magister's. "I think I was about to kill you. The Queen had overpowered my mind."

"Lock him in his chambers, once you know it's clear of guards," Erlich decided. "Take his weapons and two of you stay to guard the room," he added. "We need to talk to him soon."

Avalon had crossed the distance to Golan, and his features melted in relief when he saw her. He pulled her to him, and she enjoyed the crush of muscles against her. This kind of smothering felt only safe. She looked up at him, and he caught sight of the red bruises on her neck. He bent, his lips brushing her neck softly.

"I'm so sorry, Avalon," he breathed, and she felt like his love was healing the marks already. She wrapped her arms around his broad chest and squeezed him back.

"I have the peas," he said. He brought them out of his pockets. They looked so harmless and small in his large palms. Avalon didn't want to touch them.

Erlich took them instead. He smiled. "We're almost saved," he said. "Cleft is almost here with the third one."

Avalon and Golan looked at him in surprise. "You know where it is?"

"Almost always, remember?"

"Cleft?" The question came from Avalon.

"There is still much I didn't get to explain. The final pea was in Cleft. A few months ago, I entreated some of them to help us in the revolt. The Sparks had located a pea-Gifted soldier, and I contacted him. He agreed to help, but his men played traitor, and once they had our information, they tortured him into submission. They abandoned our cause and turned instead to gather the peas for themselves. I'm assuming that has something to do with why they took you, Princess Avalon."

"But now they're bringing their pea here." It was a statement, but questions still filled her eyes.

"They are. Seems one of them was true, at least. She has communicated through my Sparks, and she now has possession of the pea. She is on her way here. She replaced it with a false one, so the others don't even know it's gone yet. When they discover it, there could be another battle, but I think they are too small a group to risk a fight against us. Besides, we have leaders from both Haven and Ethereal on our side, do we not?"

He motioned to Avalon and Golan and smiled, but it was grim. "This is our first victory, but the war is far from over. Unless..." he cocked his head, his voice fading. His eyes narrowed on something that couldn't be seen.

C HAPTER 37

Give Me a Love Worth Believing

A valon opened her eyes and looked around the bedchamber. This room was much prettier than the one she had been staying in. In fact, it was probably the prettiest room at Blackstone. Her bed was comfortable, the bedclothes a powdery pink edged in lace. A vase of fresh flowers stood on a small table beside her bed. There was a red tapestry on the wall, gauzy curtains on the windows, and a thick rug on the floor. It felt almost as fresh and bright as her room at home.

She felt a stab in her chest. *Home.* She still needed to get there.

To her surprise, a girl came in to help her wash and dress when she pulled the servant's cord without believing anyone would hear it.

"Are you hungry?" the girl asked timidly.

"I'm famished. But how is everyone? Is anyone able to prepare breakfast today?"

"It's too late for breakfast, Your Highness, if you'll pardon me. But the cooks have prepared a cold lunch. I'll bring some up for you."

After Avalon had eaten the cold meats and cheese, she ventured out of her room. There was no one in sight, and she wasn't sure if she was reassured by that or not. Of course, most of the castle guards had been put to sleep the night before and would probably just be waking up now. Besides, their oath was to the King, and without his orders, they had no obligation to guard her or anyone else in the castle.

With the shift in power, she wasn't sure which staff they could trust yet, though apparently some servants were working. She headed to Golan's chambers. She'd slept in a room in the same wing as him. That's probably why the room was so lush; it was part of the royal family's suites. Erlich had commanded the two of them to rest as dawn had neared. He'd said that everything was under control for the time, and they would deal with picking up the pieces in the morning.

She knocked on Golan's door. He opened it immediately, like he had been waiting for her.

"Good morning," she smiled.

He was dressed in fresh clothes as well. The black tunic stretched tight around his wide shoulders, and she blinked her gaze away. He smelled like pine and mint, and she felt heady. He'd kissed her last night. She'd kissed him.

"Did you sleep?" he asked. A new flatness tamed the usual earnestness in his voice.

"Yes, actually. I was exhausted. Did you?" The mundane pleasantries felt strange in the air, which was thick with something else that made her insides hum.

"A bit." He looked haggard, deep shadows under his eyes, and her heart went out to him. "How are your injuries feeling today?" he asked.

She brushed her fingertips over the soreness at her throat. "I just feel bruised–everywhere, really–but I'm going to be fine."

He nodded. His fingers reached out tentatively toward her, and she stopped breathing. He let his hand slide from her cheek to her shoulder. The light touch made her skin prickle with awareness, every nerve coming alive for the sensation.

She met his gaze, a pleasant shock wavering through her when she saw his green eyes heavy with grief and...was that need? He focused on her mouth.

Something was bothering him. And it was making him...weak.

She threw aside all her lessons on propriety and let her shaking hands curl around his tunic and tug him closer, her lips already meeting his.

They kissed wildly, the hungriness in their lips surprising them both. But Avalon embraced it. Instead of cowering away from the unknown, she sank into the feeling and let it carry her. She roamed against his mouth. His sturdy arms braced her back and fingers massaged circles on her neck and in her hair, and she only wanted to press closer. She wanted him, every inch of him, and her mouth told him so. He groaned and tugged at her bottom lip, and the pain only made her hungrier.

When they finally parted, her lips felt swollen. And wonderful.

She tried to catch her breath, everything else forgotten but him. And she knew he wanted her as much as she wanted him, but it was Golan who shuddered and wiped his hand over his face.

"You," he breathed, but his tone held only desire.

Still, he turned away and paced to the window. He put his hands on his head and clenched his fists in his hair. After a deep breath, he faced her.

"I love you, Avalon. I love you so much." His voice shook. "That's why I won't make the mistakes my parents did. I love you, and I respect you, and I won't take you before you're mine."

His jaw tightened, but Avalon saw the desire still swimming in his eyes and knew he was fighting an internal war. She wanted to sink her mouth into his again, press close, and help him decide. The images in her mind alighted her insides in a new and exciting way, but she blinked to clear them.

Golan was honorable, and he was fighting for her honor. She respected that. She loved that. Yes, she *would* help him decide. Her heart warmed from his respect, gratefulness overcoming her other passions.

"Thank you," she whispered, realizing how easy it had been to get so close to doing something they might regret.

She turned to the door. They needed to get out of the quiet chamber.

He followed her and grabbed her hand. Grateful, she entwined her fingers in his, but he pulled her to a stop.

"There is something I need to tell you," he said, pain settling deep in his eyes. "And it could change everything." He blew out a breath. "It changes me."

He threw a glance toward Joran's door. Presumably, he was still locked inside. Golan passed the room and strode toward the stairs, sinking down on the top step. No one else was around. Avalon sat beside him and waited, worry tightening her features.

"I didn't go to sleep right away last night. I guarded your door for a while until I was sure the castle was quiet and you were safe."

Her chest warmed at his devotion.

"Then I went to the prison. I had to see her myself and know she was locked up and her power was gone, or I'd never be able to rest."

He crossed his face with his palm again. "So I went up there. The cells were full. Everyone was chained securely. There were guards, men from the Forest. She was in the back room, where you were before. I asked the guards to leave to give us some privacy, and they waited at the bottom of the stairs. I had to ask her about something she'd said."

He looked into the distance for a long minute. "The King was there too, and I felt ashamed to see my father in chains. Except he's not my father."

"What?"

A muscle jerked in Golan's jaw. "The Queen told me yesterday, when she threatened me with you, that I was the son she never wanted. And I kept hearing those words afterwards. I just wanted to know why. I knew she probably said them in anger, or as a manipulation, but I was scared. After what I just learned about Benrid, I had a feeling there were more secrets. And things kept coming to my mind, like the way she only cares about Joran.

"Once, when I was little, I fell and scraped my knees. They started bleeding, and I was terrified. I was three," he clarified, giving her a warning glance, but Avalon only felt her heart squeezing. He looked so sad.

"And I ran to find my mother. She saw me crying, and pulled her skirts back so they wouldn't touch my bloody knees, and held me away from her. She told me I should have gone to my nursemaid, and that I should never bother her with things like that, and then she walked away."

He shrugged. "It doesn't sound like a big deal, but I still remember it."

His voice got even lower. "I remember because Joran's tooth was loose, and the very next day he tried to pull it out. He managed it, but his gums bled a lot. He ran to the Queen to show her, and she was delighted. She pulled him in for a hug, and her bodice was ruined with blood, but she just kissed his head and told him she was proud of him."

Fifteen years later, Avalon could still see the toddler boy's hurt and confusion alive in his eyes. She put her hand on his arm and squeezed.

"So, I just wanted to know, you know?" Golan sighed. "She was resting. Her shoulder was bandaged. I woke her up and demanded to know why she was so determined to give Joran everything, including the throne, and why I didn't matter to her. The doctor had given her something for the pain. It made her words slur, and I think that is the only reason she talked to me at all."

He snorted mirthlessly. "She told me I wasn't royalty. The King isn't my father. She said my father was a worthless merchant. Apparently, she owed the man an enormous debt for some kind of drug he'd smuggled to her. She meant to ask the amount from the King for some invented reason, or even use the pea to make him give it to her, but Dera was very sick, and she didn't have enough strength to activate the pea during that time. The merchant sent her a message threatening to blackmail her if he didn't get the gold immediately. So she sneaked away from the castle to meet him secretly. She gave him the money she had, which was undoubtedly a lot, but he was impatient. He threatened her life and told her she could give it all to him that night or give him a night of pleasure instead. She didn't have the money, so she obliged."

Golan paused. He looked sick. "And I was conceived."

They were silent.

"She was drugged last night. I wish I could say I thought she wasn't telling the truth, but I can't. It makes sense. I feel the truth. I see it." He spread his hands and looked at them. "I look like her, but there isn't a feature of the King that I share."

Helplessness flooded Avalon. She didn't know what to say to make this shame easier for him.

He sighed. "So the only tie to royalty that I have is my mother, who only married into it herself and has a selfish, dishonest heart." He shook his head.

Avalon shook hers too, trying to disagree. *It's okay, It doesn't matter,* she wanted to say, but that wouldn't help. It did matter. Even if no one else cared, it mattered to Golan.

"I'm not quite done," he finally said. "The very next morning, she tried to drink a mixture that was supposed to ward off unwanted pregnancies, but the medicine didn't help. She drank it again once she knew she was with child, and later she took some kind of herbal tea that the midwife told her would flush the baby from her. It came close to taking her life, but not mine." His voice was husky. "That's how much she didn't want me."

Avalon felt the sting in her own soul.

"She had to pass me off as the King's, of course. She couldn't risk her unfaithfulness being found out, and especially her drug use. But it wasn't the only time she had been unfaithful. She said she had a 'friend' on the council, a man she actually loved. I don't know if she was ever capable of love or not, but this man stopped seeing her once she got pregnant. He was angry that she was still with the King like that. She says I cost her everything. I took her true love away, and I complicated Joran's right to the throne, and I almost took her life. She was even using the drugs when she first carried me, but they made her so sick she almost died. When she realized she couldn't end the pregnancy, she had to stop taking the drugs to protect her own life. She was miserable."

He rubbed his face. Tears had risen in his eyes and slipped down his cheeks.

Avalon felt wetness on her own cheeks. She hadn't told Golan that she loved him, but she realized she did. She didn't care who his father–or mother–were. She knew who he was, and he was strong and honorable and kind, and she would always love him.

Her voice trembled. "Golan, I love you. I love you for who *you* are–and you're still that person, no matter what you found out about your past. You're not a mistake, no matter what your mother thinks. You were made for me. And for this kingdom, and for the magical realm. I love you for how you've been my friend. I love you for how you've risked everything for me and protected me. I love you for how you help those who are oppressed. I love you for your honor. I love you for your honesty, for telling me every single hard detail. I've never known a better man than you, and I do not deserve you."

His eyes were red and full of raw emotion that hurt almost too much to look at. "Do you mean that?"

She nodded solemnly. "I do."

Then she leaned forward and put her lips on his. It was a gentle kiss. Their lips were soft and understanding, and healing.

She pulled back, a small smile twitching at her lips. "And I love you for your kisses." Mischief danced in her tone.

But Golan didn't smile. "Avalon, you can't. You're a princess. The firstborn of Haven's royals," he reminded her, protest and pleading in his voice. "Your parents would never allow this. And you have a duty to your people."

"I care less and less for traditions every day, Golan. And you're the one who taught me that. You taught me that I can be addressed as simply 'Avalon' and not vanish in smoke. I can be *me* and still be good and do what's right, even if *me* doesn't follow everyone's every expectation."

He lifted an eyebrow, and she smirked. "And *me* loves you, Golan. No matter what."

CHAPTER 38

Calm after the Storm

Three riders galloped up to the main gates just before dusk. They were dressed as Cleftan soldiers, but Erlich had been waiting for them, and when they were inside, the middle one took off her helmet, releasing long black hair. She inclined her head to Erlich. "We've made it, Great Magister, and it does not appear we were followed. These soldiers are friends."

She put out her hand to the soldier on her right, and he handed her a small box from his bag. Avalon knew what was inside.

Erlich's tall face eased into a wide smile. He took the box and shook the girl's hand heartily. "Everyone, this is Petra of

Cleft. Petra, this is us." He gestured to those gathered around. "She stood up for justice when the rest of her band betrayed us, making her only braver in the face of the secret mission she undertook. She has brought us the final pea."

He eased the box open. The green ball was small and dull, a crude circle with rough edges that weren't shaped or sanded.

"This is the pea of pleasure. Our set is complete."

He gathered the other two, one from his pouch, and the other from his vest pocket. He held them separately and gazed at the faces watching him. Petra stood with her helmet under her arm, smiling.

The other two soldiers stood at attention beside her. Avalon stood with her fingers laced in Golan's. The four quadrant leaders were there, as well as several of the Sparks. Two had flown in with Petra, and they danced in the air with their friends, tails blazing brightly.

"Friends, I have reached a decision. These peas were given as a gift to mankind by the Great Magister of the Beginning. Even in his lifetime, power and greed corrupted their use. He thought to curb the power by separating them. For generations, they have been apart, but even singly, they have often caused more harm than good. People are lustful, and they often see only selfish opportunities with this power."

He took a bag of crystals from his neck. Avalon had returned hers to this collection already. He shook it, emptying the colorful rocks on the table.

"I no longer see the need for such magic in our world. Magic was a privilege from The One, never intended for evil, but people are inclined to take this wonderful gift and use it for themselves. I have seen too many people get hurt, just in the last few days, to allow this to continue. The One sends personal Gifts to people even more often these days than He used to. Those gifts are magical and wholesome. People grow up with a healthy respect for their ability and are humbled by it. Most times that means they handle it responsibly.

"Just as this was the time to free our Gifted people from the Forest, now is the time to destroy the outward magical sources. We will leave the Gifting in The One's hands and accept that those who are not Gifted have no need of magic. So, today I end this corruption and this very war. Today I revoke the magic from these peas. I revoke the magic crystals, and the spells and incantations. I revoke all magic except for the Gifts!" His voice thundered and echoed off the tiled walls.

The Sparks left, unable to withstand the force of the magic about to happen. Everyone else stepped back. Avalon could feel her own blood rushing, answering to the energy in the room, but she forced herself to stay still and watch.

Erlich gathered all the gems and crystals together. The peas immediately sparked to life in response to his power, but the Magister spread his hands over them, containing the magic. He bowed his head, whispering, his eyes closed in total concentration. The light from his purple band was blinding.

There was a roar, and everything began to swirl around him. Furious winds picked up the jewels and Erlich was barely visible behind the cloud of fog and wind and objects.

The whirlwind was deafening. Petra's mouth fell open. Golan tightened his grip on Avalon. No one dared breathe as the breeze whipped their clothing and hair with ferocity. Avalon wondered if everyone else felt the pressure in their heads and the roaring of blood in their ears the way she did.

The storm raged and seemed to drag on eternally, just a fury of whirling wind and noise. But quietness finally descended with a whoosh, and then the only sound was the clink and thud of objects as they dropped from the air. The crystals lay scattered on the stone floor among everything else. Erlich had his arms raised to the heavens, high above his head, his face thrown back. He was shaking violently, but he stood strong under the power that rocked him. Finally, he, too, stilled.

When he opened his eyes, he looked haggard. His voice was heavy.

"It is done."

CHAPTER 39

Smell the Roses

Avalon had joined the others in the council room, awaiting the King. She'd expected Erlich to be there already, but he arrived a few minutes later. Jenna and Alice trailed behind him with trays of tea, which they served around the table. Avalon smiled. *Erlich and his belief that all discussions should be had over tea. He was probably in the kitchen instructing them how to make it.* She hoped it was the delicious tea he made at home.

She curled her hand around the warm cup, watching the steam until the King's entrance diverted her attention. Guards escorted him into the room. He wore clean clothes and wasn't in chains. He had not been given his crown back yet, but Erlich rose and bowed respectfully before asking him to take a seat with them at the table.

King Henry took his seat with dignity, and Avalon was surprised to see his eyes were alert and keen. How much of the time had he lived under the fog of the Queen's power, she wondered. She remembered his absent-minded jovialness, the way he seemed unbothered by tensions in the room, and she grieved for him. What most people probably ascribed to the obliviousness of age had actually been the Queen's tactic to make him mindless.

Erlich began, "Your Majesty, we are grateful that you have agreed to have this discussion with us. Obviously, we all have power here–you, as our King, and we, as your captors." Avalon winced, but the King received the pointed hint with grace and inclined his head.

"We must reach a decision about several matters."

The King shifted slightly. "Magister." He continued his glance around the table, "Men, ladies. I have not ruled my kingdom for years. I have been only a shadow, a face to the world, whose mind and will was completely smothered by the Queen's possessive power. I am ready to catch up on the affairs of my kingdom, to begin to right the wrongs and rule with competence."

Avalon's eyes met Golan's, and his were wide too. Never had she heard King Henry speak with authority like that. She studied him again. The creases gathering at his eyes still gave him a pleasantness, but his blue eyes were dark and focused, and the air around him felt regal. She rather liked the real king.

Erlich explained the Queen's part in the war against magic, and the way she had kept magic only for herself and banned it from the rest of the kingdom. He did not pause as he exposed her doings–the lies, the drugs, the unfaithfulness, the truth about Golan, the abuse of magic, and, finally, the way she had enslaved Dera and Mava and recently killed Dera.

"Benrid is your firstborn, but borne by Dera," Erlich finished, bringing the events full circle.

The King kept his head straight, but his mouth was drawn in a tight line, and his hands trembled slightly.

"I know this is a lot to learn, and a lot to bear," Erlich added quietly. "But I must judge your response to these matters before I can tell you whether I will reinstate your power on the throne. I know you would rather decide the fate of Lilian, Benrid, Joran, Golan, and the Gifted with your council members, but I cannot allow you to act in the position of king just yet. You must decide on your own."

King Henry finally spoke. "I am...sorry." He hung his head. "I am sorry for failing my sons and those who truly loved me, and allowing Lilian's poison to take over me and my kingdom. She must die."

His face paled even as he said it, but he didn't pull the words back.

Erlich's look was grave, and he nodded once. "Tomorrow. At sunrise." He jotted notes down.

"I will need to speak with Mava at some point," the King mused aloud. A cloud fell over his features. "I was foolish. I was a new king trying to win the trust and respect of my council and my kingdom, and I was too cowardly to face Dera or her child.

I tried to locate her so I could provide for them, but she had disappeared. I had hoped she had started anew somewhere else. There is no way to make those wrongs right now, but I must find a way to show Mava my regret."

Avalon stole a glance at Golan. He seemed less concerned with his mother's execution and more concerned with the King's attitude toward him. She wondered if he'd been included in the "sons" King Henry mentioned earlier. Golan watched the King's face with guarded features, but his apprehension bled right through his eyes.

Across from them, Joran muttered a curse under his breath. The King looked at him shrewdly, one eyebrow raised, but Joran refused to meet his gaze. He looked wretched.

Avalon had heard they'd found him collapsed in his chambers, exactly where they'd left him after the battle, a pouch of jacin on the floor beside him. The physician had to rush to revive him. The man had barely been able to counter the effects of the jacin, the strongest drug on the black market, before it took Joran's life.

"I've confiscated it before," his oldest guard, Dunn, had said, scowling when questioned. "He finds ways to acquire it."

"And you. Were you intentionally trying to end your life, *son*?" the King demanded now.

Joran's eyes were bloodshot. "Doesn't matter," he mumbled.

"That's not an answer," the King thundered.

Joran scowled at him. "I got carried away, okay? But death wouldn't have been a bad ending."

King Henry's eyes flamed. "Where did you get the substance, Joran?"

Joran's hand fluttered limply. "There are many sellers in Ethereal."

"How did you afford it? Your expenses are monitored."

Joran squeezed his eyes shut and rubbed his forehead. "This isn't the issue. None of this has to do with me," he spit through gritted teeth. A volley of curses poured from his mouth, then he stomped from the room.

Avalon caught the disappointment on the King's face before he straightened his features. "It seems I have much to work through with him," he admitted.

"He saved your lives," Avalon volunteered, feeling Joran was due gratitude for at least his one good deed. He was such a confused young man.

"But first he tried to end yours," Golan reminded her.

"He's been hurt by his mother," Erlich reminded them. "He hasn't processed his grief properly. I have a suggestion, but I'll speak to you about it later, Your Majesty."

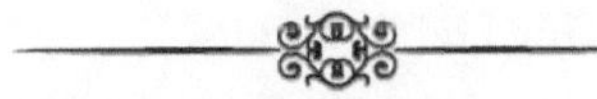

Hours slipped by as the King and the Magister reorganized Ethereal's affairs. None of the guards had been disloyal, and those who had obeyed the Queen had still been following orders, and could not be held responsible for her power to control them. The only one who would have to be tried was the guard who had tried to hurt Avalon in the prison.

Avalon's muscles tensed as Erlich mentioned that man. Should she add the other part of the story? Surely his slamming her unconscious and the still-visible bruise on her face was enough to incriminate him. *But who else might he hurt in the future if I don't tell?*

"M–Magister? Your Majesty?" She bit her lip and avoided looking at Golan. She had done things she never thought possible over the last few days. She could do this too. She took a breath. "That guard didn't only hit me. He was also going to hurt me...in other ways." Humiliation burned her face. "He didn't. Nothing happened," she added in a hurry, "But only because Magister Erlich and Golan arrived then. That's actually why he knocked me unconscious. We heard noise on the stairs, and he got scared."

She still didn't look at Golan, but she could feel his burning gaze. *Did I do the right thing?*

The King's look was dark. "Thank you for bringing forth that information. I will not tolerate such things in my household. I assure you I will deal with him. As for the rest of the men, I'll ask them to renew their oaths to me and reinstate them as soon as possible," King Henry decided.

Golan reached toward her and squeezed her hand under the table, and she relaxed. She realized The One had answered her cry for help, after all. Erlich and Golan had arrived at just the right time.

Next, King Henry sent word to Cleft that the peas had been stripped of their power and were all being held by the High Magister in Ethereal, hopefully thwarting any plans anyone there might still have. He also sent men to catch up to the soldiers the Queen had sent away the morning before the attack. He penned his own message to them, his lips moving as he wrote. "There is no battle, and we are not in danger. You may return, but there is no need for reinforcements."

Alice and the other maid came back to refill everyone's mugs with fresh hot tea. Avalon smiled and whispered to her friend, "Good things are happening, Alice. You'd never believe how wise the King is."

Alice beamed. "Then I think refreshments are in order the next time around."

"My dear," the King said to Avalon, some of his warmth coming back. She quickly turned her attention back to him. "I'm going to dispatch messengers to Haven at this very moment to inquire about their welfare and bring them news of you. I highly regret my failure to understand your situation and help you. I will arrange for your return to your kingdom as soon as you'd like. I can send servants and guards and whatever you need for the journey. I'll be sending orders to my troops in Lilt to secure our borders just in case Cleft is planning anything else, and I will make sure you are royally guarded." His eyes were still sad, but the edges crinkled at his pun. Avalon hoped he'd get his joy back one day.

"I'd like to go with her, Your Majesty," Golan interjected before she could respond.

She glanced from him to the King, who was staring at the Prince, his lips pursed in consideration.

"And, you, son of my wife." He said the words slowly, as though trying to comprehend them. Golan's eyelids flickered, but he kept his head up and didn't drop his gaze.

"Son of my wife." King Henry repeated the words quietly, nodding to himself. "You're not my blood, but you have been a son, nonetheless. I do not hold you responsible for your mother's actions, of course." He tilted his head at Erlich. "There is liberty for adoption, isn't there?"

Erlich nodded quickly.

Hope surged through Golan's eyes, but he bowed his head respectfully, hiding the rest of his emotions.

"Would you like him to accompany your journey, Princess Avalon?"

Avalon bit her lip to keep from smiling too widely. "Yes, Your Majesty."

King Henry smiled. "Then I appoint you, Golan, as custodian of the Princess of Haven until her safe return to her home. And you will act as our ambassador to Haven while you are there. I will give you my authorization to draw from our funds to help Haven with repairing their damages. We need to restore our long-lost relationship with them. Keep quiet for now about your heritage, and act wisely, because you will act in my name," he cautioned. "You will return to the Academy in the fall, but we have a few weeks to work on all this before that."

Golan blinked. Avalon bit her lip again, trying to control the happiness she felt.

"Thank you, Your Majesty," Golan finally managed.

"We shall talk further upon your return."

Golan nodded.

King Henry told Erlich he needed to return to Lilt as soon as possible. "I'd like all of us to leave Blackstone as soon as possible. I need to see to Benrid's condition and see if he has continued to sulk in despair or not. He must learn the truth about his mother." Regret and guilt shadowed King Henry's face. "I'd like you to go with me, if you're able, Magister."

"I would be honored, your Majesty. I feel fully satisfied in granting you full power to the throne, now that I've seen your heart. I will help you deliver the news to your kingdom and to your eldest son."

"And your followers, the Gifted ones. What will they do?"

"My hope is that you will allow them to integrate into society. Some of them still have families to return to, and some have been hiding most of their lives and will need to start anew."

"Granted," the King agreed. "Gifts are welcome in Ethereal, and the Gifted have the same rights as everyone else. May freedom and equality reign!"

"We are grateful. I will need to gather everyone and help them prepare to re-enter the kingdom," Erlich said.

"We will help with funds and any other way we can to make their re-entrance as smooth as possible," the King added.

"Thank you, Your Majesty. We may be able to repay you. I have a very gifted healer who could possibly help His Highness, Benrid," Erlich offered. "His name is Tiden."

Erlich and the King went on to discuss the war against magic two decades ago. They compared their suspicions and concluded that Queen Lilian had been approached by Magister Ferin about her abuse of power as soon as she had taken Dera and Mava and the pea. Resentful of his interference, she had started rumors about him. He had unexpectedly given the title of Great Magister over to his son, Erlich, around that time, but he had not told Erlich the full story of her wickedness. Still not satisfied, Lilian convinced Henry to strike out against magic, twisting the story of Aspenia's evil infection against Ferin and Erlich, and using her own stolen powers to back up her claims.

"Avalon." Erlich drew her attention. "You may wonder about your magic, now that I've taken the power from the peas and crystals."

She nodded.

"Which powers did you activate before?"

"I practiced with the fire and shape-shifting when you taught me. I used the sleeping crystal on the guards, and I tried to use the death one on the Queen, but I didn't have the time to ignite it."

"Then those are your powers. They still exist in your energy, and they are your Gift. You will be able to wield those things without the crystals in your hands."

Avalon's face drained of color. She didn't want the power to hurt people or kill them. She was content without having power at all.

"I can tell by your expression you will use them carefully."

"Y-yes, sir," she stammered. "The only one I foresee using is the sleeping one," she said, honestly, and the King and Erlich broke into chuckles.

"We have much to do, and then journeys to make," Erlich said. "We should adjourn. King Henry, with your permission, I'd like these peas to be kept on display in Lilt. A warning and reminder can be posted beside them. Magic is a Gift, but people are greedy and prone to misuse it."

CHAPTER 40

After the Rain

Avalon grew silent as night fell. Although this carriage was much more comfortable than her last journey, and the man she loved was sitting across from her, she couldn't help remembering her terrifying nights alone, fearful and desperate in a carriage by herself.

Servants came to lay sleeping pallets on the floor when they stopped, and Golan retreated to his own carriage. She felt the solitude immensely. It felt like ice under her skin, but she couldn't ask him to stay.

I'm safe, she kept telling herself. The guards outside had pledged their lives for Golan and her.

She closed her eyes.

The carriage was completely enclosed. There were no windows, the door was shut, and the walls suffocated her. Queen Lilian sat across from her, her eyes glowing ferociously. She looked lethal. Avalon cowered in the corner, trying to make herself invisible, but with every bump of the wheels, the Queen grew more agitated. She glared at Avalon as though it were her fault.

Then, from somewhere outside, Avalon heard Amelie scream. "Don't touch me! Please. Please!" Her shrill cry ended in sobs, and Avalon leaped to her feet, already searching for the voice. She ripped open the carriage door, but someone grabbed her by the collar, pulling her back inside. The fabric strangled her throat.

The person threw her to the floor, but instead of the Queen's face, she saw Joran above her. He had eyes like his mother and a dagger in his hands. Amelie screamed in the distance again. Avalon cried out for Golan, but Joran threw back his head and laughed.

"He's dead," Joran said, the dagger lunging toward her heart.

She woke with a start and scrambled to sit up. The blackness lurked around her, and she expected a face to snarl at her. Her breaths were fast and tight. A dream. *Just a dream.* She hugged herself and clenched her teeth.

Her carriage door flew open, and she saw a figure. The shadow rushed her.

She screamed for real.

"Shhh, it's me." Thick arms wrapped around her. She struggled against them until the words sank in. "What happened? Are you all right? I'm here now."

Golan. She buried her face in his chest and clung to him, letting his heat burn away the chills on her neck. He stroked her loose hair, following the long strands all the way down her back.

"Did I wake you? I was dreaming," she whispered, embarrassed, but relieved he was there.

"You called my name. I'm glad you did. Do you want to tell me about the dream?"

Her lips trembled. "No. Y-yes. He was trying to kill me again." She didn't need to explain who. "And I heard my sister screaming, but Queen Lilian was here too, and she stopped me from finding her." She shook her head, trying to shake away the images.

Golan hugged her tighter. "She's not queen anymore," he said into her hair. Avalon nodded against him. Queen Lilian had been executed yesterday morning. Avalon had closed her eyes, unable to watch the deed, but she knew Lilian was gone.

"Joran will soon be gone too," he answered her thoughts. The King planned to send him away for a while, hoping a year at sea under the watchful eye of a military captain would help him mature and get a grip on his life.

"And you're here," she whispered.

He kissed the top of her head.

"You don't wish you were with Lady Hahly instead?"

"What?" Golan laughed. "What are you talking about?"

"The Queen said you were going to visit her. It was her excuse for your absence the night she'd locked you in the prison tower."

"Is that where she sent me? I couldn't remember anything except racing away on horseback until Erlich intercepted me."

"I've figured by now it was her manipulation, but I thought maybe there was some truth to it."

"Truth, like maybe I did love Lady Hahly?"

Avalon nodded against his chest, still clinging to him.

"Not at all, my love. I barely know her. The Queen overestimated her own wits sometimes, didn't she? It's hard to build a life on so many lies without getting twisted up by them."

Rain began to fall, splattering against the roof of the carriage, and the wind picked up, rocking them gently.

"Do you miss her? Queen Lilian, I mean. She *was* your mother."

Golan was quiet for a minute. "It's not easy to comprehend everything that happened. It will take a while, and it may never make full sense. But, no, I don't really miss her like that, as a mother," he said sadly.

"How did you turn out so different from her and Joran?"

She could almost feel Golan smile. He tightened his arms around her. "A good nurse, I guess. Old Anna truly cared about me. She made me feel loved when no one else did, and she taught me to pray. She passed away when I was seven. Now her, I *do* miss."

"I wish I could thank her. You're a good man. She'd be proud."

He answered her with another soft kiss.

"I'm scared, Golan," Avalon whispered a few minutes later. The cover of darkness gave her courage to admit her fears.

"I'm scared to go home. I'm scared my parents may be dead, and my sisters are gone, and I won't know what to do."

"Whatever happens, and whatever needs done, we'll do it together."

She stayed in his embrace until she felt drowsy. He eased her down to lie on the cushion.

"Don't leave me. Please," she whispered.

"I won't." He stretched himself beside her and wrapped his arms around her again. She inhaled his minty scent, enjoying the feel of his muscles under her cheek, and let her eyes drift closed.

CHAPTER 41

He Makes Everything Beautiful

They were close. Avalon could smell the sea on the breeze already, and the land was green and rolling. When her yellow sandstone palace came into view, she caught her breath.

She didn't speak until they pulled up to the gate. The guards came to question them and inspect them before giving them entrance. She opened the door of the carriage and stepped out.

"It's me," she said, searching the face of the guard. "Princess Avalon."

He dropped into a deep bow. "Of course, Your Highness. Welcome home!"

He signaled the trumpeter, who blasted an announcement on his instrument. "The Princess has returned!"

The gates opened, and everyone gathered to watch the carriage pass.

Avalon fell into her mother's arms, hugging her as tightly as her arms could go. "You're alive," she whispered, overwhelmed with relief.

Queen Heather had tears running down her face. "*You're* alive, Avalon." A sob caught in her throat.

"Do you know where Amelie and Raine are?" She was afraid to ask the question, but she had to know. "And father? Is he..."

"He is fine. Or he will be now that you're here. Your sisters are recovering. Our troops overtook them a few days after they were captured and rescued them. But you weren't there. Our men caught the group of Cleftan rebels, but those men wouldn't admit anything about you. Amelie said she had seen you the night they took you all, but not after that. We weren't sure where to search. We sent messengers to the other kingdoms for news, but no one had heard of your disappearance. And we never got a ransom note. We feared the worst until yesterday when we got a message from the Magister Erlich in Ethereal telling us you were alive and safe and would be home soon."

Avalon's mind skipped back to the first time she'd been locked in her room and Queen Lilian had mentioned soldiers. Had they been inquiring about her? Her ears felt hot with anger as she thought of the former queen's wickedness. Lilian had made it seem like she was trying to protect Avalon from Cleftan soldiers who had come to claim her, not her own people from Haven. But then, she wouldn't have discovered her Gift or fallen in love with Golan if she had left that day.

"I'll tell you everything," Avalon promised, relief leaving her feeling light. "But I want to see everyone first. I've been so worried."

Everyone fussed over Avalon that afternoon. The Queen seemed reluctant to leave her side. Penli, her maid, bubbled with joy as she prepared a bath. "Which oil today, Your Highness? Lavender, jasmine, or rose? Gerta heard you were back and made me bring them all." She giggled, something Avalon had never heard her do before.

Raine came through her door as soon as Avalon was dressed. Her sister squealed and threw her arms around Avalon. "You're home. Oh, we thought...We were so scared. Oh, praise The One!"

Penli, who would usually shoo her sister away, claiming, "Wrinkles!" or "Her hair!" merely laughed again.

"I'm going to bring something to nibble on. All your favorites. I'll be right back." Raine squeezed Avalon in another half hug and left.

Amelie burst into tears when she saw her big sister, and Avalon started crying with her.

"Amelie. Thank The One you're here. I have been so worried about you. I ran away to get help for you and Raine, but I got caught."

"What happened?"

Raine came back through the bedroom door, a large tray filled with cakes and fruit in her arms. She plopped down on Avalon's bed, filled her mouth with grapes, and added with her mouth full, "Please tell us everything." Queen Heather didn't even throw her a disapproving look.

"Will you tell me what happened here first?" Avalon asked. Her story included the revelation that she possessed magic. She knew that fact would be a lot for her family to take in, and she wasn't ready to share it yet. She wanted Golan with her for that.

The Queen spoke in her soft voice. It fell in waves over Avalon, and she soaked in the warmth and familiarity of it, wrapping herself with the comforting sound like a blanket. Queen Heather told Avalon that the Cleftans who had attacked had not been the actual army, but a group of rogue soldiers who had found out that Cleft had a gem with immense power. They gathered information about the gem, discovering in the process that there were more pea-like gems in Haven and Ethereal. Together, they formed their own band. They had worn their Cleftan uniforms, but sneaked away from their commander, stealing the gem from their kingdom, and using it to gain entrance to the palace at Haven. Their gem subdued everyone in a stupor of pleasantness and happiness and made them unaware of anything disturbing going on.

"They meant to ransom you girls for our pea gem, but I had no idea they wanted the pea, or that they would take you. I knew the pea was supposed to have power, but I'd never dared try it. When I realized our palace had been infiltrated, I wanted to give the gem to you to keep it safe, or to protect you if need be. You see, I discovered you had magic blood when you were just a toddler, Avalon. The pea glowed one day when you got near it. I grew up in Aspenia, and, as you know, Aspenia is full of magic, but when their magic turned dark, I decided it was safer to abstain from magic completely."

"Even though magic is a Gift from The One?" Avalon asked quietly. At least her powers wouldn't be a total surprise.

Queen Heather sighed. "I realize that now, but I've seen it twisted and misused, and I didn't want that to happen here. I'm sorry. The pea was a gift to me on my eighteenth birthday, but I never tried to use it because I was afraid of the woman who gave it to me. She was a sorceress, important to the Aspenian court, but later condemned for twisting the power for her own intentions. I was afraid that using the gem would open the door for whatever evil was in her heart to hurt us here. I often considered discarding the gem, but when I realized the pea responded to you, I knew I couldn't do that, and one day I'd have to tell you the truth. I planned to pass it on to you on your eighteenth birthday and explain to you then about your power. Then the attack happened, and I knew I might be out of time and had to do it sooner. I tried, but I was too late."

Avalon was hurt that her own mother had hidden her Gift from her all these years, but she couldn't actually be angry. Queen Heather had been doing what she thought was safest.

"The Cleftan men killed eight of our guards, but they managed to subdue the rest with the pea," Queen Heather continued. "Two of them stayed here and continued to use the effects on the rest of us for a day or two so the others could get a head start with you all. The magic clouded our minds, making us feel content and relaxed, even with our children missing. When at last they left, taking the pea with them, the spell disappeared, and we pieced together what happened. Then we were frantic with worry about you all. Your father and his men rode hard, tracking your path, and praying the whole way. The One led them straight to the attackers. One of them, a young woman, admitted they were going to ride on Ethereal next, until they lost you, and it threw their plans off. They couldn't afford to lose men to search for you, but if you got away, and their secret got out, they could be destroyed. So they abandoned their plan to attack Ethereal and were headed straight back toward Cleft to hide when our men caught up with them. Amelie and Raine were weak and terrified, but as soon as they got home, they improved. Amelie has bad dreams, but she has moved into Raine's chambers, and being near her sister has helped."

"I prayed too, but it just seemed like everything got worse every time I did," Avalon admitted. "A lady named Mava told me that things always come right in the end, and she was right. The One did hear my prayers after all."

"Always." Queen Heather smiled. Avalon knew Mava's ending hadn't come right yet. She was suffering terribly with grief, but she was strong. *I'll pray for her too,* she decided.

"I saw fire the night I was taken," Avalon remembered.

"They burned the palace's fields," the Queen admitted, "as part of the distraction while they infiltrated. But our kingdom is fertile, and we won't go hungry. Now, my daughter, your story."

Avalon stood and smiled at the loving faces around her. She straightened her yellow skirt and nodded to Penli. It was so nice to feel like herself again.

"I'll share my story when Father is there to hear it, and Golan, the ambassador from Ethereal," she said. "Over dinner perhaps?"

They rose to follow her.

"I saw the ambassador," Raine commented as they walked down the corridor. "Handsome in a serious way." She threw a sideways glance at Avalon. "Do you know him well?"

Avalon wasn't sure if her mother caught the faint surge of blood on her neck.

But Amelie sighed, her eyes on the ceiling, before Avalon could answer. "I love a handsome man," she said with all the exaggerated swoon of a twelve-year-old.

Avalon giggled at her little sister. "So do I," she admitted, with a smile.

Acknowledgements

Thank YOU, friend, for choosing to read this book. Writing stories is fun, but publishing stories and displaying my babies for the whole wide world to see is downright scary. The fact that you gave my book a chance and made it to this page means a lot to me. Every time someone chooses my book, I consider it a gift.

I hope you loved your adventure in Kerrynth and that you fell in love with these characters the way I did. If you enjoyed any part of Of Crystals and Peas, please consider leaving a review on Amazon or Goodreads, or wherever you go to buy books. Even if it's just a line or two, reviews are kind of like gold to independent authors like me. They're how our books get seen in the big, busy world of readers. If you haven't read my other book yet, Of Oceans and Pearls, consider checking that one out as well, and diving into Prince Joran's life.

Of course, writing a book takes a village, and I owe many people thanks.

As mentioned in the beginning, I wouldn't be here telling stories if it weren't for my parents, who not only gave me life, but reared me with books. They taught me to love them from the time I can remember, and books were as close companions to me throughout my life as my friends and family were.

I'm grateful to Joyce at ReJoyce Literary Editing for once again taking on my rough draft and helping me polish it into something worth sharing. She asked all the hard questions, and I'm grateful for the ways she helped challenge me to think deeper about my words. Thank you most of all, Joyce, for continually cheering me on through the whole process.

Talking about cheerleaders, my daughters are up there at the top! They believe in me more than I do most of the time, and their whole-hearted enthusiasm for everything to do with Princess Avalon and Prince Golan gave me courage to keep going when I felt unworthy. Thank you, Mercy and Selah, for loving me so very much. Nurturing you is a gift in itself, but being loved in return is more than I deserve.

My own siblings always make me feel amazing too. Following my posts, and sending all the heart eyes when I share my progress with them means more to me than they might realize. Thanks, Rydal, Gretel, Elsie, and Nolan, for being proud of me and telling me so.

My Josh has supported me in ways no one else will ever see, whether by taking over extra duties, watching the kids, or staying up late with me when I need to get work done. He's always behind the scenes, making my life easier and better and loving me well. Thank you, Love, for letting me be a writer.

My Instagram family has grown, and I've met so many special friends there. I'm thankful to social media, despite its flaws, for giving me a place to interact with other writers and readers. For those of you who I've become close to through that platform, thank you for being there with prayers, messages, and encouragement. I truly don't think I'd be at this stage without you.

Thank You, God. You are the foundation for every part of my life. May my words serve others in some way, and, in that, please You.

You can follow me on Instagram at @reneeknightauthor

Or sign up for my newsletter by going to https://form.jotform.com/232853465596570

I truly love building lasting connections with readers, and I would love to hear from you.

About the author

I'm Renee Knight, and I believe in fairytales. I think they help promote truth in a lovely way, a way that sticks with us. Living with my husband and our two princesses as missionaries in South Africa is what I call my real-life fairytale, and I am in love with it! Also, I eat too much chocolate and stay up too late reading–basically every single day–and write stories that always include love and redemption.

REAREVGARD
FAMILY TREE

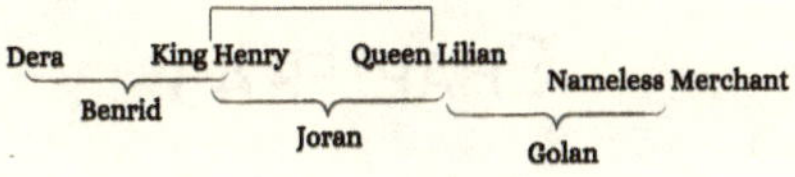

Sneak Peek Bonus Chapter

THIS IS THE UNEDITED FIRST CHAPTER OF BOOK THREE, WHICH IS SUBJECT TO CHANGE

Benrid paced to his door, opened it a crack, then closed it again when he was sure no one was around. No one other than Bertram, his guard, but he hadn't spent a morning without Bertram around for the last decade at least. Bertram was on duty from breakfast until dinner, and he was probably the best friend Benrid had, despite his being a glorified servant. True, royal guards had years of training and were highly skilled with weapons, but he worked for the Rearevgards just like anyone else in the castle. Bertram was a few years older than Benrid, and Benrid looked up to him like a big brother. It helped sometimes to have a friend like that, someone who could help ease the responsibilities Benrid shouldered, especially since his own father, the King, was oddly distant.

But Benrid was glad Bertram was stationed outside his room in the hall right now. He needed to be completely alone, even from his guard. He tugged his ear nervously. What had he just done? He was half afraid to try it again. He was afraid it wouldn't work, and, truthfully, more afraid that it would.

He'd only been home for two days since graduating from the Military Academy. Maybe with the strenuous preparation for graduation and then the trip home he was so tired he was imagining things. *But I have to know*, he decided.

He walked to the window again. His room overlooked the back of the castle grounds, just a sprawling lawn edged with trees before the walls. Beyond that, the River Lilt, for which the town was named, flowed south to the sea. He swallowed nervously. Then he squinted toward the trees. They were so far off, the colors were a mere blend, and a man would be but a shadowy form the size of a child to any normal glance.

Benrid concentrated on the spot where his eyes had fallen a few minutes earlier when he'd been thinking about his brother, Joran. At first, he saw nothing except the shadowy forms of the trees through the early morning mist, but as his concentration grew, it came into focus. *He* came into focus. Benrid could *see* Joran—and not just in his mind's eye. Joran was actually there, sunk down behind a tree, his head in his hands. The embarrassment of being involved in someone else's private moment pricked at Benrid, but he couldn't tear his eyes away. Joran's shoulders shuddered slightly. He finally looked up and rubbed his forehead before leaning his head back against the tree trunk, staring off at nothing. His face was wet with tears.

Benrid inhaled sharply and blinked. Heat rose up his neck. He'd spied on his brother's grief without him even knowing, and...and he had a Gift. *I am...Gifted.*

Emotions surged through him. Excitement, curiosity, fear. Mostly fear.

How did one get a gift? And more importantly, how did one have a gift and not know it until he happened upon it by accident? Benrid sank into a seat, staring at the wall in stunned silence. A servant knocked, breaking him out of his reverie.

"Come in," he called quickly, rubbing his eyes and the guilt off his face.

Alice nudged the door open. She'd been born and raised at the castle, though she hadn't started serving from the kitchen until recently, he thought. He didn't remember her working when he'd been here on holiday a year ago. He didn't know her well, except for her name, which he was sure everyone at the Castle Lilt knew. He remembered her darting around the castle when she was younger, always everywhere, smiling up at people and wheedling things out of them. At least she seemed to have calmed down now, he noticed, as she poured his tea with her eyes downcast. She moved deftly, but softly. After she'd arranged his breakfast, she curtsied. Benrid nodded absently until an idea came to him. He bolted up, causing her glance to jerk to him.

"Alice, aren't you? Would you fetch me another–" He searched the tray for something to ask for. "Another roll?"

Alice didn't balk or seem surprised. She simply bit her lip against a grin and bobbed her head. He let her go and counted to a hundred before going to his door and stepping into the hall.

"Where is she?" He grumbled for Bertram's sake. "My tea is getting cold."

He peered down the long corridor, wondering if he could see through stone if he concentrated hard enough. He attempted to focus, but he was afraid he'd give something away by his odd behaviour, so it didn't work. He couldn't see anything until Alice appeared at the top of the stairs at the end of the hall. Seeing her clearly from there was no special feat.

He nodded to Bertram, then again to her when she deposited the extra roll on his tray, his mind racing. He needed to try again.

"Go to the stables and tell the boys to prepare my horse. Stay there while they ready him, and when they are nearly done, come let me know."

Alice kept her gaze down and curtsied, but her lips twitched so much Benrid was appalled she might laugh. *Laugh? At me?* He went over his request in his mind, but could find nothing humorous, so he frowned at her instead.

Still smothering a grin, she left.

Benrid was too distracted to sit, so he paced again, trying to give her time to get to the stables before he honed his concentration there. He could just see the corner of the stables if he leaned out his window. He was not sure exactly how his Gift worked. Did he have to picture a person? That was how it started the first time he'd seen Joran. Or could he simply choose a spot and see into it? Maybe he could even see something only by picturing it in his mind, but he needed to practice on actually visible places for now. And he wanted to know Alice was there, so he'd know what he was "seeing" was true, not just his imagination. If he just imagined the stables, he'd have no way to know if what he saw was literally happening.

Finally, he deemed enough time had passed, and he leaned out his window. He narrowed his eyes at the gray corner of the low building, unblinking. He felt his sight focus and his mind hone in, and slowly, a fuzzy image appeared. He could see inside the stables! He caught sight of Alice's light hair, covered by her headscarf in the corner of his vision, and excitement stabbed his chest. He could do it. This was real!

But then a wave of utter exhaustion rolled over him so heavily he staggered and grabbed onto the window edge. His concentration was broken, and only the outer wall of the stables was visible now. He held on to the window frame, willing himself to concentrate again, eager to see more, to see what he was capable of. His legs began to shake before he caught sight of the vision again. He'd never felt so tired in his life before. His eyes closed, and pulling them open felt harder than lifting his sword after his first day of training. Such a sudden weakness should scare him; he knew it should, but every part of him was tired, so tired that he could not even find the mind power to feel afraid.

He swayed and didn't even realize when he crumpled to the floor.

Also by

Also by Renee Knight:
Of Oceans and Pearls

There are three things Prince Joran thinks he will never get over: the way his mother used him, the way his father ignored him, and the way an assassin murdered his fiancee.

Angry at the injustice of life and grieving his loss, Joran finds himself on a path of self-destruction. That's before his father, King Henry, sentences him to a year at sea under the watchful eye of Captain Markus, with hopes that the rigorous lifestyle will help him move forward. His guard, Peter, and Captain Markus, seem intent on teaching him what they know about love and loss, but Joran hurts too much to welcome their friendship.

When he hears about an assassin who severs the left hand of his victims, he knows he's discovered the man who murdered the girl he loved. Determined to make the man pay, Prince Joran believes he has found a new purpose for his life.

When Joran is met with an unexpected revelation involving a young woman during his travels, he finds himself full of questions and speculation. Joran must now decide if loving again is worth letting go of the past.

Available in paperback from Amazon or other retailers
Also on Kindle Unlimited